About the Author

Sue Clark worked for many years as a journalist, BBC comedy scriptwriter and PR writer. Her writing credits include TV shows such as *Alas Smith and Jones* and *Three of a Kind* and the radio show *Week Ending*. *Note to Boy* is her first novel. She lives in rural Oxfordshire.

Note to Boy

Sue Clark

unbound

This edition first published in 2020

Unbound
6th Floor Mutual House, 70 Conduit Street, London W1S 2GF
www.unbound.com

ISBN (eBook): 978-1-78965-094-5
ISBN (Paperback): 978-1-78965-093-8

Cover design by Mecob

Printed and bound in Great Britain by Clays Ltd, Elcograf S.p.A.

*To Michael, my favourite companion,
tea-maker, wine-pourer, patron – and did I
mention, husband? – with all my love.*

Super Patrons

Pamela Adams
Simon Adams
Ivan Anketell
Kevin Ansbro
Karen Attwood
Colin and Thelma Barrett
Caroline Bobby
Sue Bradbury
Ed Burrows
Lesley Byrne
Sue Chatfield
Jamie Chipperfield
Ben Clark
Matt Clark
Michael Clark
Naomi Clark
Sam Clark
Stephen Clark
Mike Coleman
Jude Cook
Andrew Crofts
Melanie Cumberland
Steph Davies
E R Andrew Davis
Daniela Dzepina
James Ellis
Louise Esplin
Caroline Fairfax Scott
Laura Fitzgerald
Terence Flanagan
Jim Fowler
Jude Fowler
Sheila Frost
Tatiana Fujiki
G.E. Gallas
Hazel Glennie
David & Rosalind Goodyear
Meg Gordon Sussman
Eamonn Griffin
Francesca Gubbay
Geoffrey Gudgion
Eileen Holmes-Ievers
Patrick Kincaid
Bethany Koblbauer
Ian Koblbauer
Ewan Lawrie
Chris Limb
Amanda Lloyd Jennings
Amy Lord
Sheila Loy
Louise Ludlow
Imogen Matthews
Paul Mayhew-Archer
Alice McVeigh
Virginia Moffatt
Anthony Mulville
Victoria Nixon
John-Michael O'Sullivan
Jennifer Pierce
Anna Pitt

Janet Pretty
Cliff Purrington
Barry Reeves
Dee Reeves
Sarah Rowe
Charlotte Rushby
Nicola Smith
Susan Smith
Jean Sullivan
Mark Vent
Angela Vincent
Julie Warren
Claire White
Philip Whiteley
James Wilkins
Tom Woodman
Charli Young
Nigel Young

1.

BRADLEY

She ain't a bit like I'm expecting.

'Kindly remove your headgear,' she goes, 'in the presence of a lady.'

Well, that's me done for, I think, pulling off the beanie. *Just when everything was going smooth as.*

It's a miracle I get there at all. Never go in that newsagents no more. On the Parade. On account of the creep behind the counter. He's a gawper. One of the worst. That's why I always wear a beanie or a hoodie when I'm out. Both sometimes. On account of the gawpers.

His fingers is black from the papers, except for the one always up his nostril. That's pink, glowing pink. One minute he's snot mining, the next he's serving sweets to little kiddies. Makes me want to vom.

2.

ELOISE

He was exactly what I expected. Skinny with a pinched face, as if a square meal would choke him. Restless brown eyes. Not shifty exactly, more watchful, though whether readying himself to pounce or to flee it was hard to tell, as most of his face was hidden under a woolly hat and a stringy fringe. Nice eyes though, deep and dark. Nose, biggish; chin, weakish – though that could have been my varifocals.

Smartly turned out by today's slack standards in well-pressed black t-shirt and jeans. A pity they were several sizes too big, swamping his underfed frame.

Functionally illiterate, of course, but a distinct improvement on the last one. She didn't have a word of English, not a word. Not even the essentials like 'gin' and 'tonic'. I don't know *what* Tabby was thinking.

3.

BRADLEY

Like I say, it was a stroke of luck I saw it. Sellotaped in the corner of the window.

'Wanted!!! Urgent!!! Refined, respectable lady authoress seeks domestic assistant of same ilk. Usual rates.'

And a mobile number.

Well, I get the 'domestic assistant' bit. That's a cleaner, right? But I don't know nothing about no ilks. Still, what have I got to lose? I break my rule, nip into the newsagents and pretend to be browsing in the gardening section. I glance over. He's got his elbows on the counter, head deep in a mucky mag. As I'm leaving, I feel his dead, gawping eyes follow me to the door. Don't matter 'cause I got the card in my pocket. Well, don't want no one else going for it, do I?

I go home. Just my luck, Dom's up. He's in the kitchen, ramming a sarnie in his gob like he ain't ate for a week. Raspberry jam dripping everywhere. Right off, he eyeballs the card. Next thing, he's snatched it.

'Watch it,' I go. 'You'll get jam over that.'

'You'll get jam over that,' he goes, in a stupid whiny voice what's supposed to be me.'What's this then, Bradley? Postcard from your boyfriend?'

He's always saying stuff like that.

'It's a job,' I tell him. 'Leastways, could be.'

'You stupid or something?' he snorts. 'You know Ma'll go mad if you get a job. Messes up her benefits.'

'No, it's sound,' I go. 'Cash in hand.' Leastways, that's what I'm hoping.

'What kinda job?' He squints at the writing. Never were much cop at reading, our Dom.

'Dunno till I call, do I?'

'Cheeky,' he goes, cuffing me one round the ear. I take my chance and reach for the card. He grabs my wrist, twists my arm up my back and shoves his gob up against my ear. 'You come across anything interesting, you be sure and let your big brother know,' he hisses, spraying jammy paste over my cheek. 'No sneaking behind my back, you little freak.'

He loosens his grip and for a sec I think that's it. Then he comes back at me, jabbing me with a nasty little John Wick punch. He strolls off, still chewing. I hear the flat screen fire up and stand there, wiping jam off of my face.

Been practising what I'm gonna say on the phone, but when the woman answers, she ain't in the mood for no chitchat.

'You can ask all the questions you want tomorrow at the interview,' she goes. 'Lancaster Gate. Ten-thirty. Don't be late.'

'See you tomorrow morning then,' I go, all chirpy.

'You most certainly will not. I'm merely the dutiful daughter in this equation. I've done my bit by getting my housekeeper to go halfway across London to put that wretched advert in a shop window in Kilburn. The rest is up to my mother.'

I'm thinking, *Why get the poor woman to schlep all the way to NW6? They got newsagents in Lanky Gate, ain't they?* Then I get it: posh Lanky Gate or scabby South Kill? No sense paying over the odds for a cleaner, is there?

'I hope you're accustomed to dealing with dotty old ladies,' she goes on, 'because, if you shape up, she's the one you'll be working for – God help you!' And she's hung up.

Ain't no skin off of my nose. Doddery old dear or her stuck-up, skinflint daughter, long as I get the gig.

Next morning I'm out of our house by nine. Good thing about getting up that time is, ain't no chance Ma nor Dom will be stirring, poking their noses in, asking awkward questions. Takes me best part of an hour to walk it but I'm there, good and early, outside her address.

Big old red-brick building it is. I'm looking up, taking in the curved steps up to the front door and the fancy stonework round the windows when I see it: the crest over the entrance. Courtland Mansions. It's only a flipping mansion. I rub my hands.

Not so fancy inside, mind. No lift for starters and cold, concrete steps. A sickly smell like someone's been boiling tomato soup on a stove for about a fortnight. Anyways, I walk up to the second floor, like I was told, and ring the bell. No answer. I knock, quiet at first. I call through the letterbox. Still nothing. I knock again and put my head to the door. Can't hear no one. I'm well put out. Seems I've come all this way for nothing. Bang my fists on the woodwork hard enough to hurt. I'm getting in a right strop. Then I hear something. A voice from inside. An old lady's voice. I flip up the letterbox.

'Do come through,' she warbles. 'You'll find the key under the mat.'

This is gonna be a doddle, I think, letting meself in.

'I'll receive you in my *boudoir,*' she goes. 'Proceed along the *foyer* and it's the second door on the right.'

I go up the hallway to the end and turn left, following my nose. The smell I mean. It's her kitchen and it's in a right state. Don't hardly like to walk across the floor. I'm wearing new kicks, see. OK, so they're hand-me-downs and a size too big but sharp black Nike Blazers, right? I take the biggest strides across to the cupboards, the soles of my shoes making a noise like ripping Velcro.

That's when the stink really hits me. Like when you're on a bus stuck behind the bin men. Rank. Brown slime trails out through a split in the bin. Towers of dishes is stacked up on worktops covered in tea rings. I go to pick up a plate. Two come away, stuck together with what looks like baked bean juice.

One thing I cannot stand is dirt. Even if you ain't got nothing, even if you're stony, it don't cost nothing to wash your pots and mop your floor. Dom says I'm OCD. Dom says a bit of dirt's good for you. But he says a lot of div things.

It's all I can do to stop meself from getting down on hands and knees there and then, and giving the floor a good old wash. I don't, though. I Velcro my way over to the fridge. Rip, rip, rip. Big old thing it is, stood against the wall. Used to be white. Now there's grey grime round the silver handle and red rust coming through chips and scratches. I grab at the handle and yank. It don't move. I give it another tug. Seal comes apart with a crack. A dim light comes on.

What am I looking at? Small, furry animals crouched on plates and in bowls. Then I twig and my head jerks back. It ain't animals. It's mould. Greyish-green mould covers everything. You can't tell cream buns from lamb chops. Black spots is spreading up the walls and down the insides, like the fridge has zits. There's a different stink. Like Dom's most cheesiest socks. Out the corner of my eye, I see something move on the top shelf, behind a burst yoghurt pot, something that really is alive. I slam the door sharpish.

She's calling me again, more tetchier now. 'What's going on out there? What are you doing?'

'Just taking off my coat an' that,' I go. She ain't to know I got no coat. That's top of the list when I get some readies. Nice warm Puffa. 'Won't be a mo.'

I edge my way down the hall and push a door. Bathroom. Don't go in. One sniff from the doorway's enough. On the other side is her sitting room. Poke my head round. Busted red settee. Cushion on one side squashed and worn pale, where a big, fat, lonely old backside has been parked on it. Long grey hairs stuck to the back. Little table covered in puzzle pieces and four mugs in need of a good soaking. Old-style telly, big as a Mini. Dead flowers in a dry vase. Dining table, piled up with papers and photos. Run my finger through the dust. Scrub the muck off with a wet wipe. Always keep a sachet or two in my pocket. You never know.

Next to that's her bedroom, where she's waiting. Door's ajar. I sneak past to another bedroom, smaller this time, with a single bed and a dusty bookshelf. One more door left to recce. Across the hall. I try it. It's locked. *Interesting.*

'I say,' the old lady shouts. 'Do you want this sodding job or not?'

'Sit here and let me examine you properly,' she goes, pushing away an eggy plate and patting the tatty bedcover. 'I like to get to know my staff.'

Not falling for that one. I plonk meself down on a chair well away from the bed. I know her game. Women can be pervs too, you know. Dom told me.

'Don't mind if I do, missus.'

'How quaint,' she laughs, giving me a view of pink tonsils and black fillings. 'But you must call me "Miss Eloise". Everybody does.'

Who's everybody? I think.

I get a good look at her for the first time. She's no fluffy-haired Werther's Original sweet old lady – and that's the truth. Not at all. Even though she's lying in bed, propped up on a pile of filthy pillows, she's painted up like she's on stage or something. I got sort of used to her after a bit, but back then, that first day, I'm pretty much gobsmacked. And believe me, I'm used to old dears what cake on the slap. Ma on karaoke night for one.

Her face is thick with powder, her cat's-arse lips is painted over with sticky pink stuff and she's drawed wobbly black lines round her eyes. A few wisps of grey stick out from under a red and orange scarf she's wound round her head like a bandana. Only she ain't done it right and it's dangling down over one eye, like a pirate. She looks like Captain Jack Sparrow's mad old granny, to be honest with you.

'The last one was useless,' she goes, struggling to pull a shapeless purple cardy round her big, saggy wobblers. 'You can hardly be any worse.' She frowns, making wrinkles in them wrinkles, and then goes chatting on about some foreign girl. I do my best to look interested but I must have been staring too hard, 'cause all of a sudden, she stops.

'Oh, you're admiring my lashes,' she goes, fluttering them up and down like flapping vampire bats. *Heck,* I think, *is the old girl flirting?* 'I do all my own styling, you know. Have done for years. And this peignoir' – she pulls at the purple thing again

– 'is from my collection. I remodelled it with my own fair hands.' She strokes it like it's a cat. 'It's the very one she wore that night… you know, the coat hanger. The bride.' She goes silent, drifting off. I wait for her to explain. I clear my throat. And she's back in the room, like someone's plugged her into a charger. 'Ah, but that's a day for another tale.'

She turns to me and that's when she says it.

'Now, kindly remove your headgear in the presence of a lady.'

There's nothing for it but to do like she says. I take a deep breath, sweep the beanie off and stand, twisting the life out of it, waiting for the inevitable. Don't know what gives me the most aggravation: the gawpers, the smart-arses, or the head-on-one-side, sad-faced do-gooders.

This old dear ain't any of them. She looks me straight in the eye, like most people can't bring theirselves to. Her eyes narrow and I see she's weighing me up. Not grossed out, nor no bleeding heart neither. Just curious. She's sharper than I thought, I reckon.

'That's better,' she goes, without a flicker. 'Now I can see to whom I'm speaking.' If she notices anything, she don't say. All she does is lift one bum cheek and squeak out a little fart. 'Tell me about yourself,' she goes.

I just about die on the spot. 'Name's Bradley,' I splutter, trying to hold it together. 'I'm seventeen and—'

'Bradley, hmmm?' she goes, interrupting my spiel before I can even get going. She presses a finger to her chin. 'It smacks somewhat of the council estate but I suppose it will do. Bruno took me to a council estate once, you know. Where he was born. Somewhere up North. Ghastly place. Dreadful people.'

And she's off, hardly pausing to take a breath, lah-de-dah-ing on about people and places I ain't never heard of. I'm losing patience.

''Scuse me,' I go, when I've had enough, 'do I get the job or not? Your daughter's said I had to have your say-so before I could get stuck in.'

'Dear, dear Tabby,' she goes. 'How I long to see her, but, as she says, Greenwich Park to Lancaster Gate is *such* an awkward journey.'

No worse than Kilburn, I think. *And I had to walk it.* But I don't say.

'Look upon today as a trial run,' she goes. 'If you perform satisfactorily, then we'll see about making the arrangement permanent.'

I'm well chuffed. 'Where do you want me, in the kitchen or here?'

While I'm talking, something's bothering me. Underneath her fart, and the fruity-floweriness of the powders and paints spilling out on her dressing table, my nose has picked up another smell. Something not nice. Coming from under her bed. I bend down and – guess what? – there's only a pink plastic potty there. Like they has for little kids. Brimming, it is. With a rainbow skin an' everything.

'I'll just get rid of this,' I go, sliding it out and wafting away the ripe old pong.

'As you wish,' she yawns, not one bit put out I'm standing there holding a pot of her stale piss. When I get back, she's slid down the bed and a dreamy look's come in her eyes. I wonder if she's been on the booze. Know the signs, see.

'I asked for Martin Bashir, you know,' she murmurs, half asleep. 'A man with his track record would've been ideal.' She gives a gynormous sigh. 'Sadly, he's in America, Tabby informed me. So you see, like it or not, we're stuck with each other. Are you ready?'

I'm confused. Who's this Martin bloke? What is she wanting

me to do? I don't like the weird way this conversation is going. And I definitely don't like the look in her eyes.

I stick out my chest and, putting a bit of macho gravel in my voice, like I ain't someone to be messed with, I go, 'It's me, Bradley. Remember?' All the while keeping the door in view over my shoulder. 'I spoke to your daughter? About the cleaning?'

She ain't listening. 'Be so good as to bring over my clippings from the *escritoire,*' she goes. 'And my spectacles on the *chiffonier.*'

From the what? On the where? Wish she'd stick to English. After a search, I find her glasses on the dressing table and a battered blue photo album on a spindly table in the corner.

As I get a hold of the album, a bunch of loose photos slides out and slaps to the carpet. I kneel to pick them up. Stacking them like playing cards, I grab meself a dekko. They're a weird yellow colour but I make out people mucking about in the street, arms round each other, jumping in the air, throwing back their heads, looking like they's having just the best time. The girls is stunners. Long legs and wide eyes. The boys, their hair long and their shirts frilly, is almost as good-looking.

When I come to the last of the photos, I do a double take. Right in the middle, reaching out to write on this piece of paper someone's holding up, is a baby-faced dude with a thick fringe and a cheeky grin. I kinda recognise him. *It couldn't be, could it?*

I turn to her and say, 'Excuse me for asking. Is this one of the Beatles?'

'Give the boy a coconut!' she shouts, making me jump. 'A glimmer of recognition at last. Yes, that's Paul with some of the gang. Pretty, isn't he? Too pretty to be a boy.'

'Did you used to be famous, then?'

She gives a filthy laugh. 'Better than that, young whatever-your-name-is, I used to be *infamous.*' She flicks a hand at me, impatient. 'Give me those Polaroids.' 'For pity's sake – the photographs you're holding.'

I do like she says.

'I wondered where these had got to. Such memories,' she goes, crushing them to her chest. 'Now, enough of your timewasting. Time to get to business. Pin back your ears, Boy, and prepare to be amazed. We're about to set off on a journey through the life of Miss Eloise Slaughter.' She throws out her arms, bingo-wings flapping, photos flying. 'Style supremo and fashion phenomenon.' She snaps her head round. 'Well, what are you waiting for, what's-your-name? Get scribbling.'

At last I get it. I scrabble about in the scrunched-up tissues on her bedside table until I find a chewed-up biro and an old envelope. Sitting down, I smooth the envelope on my knee. 'Ready,' I sing out. 'Oh, and the name's Bradley, by the way.'

She clears her throat and, staring at the ceiling, starts up in that funny, fruity, whooping voice I get so used to.

4.

ELOISE

Ahem. What do you think of, dear reader, when you hear the name, Eloise Slaughter? Outrageous fashions? Extravagant parties? A bit of how's-your-father with every popstar and actor of note in Swinging London? Ah, but there is so much more to my life, as will become apparent as this, my poignant tale, unfolds.

I've always fancied myself as a writer, you know, even though I've never written anything longer than a cheque before. I have bestraddled the fashion world – if that's not too explicit an image; surely I can dictate a few thousand riveting words to a goggle-eyed boy?

That's you, by the way. My little joke. What are you staring at? Eyes down and get scribbling. Is that the best you can do? In your lunchbreak – half an hour and not a minute longer – buy yourself proper implements. A notebook and some pens. In fact – hang it – a pack of notebooks and half a dozen biros. Go to Woolworths. Always good value. What, no Woollies? What is civilisation coming to? WHSmith then. They haven't gone down the pan too, have they? Now, enough of your mindless chitter-chatter. To work.

Where to begin? Carnaby Street? The Hot Spot? *When* to begin? The sixties, when I was the grooviest chick in town? The seventies, when I was at the height of my powers? No, the eighties. That's what you want to hear, isn't it? When everything went tits aloft. I could start there. Get it over with. Grasp the bullet. Bite the nettle. But no, impatient reader, you'll have to wait. I'm going to begin with my birth, way back in 19… oh, let's not get bogged down in boring little details like dates.

You ready, Boy? Pen poised? Good.

Meat pies. I owe everything to them. They paid for my childhood ribbons and tap shoes, my education at St Jude's and my elocution lessons. It is thanks to them that you won't catch a trace of Coventry sing-song in my accent, except perhaps when I'm a little squiffy.

From the beginning, my parents, Terry and Urse Armitage, adored me. And who could blame them? 'My angel,' Terry used to call me. Cherry lips, lavender blue eyes, cascades of blonde curls – I was delectable. Thinking back, it was probably from my father – known throughout the meat processing industry as the Pie King of the West Midlands – that I inherited my instinct for business. My good looks I got from my mother, a renowned Coventry beauty.

Some might say I was a spoilt child. I prefer to think of myself as blessed with a sensitive and creative nature. Like many gifted children, I was prone to the occasional tantrum. To this day I can turn ratty if I'm not the centre of attention.

Terry always knew how to handle me.

'Oi'd chuck yow over me shoulder and tek yow 'ome, kicking and screaming, to Mother,' he used to remind me, in his heavy West Midlands tones. 'Remember when yow blacked my eye?' What a card he was.

Where Terry was a man of hearty appetites, Mother – Urse – was the opposite. How best to conjure her up for you? Never a party girl, my mother, but always well turned out – for a butcher's wife, at least – and admirably thin. No lipowhatsit or gastric whojamaflip back then. Urse kept her figure by the simple process of hardly ever eating. And so house-proud. I almost never saw her without a duster or a broom in her hand.

Standoffish, I suppose you could call her, or, as the family fortunes improved, an out-and-out snob. 'Do I look like the kind of person who'd pass the time of day with the likes of *you*?' I overheard her say one day to a neighbour whose husband was a mere milkman.

Yes, dear reader, hard though it is to credit, the woman who was to become the fashion queen of the sixties – that's me by the way – began life in a humble flat above a butcher's shop in Coventry.

All in all, life was good. I was happy. Then Terry and Urse did a dreadful thing. They had another child. Silvia. What to say about Silvia, my dear sister? Tall, gangly Silv. Clever, hard-working Silv. Happily-married-to-the-same-man-for-more-than-forty-bloody-years Silv.

'Get used to it, ower Elaine,' I remember Terry saying, cooing over her crib. 'This little babby is 'ere to stay.'

I should explain. Terry and Urse were the only people on earth who called me by my hideous birth name. No matter how many times I forbad them.

Silvia didn't stay a 'little babby' of course. She grew fast and kept on growing. My nickname for her was the Carthorse because she was always so big and clumsy. Said with affection, of course.

Do you have siblings, Boy? Oh, for pity's sake – brothers and sisters? What's he called? Dominic? That's nice. Nothing council house about that name. Not like yours. Remind me again what it is. Never mind. Now you've made me completely lose my whatsit... you know. String, is it? I do wish you wouldn't interrupt.

Terry and Urse. Urse and Terry. What a pair. Maybe if she hadn't been so uptight and po-faced, he might not have started hopping on his bike and delivering more than pork bangers to the ladies of the district. Always one for the ladies, Terry, right up until the day he dropped down dead in a platter of Scotch eggs at a Worshipful Company of Meat Manufacturers dinner dance in Wolverhampton. Two brassy blondes with stiff perms attended the funeral, shooting daggers of hatred at each other across the grave. Who they were, one could only speculate.

Thinking about it now, that must be where I got it from, my huuuuge sex drive? From Terry.

No need to look so alarmed, Boy. My libido vanished long ago, along with everything else I had of value. You'll have to get used to earthy talk if you're going to be my aman... aman... what is that sodding word? My personal secretary. Now where was I? Meat pies. Jolly old meat pies.

Terry made his money during the war.

'Folk en't so fussy what's in a pie, when there's a war on,' he used to say.

Never one to worry about the niceties, by the time I was eleven, he had a second shop and we'd moved to a neat Victorian semi with a walled garden and an upstairs bathroom.

'Ower brain and tongue pies is going grite and the new shop is doing a grand trade,' he said one day, a self-satisfied look on his face. We two girls were swinging our legs on the sofa, where we'd been sat down to hear a big family announcement.

'Me and yower mother,' he glanced over to the doorway to where Urse was polishing the door handle to within an inch of its life, "ave decided to send yow girls to private school.' Terry puffed out his chest. 'Next term, our Elaine, you're starting at St Jude's with the posh girls. What do yow reckon to that then, eh?'

'Oh, how thrilling, Daddy!' I trilled, throwing my arms around his neck, taking care not to come into contact with his bloodstained apron. No more mixing with girls with common accents and nits. I was going to St Jude's.

My St Jude's education didn't get off to the best of starts.

'Isn't this exciting, Mummy?' I said. 'My first school uniform.' I wriggled with pleasure as the shopkeeper removed gymslips and jumpers from their cardboard boxes. 'Oh! But they're brown,' I said, feeling a tantrum brewing.

Brown blazers, brown ties, brown skirts, brown jumpers, brown shoes, even brown knickers were spread before me. And not a rich chestnut or a vibrant copper, either. These were a hideous shade of diarrhoea not even a Marisa or a Shrimp in their sixties heydays could have carried off, let alone a delicate little thing of eleven with classic English rose colouring. That's me, by the way.

'Brown drains my complexion. I cannot wear brown,' I said, taking in a massive breath in preparation for a major bawling session.

'Stop yower blarting and tek a look at this,' the assistant said.

My jaw dropped, my tears dried and my tantrum was forgotten. In her hands she cradled the cutest, snappiest, most adorable straw boater you ever saw.

'Troi it on.'

As she placed it on my head, I knew – despite the brown – I was going to love St Jude's.

Note to Boy: I may still have that hat. You know, for the museum.

It was at St Jude's that I first got an inkling I was someone out of the ordinary. To be honest, quite a few of the girls there fancied themselves as special. It was that kind of school. They were wrong, of course. I was the only one who got it right. How do I know? Name me one other who went on to found a ground-breaking fashion empire. Exactly.

I didn't really make any friends at St Jude's. Not as such. In fact, tell you a secret. I've never really seen the point of friends. I've been friend-*ly* with many people over the years, usually when I needed something from them. Talent, money, contacts, sex. But as to friendship for friendship's sake, I didn't get it. Still don't, if I'm honest.

Though now I come to think, there was one girl at St Jude's. I'm not sure she counts. Bethany Sawyer wanted to be friends with everyone.

Bethany was a sweet-faced, sweet-natured girl with a shy, ready smile, lustrous, honey-blonde hair, peachy skin, and enormous, grey-blue eyes, fringed with thick, curling lashes. Top of the class too, without ever appearing swanky or swotty.

In other words, the sort of girl I would usually have run a mile from. I mean, who needs the competition, especially when you're going through a dumpy, spotty, grumpy phase yourself? But Bethany wanted to befriend me and for a while I went along with it, for I had, dear reader, an interior motive: I wanted to copy her homework.

Naturally, the saintly Bethany was unhappy with the arrangement. I appealed to her softer side, however, squeezing out a few tears for good measure. I've always had a persuasive nature.

It didn't work out. It turned out I was no better at copying than at studying. When our marks came back, I hadn't moved from my position at the bottom of the class. *Can't even spell*

Bunsen burner! Miss Bohenna had scrawled over my science practical in shouty red ink.

Surveying the bloody carnage of my exercise books, I knew the days of my one and only schoolgirl friendship were numbered. I dumped Bethany in the changing rooms after hockey – a sport at which, with her long legs, she naturally excelled.

For weeks afterwards, she sent me little poems and shot me sad, conciliatory looks from under those annoyingly lengthy lashes. I didn't waver. Even at that tender age I realised friendship for its own sake was a luxury I didn't need.

For five years I was happy ploughing my solitary furrow at St Jude's. Then disaster. Silv joined the school. I was by then in the fifth form. Already taller than me, Silv soon eclipsed me in other ways, winning prizes and topping tests.

I never understood why Silv was so hard-working. While I spent my time buffing my nails, giving my hair its daily hundred strokes, and devouring every word of *Vogue*, she was swotting for science competitions, captaining the lacrosse team and auditioning for school productions. It was small consolation that it was Romeo she was cast to play, not Juliet.

Silv had the last laugh, of course. University degree, career as a GP, big look-at-me house in Teddington; six bedrooms, indoor pool, the works. Solid, sensible chartered surveyor husband, who buys her flowers every Friday evening, even if they haven't had a row. Four grown-up kids. All six footers. All still speaking to her. And in August, the whole merry gang gather together for fun and frolics in their villa on the Algarve. Silv sends me postcards every year: *'Chaos here with the little ones but wouldn't miss it for the world.'* Suppose she means the grandkids.

She's invited me, of course. Many times. Generous old Silv. Couldn't face it. Just the thought of all that family togetherness gives me the heebies. But bully for you, Carthorse.

Shit, shitterty shit! I've only just started and already I've gone and depressed myself. Fix me a drink, will you? Where are you going? Tray's here, on the window sill. Allow me to introduce you. Sapphie, this is Boy. Boy, this is my very good friend Bombay Sapphire. I'd offer you one but you're on duty, so to speak. No ice, plenty of slice. What do you mean, mouldy? Don't be such a fuss-arse. Cut that bit off. Lovely. It's thirsty work, being a lady authoress. Don't drown it!

Now listen up, important staff announcement. Three things I need to keep me happy. Without them, the muse won't flow and if the muse won't flow I may lose my customary placid temperament. You paying attention? Well, look as if you are then. The three things are: Sapphie. You've met her already – top me up, a proper measure this time. That's one. The other two are Gypsies and Cameroons. They are my staples. See that I never, and I mean never, run out of any of them. You can have a good dunk with a Gypsy. Oh, and coconut on the Cameroons. I'm old school on that one.

Hush. No more of your moronic questions. Off you pop. Yes – now. I'll just close my... No, no, leave that where I can reach it. What? Tiresome child. Here you are, warm from my panting bosom. I'll be wanting change, mind.

Still here? What is it now? I suppose so. After the masterly way you dealt with my pot de chambre, *I can hardly refuse. So, yes. If it means that much to you, you can have the sodding job.*

5.

BRADLEY

Yaay! I got it. She's well wavy when she tells me, mind, but I reckon it's still sound. Drunk or sober, she's give me the job. Two mornings a week. Tuesdays and Thursdays. She don't even blink when I say, 'Cash in hand, OK?'

I go to the shops, her instructions rattling round in my brain. I take the long way round. Scoping out the area, see? It's well cold out there. Wind whistling up Bayswater Road, whipping the last yellow leaves off of the trees. No matter how deep I stick my fists into the pockets of my hoodie, my fingers is about to drop off.

When I get back, she's in her sitting room, still in her nightie, mind. Been helping herself some more, she has, and ain't too clever. Has a go at me about the shopping. All wrong, she tells me, shouting and calling me 'idiot boy'. But, honestly, how was I to know?

Gypsies, she's asked for. What am I supposed to make of that? Biscuits, I manage to fathom out in the end. Gypsy Cream biscuits. But can I find any? Not in any of the places I go. And I ask all over. Get custard creams instead. You'd think I'd tried to feed her rat poison, the face she pulls. But she still scoffs the whole packet, I notice. There's not even any crumbs left.

Then there's Cameroons. That's macaroons to you and me. Find out when I pluck up courage to go into the Waitrose off of the Edgware Road and ask. They look lush in the chiller, snuggled up together in their own little box, two pink, two pale green and two coffee-coloured. Real cream inside. My mouth waters just looking at them. But no, they're wrong too, she says. No coconut. She has a right mare at me, then manages to force down four of them.

Not that her ranting gets to me. One thing I'm good at, one skill I got down to a tee, is being given a bollocking. You could say that's my area of expertise, my specialist subject. Ma. Dom. Teachers. Coppers. Kids at school. It don't matter who it is. I can stand there long as you like, sucking it up, looking all sorry an' that. Don't bother me one bit 'cause my head is miles away. For instance, while she's giving me a right tongue lashing about what I bought, I'm wondering if the pink macaroon she's left will taste different from the green one. Waste not, want not, eh?

OK, so I get that she's bats, as well as being a juicer, but that don't matter. I'm in there and, you never know, could work in my favour, her being a sarnie short.

Let her sleep it off while I make a start on the kitchen. No time like the present. Can't wait to get stuck into that washing-up. Up to my elbows in hot, soapy water and I'm happy. Seeing them dishes and plates come out of the suds gleaming, rinsing them off, drying them on a brand new tea-towel I found in the airing cupboard – 'present from Bridgetown', still in its wrapper – wiping out her cupboards and stacking up her plates, all neat and tidy, cup handles facing the same way, glasses lined up in straight rows, well, it gives me a good feeling. Like I've done something useful with my day. Been a while since I felt like that.

Time goes quick and when my four hours is up, I go to say cheerio, though I been listening to her snoring like a pig all the while I'm in the kitchen. Still it's only manners. Like I thought, there she is, head back on the sofa, dribble snail-sliming its way down her chin. I decide to get off home. As I'm leaving, I have to pass the locked room. Rest my head against the door, wondering what could be in there. Still, there's no rush.

Ain't due back till Thursday. Dom tries to pump me, of course. I don't tell him nothing. Just about how I had to shout through the letterbox and let meself in. And how minging it all is. Funny thing is, all day Wednesday, when I should be chilling, I'm thinking about the old girl in that tip. So, when Thursday rolls around, I make sure I set off in good time.

Got enough left over from her shopping to take the Tube this time. Worked it out on my phone. Bakerloo to Paddington, then walk the last bit down Sussex Gardens, cross at the lights and you're there. Easy peasy.

When I let meself in, I get the shock of my life. She's sitting behind the front door, perched on a kitchen stool with a face like thunder. She's dressed an' all. Leastways, she's pulled on some awful skirt thing round her middle, over the nightie, and some trackie bottoms, and shoved her arms into a thick, knitted thing what's so stretched it almost reaches down to the floor. Hard to tell what colours they are. The jumper's a sort of patchwork of greys. The skirt could have been yellow. No mistaking what she's got wound round her neck: that purple thing. None of it ever seen the inside of a washing machine, you ask me. She's done her face again. I wish she wouldn't. She looks a right munter. I try not to stare. She gets the wrong idea when I stare.

'Where the sod have you been?' she goes, not hardly waiting for me to get through the door. 'Do you know how long I've been sitting here? The milk's off and I've run out of bickies. I could have died of malnutrition. I've a good mind to sack you right now.'

'It's Thursday, missus,' is all I can think of to say.

'As if that weren't bad enough,' she rattles on, not paying a blind bit of notice, 'I've had so many memories bubbling up inside my brain, I can't think straight.' She presses her fingers into her forehead like she's trying to stop her thoughts escaping. 'And who did I have to tell them to? No one.'

Her voice wobbles and round her eyes, watery at the best of times, it's all wet. She's been blubbing. I understand now. She ain't vexed at me. Not really. She's upset because she's scared. Scared I'd scarpered. Scared she was on her own again. File away that little gem in my noddle for later.

'I come here Tuesdays and Thursdays,' I go, my voice gentle. I move more closer and get a vinegar blast of old lady hum up my nostrils. 'That's what we agreed. Yesterday was Wednesday. Today's Thursday.'

'You sure about that?'

'Hundred per cent, Miss E,' I go, wanting to get the chat over with. 'Shall I get you out of this draughty old hall and into a comfy chair with a nice cuppa?'

'What did you call me?'

'Miss E,' I go, straight off regretting it. 'That's probably disrespectful. Sorry.'

'On the *contraire*,' she goes, wiping her eyes on her baggy sleeve and getting to her feet. 'I like it. You should always address me thus.'

Ain't never seen her standing up before. She's not what

you'd call tall. As I'm helping her along, she don't hardly come up to my shoulders. Five foot at most, and almost the same around the middle, I reckon. Like a squidgy old ball, balanced on a pair of tiny, high-heeled slippers. If you was to give her a good push, reckon she'd roll.

'Miss E,' she murmurs, trying it out for size as we trot along together. 'I like it. I like it very much.' And she flashes me a big old smile.

Takes me a long time to get used to them mood swings, I can tell you.

'Do you have to do that when I'm trying to concentrate?' she grumbles.

I'm not even in the same room as her. She's in the sitting room listening to some bloke on the radio yapping on about gardening. Why she bothers beats me. It's not as if she's got so much as a window box. I'm in her hallway, dusting the row of black and white photos she's got hanging on the wall. The more I look, the more filthier they are. So I take them down from their hooks and give them a good spray and a wipe.

While I'm doing that, I have a nose, of course. Took years ago, judging by the girls' short skirts and the blokes' long hair. No Beatles this time. Just girls and blokes enjoying theirselves. Holding up glasses at a party. Arsing about on a beach. Posing on the bonnet of an old-school motor. Can't help but smile. Looks like they'd be a fun crew to hang with – if they wasn't OAPs by now.

One blonde girl grabs my eye. She's in a couple of them. Despite the old-fashioned hair and the clothes, you can tell she's a looker. I pay one photo particular attention. It's of her on her own. She's sitting curled up, making long, black shadows across a wood floor, bare legs tucked under. Her hand's on her shoulder, chin resting on her arm, and she's tilting her head, half-smiling at the camera. What with the dark shadows and the way she's sitting, you can't tell if she's naked or not. I think she is. Her face is beautiful. Glowing. Eyes wide and pure like a little kid's. Mouth half-open in a wicked smile that's anything but pure. Man, but she is hot.

Some supermodel. Gotta be.

I pop my head round the door. 'Miss E. Who is…?'

A long piggy snore cuts me off.

Takes me ages to rehang them pictures. I line them up with a tape measure, so they's spot-on.

I'm working in her kitchen, on my hands and knees, scrubbing the floor.

'Boyeeee,' she calls out, in that way she has. 'I've been thinking.'

I go through to her sitting room, wiping my hands on a clean cloth.

''Bout what, Miss E?'

'Your shopping skills leave much to be desired, but I have to admit you've done an adequate job on the cleaning. Furthermore, I can see that, with my guidance, you could have potential. So…' – she folds her hands together like she's praying – 'we said two mornings a week, I believe. What if we made it every day, Monday to Friday? There's so much to be done. Say, ten till four? Would that suit?'

'Every day?' I gawp, not taking it in. 'You mean, a full-time job?'

'Of course, if you have other calls on your precious time…'

'No, no,' I jump in. 'I mean, yes. That would be prime.'

'I'm assuming that's a "yes".'

'Cash in hand?'

She bobs her head.

'Quality.' I have a thought. 'Is it for the book? You wanting me here full-time so we can get on with writing this book?'

'That – and the occasional errand.' And she's off, going on about how she's told her girl to cancel her Waitrose delivery on account of how they was always getting it wrong. 'If I've told the little man once, I've told him a dozen times, my digestion cannot tolerate own-brand gin,' she goes, sticking out her tongue and gagging, like she's chugging cough mixture.

I smile but there's something on my mind. Something I gotta get out in the open. 'Thing is, I don't hardly like to say this but, looking round an' that, I was wondering, have you got the readies – for full-time wages, I mean?'

She startles me by tipping her head back and laughing. 'You've found me out, Boy. I'm skint. Broke. Haven't a bean. You've hit the hammer right on the whatsit: I can't afford you.'

My stomach drops to my kicks. *That's it then. Batty old girl's just been winding me up. There ain't no full-time job.*

'Might as well be off then,' I go.

'Look at his face,' she coos, screwing up them wrinkly lips. 'Don't look so miserable. *I* may not be able to afford you but *Tabby* most certainly can. Have you any idea what corporate lawyers make these days? Of course, you don't. As much as premium league footballers, I should imagine. I'd rather see my darling daughter in person, of course, but in her absence, her generous monthly allowance comes in very handy.'

'Why the heck didn't you say that in the first place?' I mumble under my breath. I'm well teed off with being messed about.

She hears. 'What did you say?'

'Nothing. Just wondering if the deal's still a goer?'

'The deal is most definitely a "goer", as you so vulgarly put it. Now, sit,' she orders, like I'm her pet Staffie. 'I feel another of my tales coming on.'

'Fire away,' I tell her, perking up. 'Ready when you are, Miss E.'

6.

ELOISE

I couldn't stay at St Jude's forever, much as I'd have like to. It was left to Terry to break the devastating news. I'd have to leave and get a job. A job! Me! The thought had never crossed my mind.

Terry sat me down. 'What do yow plan on doing with yower life, ower Elaine? What do yow want to be?' he said, wiping bloody hands down his apron.

Horrified at the red imprints, that hideous name and the thought of getting a job, I was rendered speechless.

''Cause, there's not many as'll tek on a wench with no qualifications and no love for 'ard graft,' Terry went on.

'I could take highers,' I said, recovering my voice. 'Go to university… or something.'

Terry exploded into laughter. 'That's a good 'un. Our Silv, mebbe. Not yow, angel. Yow're a lot of things but university material yow en't.'

'Or stay here and help you and Mummy?'

Another explosion. 'Drive Mother round the bend and me into bankruptcy, more like. No, angel. Yow're coming up for seventeen. Me and yower mother both left school at fourteen, yower mother for the New Street pickle factory, me for the slaughter house.'

I squirmed. I didn't like being reminded of my parents' lowly beginnings.

'The time 'as come, he continued, 'for yow to mek yower own way in the world. Yow'll thank us for it one day.' Terry stroked his chin thoughtfully, leaving a crimson streak across the stubble. 'If yow've no suggestions, 'ow about working in an office? Nothing too fancy. Just office-fodder. If I was to shell out for yow to go to secretarial college for a year, learn shorthand, typing and filing, 'ow would yow like that?'

Shorthand? Typing? Filing?' The words sounded strange to my ears. 'But Daddy,' I said, 'that's the sort of work the sec mod girls do.'

'Aye, angel, yow're right,' Terry sighed. 'Yow'd never manage it.'

I proved him wrong. I *did* go to secretarial college, a nasty red-brick establishment, and, a year later, left with certificates in filing and general studies. Never got the hang of typing or shorthand.

It was, all in all, a dreary year but my time there opened my eyes. Just as St Jude's had given me the taste for a more refined lifestyle, Spon End Secretarial College made me realise that the West Midlands was too small a stage for me. I needed somewhere bigger, better and more sophisticated. I needed London.

As soon as I could, I wiped the grit of Coventry from my brown suede, kitten-heeled Mary Janes and boarded a train for the capital, heart full of hope, head full of dreams, handbag full of ten bob notes from Urse's emergency housekeeping tin.

Note to Boy: Splendid. Now we're on our way. You'll like

this next bit. The Metropolis. The world of work. The losing of cherries. I do love a good cherry popping tale, don't you? Seduction. Deflowering. Losing your virginity. Oh, look at him blush.

But that's for later. I have something else up my sleeve now. Ever heard of Osh, Boy? Osh. O. S. H. No? Well, you're in for a real treat. To the kitchen. Chop chop!

7.

BRADLEY

Beginning to wonder if this job was such a great idea.

She's got me cooking, see. Leastways, her version of it. She's hyped. Keeps going on about this stuff 'osh'. I've never heard of it. She spells it out. O.S.H. Tells me how delicious it is, how much fun we're gonna have making it. I imagine all sorts but what I don't imagine is what it actually turns out to be: a pudding. Just a pudding her old ma used to make her back in the day.

Sends me shopping. Only two things on my list. *Blackcurrant poorie. Eevap.* Don't have the foggiest what neither of them is. Drones in the supermarket can't help with the poorie, so I get jam. Not the cheap stuff. Extra fruity preserve. Have more luck with the eevap. Turns out to be milk in a tin.

You has to whisk and whisk the eevap, she tells me, till it goes thick. After about a half hour with a fork, my wrist is about to drop off and nothing is happening. Milk runs off like water. I give up. Ain't got the patience. Not with her at my elbow, getting on my nerves, making out like this is the most excitingest thing anyone's ever done, telling me to 'put more effort in' and how 'scrumptious' it's gonna be.

In the end, I put the radio on to drown her wittering. Just

my luck, it's a sixties show. Before I know it, she's jigging round the kitchen, singing along to some ancient old song from before the war or something.

'*I whatsit it. I whatsit it,*' she warbles. 'Oooh, I remember this one. *I… dum-de-dum-de-dumdy-dumdy-dum.* Perry and the Face-achers. They were fab.' She holds out her claws. She only wants me to dance with her.

What the heck, I think to meself. Only I don't know where to put my hands.

'For goodness' sake,' she goes, taking them and plonking them on her waist – at least, where her waist should be. My fingers sinks in down to the knuckles. Then she stretches up – like I say, she's a proper short-arse – and puts her hands on my shoulders. We shuffle round the table, her jigging and humming, me feeling a right melon.

Thing is, though, after a bit I get into it. The song – proper cheery it is – gets to me and I find I'm doing some jigging meself. Then the music stops and the bloke on the radio prattles some rubbish. Her face darkens.

'Unhand me, Boy,' she goes, pushing me away. 'Such familiarity. What are you thinking? Back to your duties.'

Back and forth, her moods swing, like one of them old-style, big old clocks.

It's supposed to go in the fridge to set, the osh stuff. No way am I gonna put food anywhere near that filthy thing. Stand the bowl in the pantry instead. It's cool in there. She keeps opening the door and lifting the cloth I put over it. 'Just checking,' she goes. I know what she's up to. Having a sly dip. Disgusting.

Course it don't set. In the end, to keep her happy I pour some into two cereal bowls. She takes a gynormous spoonful, making 'mmmmm' noises. I get a teaspoon and have a little sip from the edge. Almost vom in my mouth. She clocks my expression.

'It's an acquired taste,' she goes, swallowing her spoonful in one big gulp. 'Like black pudding and modern jazz.'

The osh sits untouched in the pantry for a coupla days. Then I swill it away. She never mentions it again, I'm happy to say.

Funny thing is, long after the osh is history, that stupid song stays with me. Keep finding meself humming it, as I'm cleaning and putting stuff away. And a few days later when I put my head round the living-room door when she's supposed to be listening to her afternoon play, I catch her at it too.

'*I whatsit it, I whatsit it…*'

Me and my big gob. I don't mean to tell Dom nothing but I'm that stoked when I go home, he's onto me straightaway. Stretched out on the settee, he is, telly blaring, skinning up a J. Ma, as usual, is nowheres to be seen.

'What's that stupid face for?' he goes. 'You up to something?'

'Started the job, that's all.'

'Oh yeah?' That look comes across his face, that scheming look. 'So, spill. What is it?'

'Just cleaning. Old lady's place.'

He sits up. 'Where's her crib?'

'Up West.'

'That so? She minted? Sounds like she's minted.'

'No. She's old, like I said.'

'They can be crafty, them wrinklies. Make out they only got their pensions, arses out their knickers, cat-food toasties for their dinners. Then you poke around in the back of the wardrobe and – whaddya know! – you happen upon a tea caddy bursting with folding stuff.'

'She don't have nothing, I'm telling you.'

'You're kidding, ain't you? Don't believe in banks, them greyheads. She must have something. What about jewels? Them old tarts love their rings and bangles. You checked? You haven't, have you? First chance you get, you take a proper look – wardrobe, dressing table, back of her cupboards, under the mattress, inside the cistern – everywhere you can think where a sly old witch might stow her valuables. You find anything, I'm the first to know.' He shoves his face in mine. 'You get me?'

I try to stare him out, but he just laughs and goes back to skinning up. 'Now we got that cleared up, three sugars in mine, bruv,' he goes, lolling back. 'Thanks for asking.'

Go by bus this time. Number 16 to Marble Arch, then it's just a stroll along the Bayswater Road.

I'm in a good mood. Been looking forward to tackling that fridge ever since I seen it. It's gone ten but she's still spark out in bed, so I make a start. It ain't such a shock the second time, though the mouldy smell still knocks me back. But this time I'm ready for it. Locked and loaded. On the way over, I've ducked into the minimart and got tooled up. Marigolds, bleach, sponges, a fat roll of bin bags and a whole tub of wet wipes. First off, I dump the food, dishes an' all, in the bags. Then I set to.

Black, the sponges turn. The muck is that bad. Pretty soon, I'm getting there. That fridge's insides is beginning to shine. I weren't wrong about something moving in there neither. I walk the fridge out from the wall and squint round the back. There's this tube and round it, a jagged hole where the plastic's been nibbled. It's one hell of a mess. Bits of chewed-up plastic and something what looks like chocolate hundreds and thousands. Know what that is, all right. Mouse poo. Better get a trap.

I clean up best as I can and stuff a piece of cloth in the hole. Don't suppose it will stop the little beggars for long but I can't just leave it, can I? I'm giving the fridge door a last polish when I hear her from the bedroom. A wet cough. A little guff. She's awake. Bedroom door clicks open and I hear the tap-tap of her slippers – mules she calls them – on the lino. *Going for a jimmy,* I think to meself.

'Morning, Miss E,' I call out over my shoulder, still polishing away. 'Anything I can get you from the shops, only I—'

'Morning, Boy.'

She's right behind me. I jump out my skin. *How'd she do that?*

'Surprised?' she goes, a twinkle in her eye. 'Just making sure you're not up to anything. You know, poking your nose into my private things, having a quiet wank in the pantry.' I blush to my roots. 'That's what you young boys get up to, isn't it?' she goes. 'When no one's got their eye on you.' She sighs. 'Evidently not in this case. Here you are, slaving away like the little goody two-shoes you are.' She plonks herself down at the kitchen table. 'Be a dear and make some tea. I feel like a chat. Some sophisticated conversation. Come on, chop chop.'

I get a brew on.

'So,' she goes, arms crossed. 'About what shall we converse?'

Search me, I think, and carry on fiddling with the kettle an' that.

'What are your hobbies, Boy?'

'Hobbies?'

She sighs. 'Interests, past-times, leisure pursuits? I assume you have some?'

'Well,' I go, 'I like wildlife.'

'Chasing through the hedgerows, searching for birds and butterflies? Taking long walks through the meadows?' She takes in a gynormous breath, like she's inhaling a lungful of countryside. Then she lets it out with a cough. 'Never cared for that sort of thing myself.'

'Watching it on the telly,' I go. 'That's more my style.'

'Oh,' she goes, sagging. 'How's that tea coming along?'

I pour and we sit in silence. She taps her finger on the table.

I feel I've disappointed her, so I go, 'Yeah. I like that David Attenborough best. Lord Attenborough. He's the bomb. Thing is about Lord David, Miss E, he's dead posh and educational an' that, but he don't bore your nuts off.'

'So much for sophisticated conversation,' she goes, folding her hands. 'What about this brother of yours, Dominic, was it?'

Flipping heck. Didn't see that one coming. How come Dom manages to wheedle hisself into every corner of my life? Half the time, she can't recall my name but his trips off of her tongue just like that.

'Six years older than me, he is,' I go. 'Lives with Ma and me. He's a window cleaner.'

Well, I can't hardly say he's a psycho stoner with sidelines in dealing, housebreaking and moped mugging, can I? Anyways, it's true. Sort of. When he's short of readies, he does wander about the streets with a ladder and a bucket. But he don't have no water in his bucket and he don't wash no windows neither. I know. He gets me to tag along sometimes as lookout.

'Eight quid for one clean,' he tells the punters, big smile plastered across his mush. 'Only the best shammies, mind. Tell you what, seeing as how I'm building up the round and I've taken a shine, bung us forty and I'll do all your windows, once a month for six months. Regular like clockwork, sparkling like diamonds. Whaddya say?'

And he sticks out his hand and looks them in the eye, like he's the most friendliest, most trustworthiest bloke you could ever wish to meet. There's not many who'll fall for his line but there's enough. Old ladies like Miss E mostly. Once, he cleared two hundred in three hours.

'And the beauty of it is,' Dom goes to me one night, lying on his bed, slurping and burping on a tinny, 'it's a month before the stupid cows even catch on they been had.' He sniggers fit to bust.

Don't tell Miss E any of this though, do I? I leave it at 'window cleaner' and go back to wiping out her salad drawer.

'Maybe I should get your brother round here,' she goes, looking round. 'These windows haven't been cleaned since… they haven't ever been cleaned, as far as I know.'

'No,' I go, louder than I meant. 'There's no need for that. I can do your windows for you. No problem. I'll add it to my list.' And I hold out my 'to do' list. The one with 'buy mousetrap' on it.

She don't even glance at it. She's onto something else, one of her tales. Dom is clean forgot. While she's yabbering, I spend a good fifteen minutes getting the lime scale off of her sink. 'Shiny Sinks' it's called, the stuff. Nice orange bottle. Costs but it does what it says, all right. Sink comes up a treat. Smells nice an' all. Dead clean, like that lemony bleach. All the while I'm scrubbing, she's talking at me and I'm thinking about what Dom said. About the back of the wardrobe.

'And I haven't seen the Aga Khan from this day to that,' she goes. 'What do you say to that?' And she knocks back the last of her cuppa.

'Amazing,' I go, snapping off the Marigolds. 'Better get meself down to them shops sharpish.'

'Oh no!' she goes, clapping a hand to her mouth. 'You didn't write any of that down. Why didn't you stop me? Naughty, naughty.' She leans over and gives the back of my hand a slap. Quite hard. It's all I can do not to laugh.

'Not to worry. You can tell me about Mr Kahn again when I

get back from the shops. With your shopping an' that.' I don't move. I'm waiting for her to cotton on.

'What?' she goes, raising an eyebrow. 'Oh, I see. Another cash injection. What happened to the money I gave you yesterday?'

'Had to buy all this cleaning stuff, didn't I?'

She hesitates, screwing her mouth round, like she's got something stuck in her teeth, then she says, 'Oh, take it. Tabby can afford it.' And she peels off another coupla twenties from the roll she keeps down her front. This rate I'll have that Puffa by next week.

8.

ELOISE

London – what a shit-hole. Instead of attending garden parties at Buck House, taking tea at the Ritz, or shopping for caviar in Harrods Food Halls, I found myself homeless on a windy corner of the Euston Road, drizzle ruining my hair and wet pages of the *Evening News* plastered against my legs. But I was the daughter of the Pie King of the West Midlands. I wasn't going to be put off so easily. Damp but undaunted, I straightened my back and sallied forth to find somewhere to stay.

That somewhere, dear reader, was the Brompton Guest House. From the outside, it was shabby and seedy; from the inside, even worse. The cracks in its walls were big enough to put your fingers in; the wallpaper peeled off like those curly wigs lawyers wear; and orange gunge streaked alarmingly from the pipes.

Heart sinking, I rang the desk bell. When the manager eventually slithered from a backroom, he was unshaven, a napkin tucked into the neck of his vest, a ciggie dangling from the corner of his mouth.

'Can't a man even finish his haddock without…?' he began. His tone changed when he saw me. 'Hello, hello. What brings *you* here this time of night?' he said, wiping greasy hands down his vest and giving me a look. It was a look I was to grow familiar with: lust. Every instinct told me to turn on my heel – but where would I go?

'I'd like a room.'

'Single, or are you expecting company?' the man asked, squeezing one bulging eye into a grotesque wink. I let him know in no uncertain terms I was looking for single accommodation and none of his backchat, thank you very much. Meekly, he showed me to a room.

I almost fainted when I saw it. Everything was awash with brown. Ye gods, was I to be haunted my entire life by that odious colour? I tried the bed. The mattress sagged almost to the floor and the bedsprings squeaked out a rusty protest as I sat down.

'Best contraceptive in the world, a noisy bed,' the manager said, risking a sly glance in my direction.

'What did I just say about you and your cheek?' I snapped.

Cheap and dismal though the Brompton was, I knew I wouldn't be able to manage the rent for more than a couple of weeks. What was I going to do when Urse's ten bobs ran out? There was only one option, drastic though it was. An office-fodder job.

First thing in the morning (well, around eleven), I set off in my best interview outfit – a tweed suit in maroon and fiery orange – for Oxford Street. Why there? Because, dear reader, those damp *Evening Standard* pages that had wrapped themselves round my slim ankles had contained an advertisement: 'The Feminine Touch Secretarial Agency. Girl Fridays wanted. 10 Hanover Street, Mayfair.'

Even fresh from the Midlands, I knew that Mayfair was where the rich people hung out.

The Feminine Touch, as you may have anticipated, was another let-down.It was located at the top of a steep flight of dark, narrow stairs above a bookies and presided over by a middle-aged woman encased in tight navy Crimplene. With the minimum of formalities, I was sent on my way to my first – and only – interview. By the next morning, I was seated in the typing pool of an engineering company off Grosvenor Square.

There was one problem. As you may recall, if you've been paying attention, I'd failed shorthand and typing. My mistake-strewn, Swiss-cheese letters did not impress the typing pool supervisor. I'd have been given the sack on the first day if it hadn't been for the bosses. They, being men, were more indulgent, overlooking my shortcomings in exchange for a winning smile or a sexy wiggle.

So. I was in London. I had somewhere to live. I had money. But I was miserable. Imprisoned in a stuffy office every day, trapped in a sordid guest house every evening – this was not the life I'd dreamed of when I'd boarded that train to the metropolis.

Luckily for me, I'd been office-fodder for only two months, when I happened upon my express ticket out of there, in the portly shape of Jolyon Slaughter.

There. That'll do for today. I simply don't have any more in me to give. It's more tiring than it looks, this lady authoressing lark. Don't think I'll be stirring for a while. I shall remain en boudoir. *Tell any callers, I'll receive them in there.*

What? Yes, off you go. Just the usual basics. Fresh lemons and tonic. Cameroons and Gypsies of course. And I have a fancy for minestrone soup and an onion flan – are you writing this down?

And for dessert, Pop-Tarts, the fudge ones. Away with you, linger no longer.

A digital what? Why? How much for this digi-thingy? How much! See what you can get for forty. My brassiere, I fear, is quite, quite empty. Of money, at any rate. Oh, what a prude he is. Here, pass me that handbag. Time for a trip to the hole-in-the-wall gang. Minicab drivers are such ill-mannered oafs, don't you find? There they sit, picking their teeth, while you struggle across the traffic to wrestle with the wretched money machine. Never occurs to them to offer to do it for you.

Oh, would you? That would be gallant of you. Here's my card. The what? Got it written down somewhere. Tabby says never to write it down, but what's a girl to do? What shall we say? Two hundred? That should tide us over for a while. Now, be off with you. I need my forty winks.

9.

BRADLEY

Tottenham Court Road, she tells me, that's the place to go. There's a little man there what she buys her gadgets from. What gadgets, I'm thinking. Her stuff goes back to the ark. But I do like she says, 'cause I ain't explored up that way before and I figure it must be worth a look. It ain't. Just a bunch of big shops like anywhere else, loads of them. I walk up and down but I can't see the one what she's on about, Gerry's Electricals. I end up in Currys. Nice little piece of kit. Should do the job lovely. It's not like she'll know the difference, is it?

After that, I do her bit of shopping in a supermarket. I'm about to head back but I still got some cash burning a hole in my jeans. She's never gonna miss the price of a coffee, I figure. I stop outside a caff. Aromazz, it's called. I blow on my hands. Wind is like a knife. Looks proper toasty inside. There's a girl serving. Girls is usually the worst but by now my hands is tingling with the cold. Drag my frozen fingers through my hair, pull my beanie down till I can hardly see out, and, head well down, push open the door. A blast of lovely hot air greets me.

'I'll have one of them. Large,' I go, pointing to the picture.

'One *cappuccino grande* coming up,' the girl sings out.

'Cuppa what?' I go, joking like.

She laughs. I like her right from the off. She don't gawp, see. Her eyes don't keep skipping up to the place just above my left eyebrow. That's rare in a girl. It don't hurt, of course, that she's small and pretty. Bit too much make-up and hair dyed dead black but friendly, greeny-brown eyes and a turned-up mouth what smiles even when she ain't smiling, if you get me.

She makes the coffee, carefully pouring in the steamed milk, taking her time. When she hands the cup over, I see she's done a pattern. A leaf with some swirls round it. Dead artistic.

'Fancy,' I go.

She laughs again and slips a little biscuit onto the saucer. 'And one *biscotti* for the gentleman.'

Feel her eyes on me as I weave my way through the tables, past half a dozen other customers. I sit down by the window and take a sip. The coffee is so hot it numbs the tip of my tongue. Sit back to wait for it to cool. Can't seem to sit still, feeling her watching me. Take another sip and this time I end up with a milk moustache. When I get up to fetch a paper serviette, I glance over to where she's wiping the tables. She's smiling but I can't tell if it's a proper one or just how her mouth turns up.

'I was wondering, Molly,' I go, clocking the name on her badge as I'm leaving. 'You being an expert on biscuits an' that, if you know where I could get hold of some Gypsy Creams?'

'Oh, you,' she goes. 'You are *such* a joker.'

I don't get it but I laugh anyhow. One of the other waitresses, tubby with dirty blonde hair, nudges her in the ribs, as if to say, 'You better watch that one.'

Molly holds out a card. 'You get points for every coffee you buy. It's worth coming back.'

'Might do that an' all,' I go. 'Laters.'

'Did you get it?' Miss E calls out the second she hears my key. She's that amped. All the while I'm undoing the packaging, she's leaning over me, having a poke, getting in the way. But when I hand it over, her face falls.

'I was expecting something bigger,' she goes. She giggles. 'Not the first time I've had cause to say that.' I don't react to her potty mouth. She turns it over. 'What does this do?' She jabs at the buttons, long white nails clicking against the casing.

'Give it here,' I go. 'State of the art, that is.'

She sniffs as if she don't believe a word. 'Where does one insert the tape?'

'No tape. It's digital. Five hundred hours capacity. Two gig memory.'

'Oh, you young people and your slang. Show me.'

I press a button and hold it out, signalling for her to say something. She clears her throat.

'This is Eloise Slaughter speaking,' she shouts. 'Welcome, dear reader, to this, my tome.' I wave for her to stop, button-punch some more, then jump a mile, as her voice pumps out full volume, loud enough to deafen Wembley. 'Wonderful,' she goes, clapping her hands like a kid at a party. 'How much?'

'Forty-nine, ninety-nine. Down from fifty-four, ninety-nine. Bargain.' I bite my lip. If she goes for it, I'll have enough for that jacket. 'Nothing's too good for your book, Miss E,' I go, pushing it.

She looks serious, having me worried. 'You're bleeding me dry but I suppose it's worth it.' Then she laughs, so I don't feel so bad.

Since then she's been at it day and night. Wants me there, of course, to push the buttons, though a two-year-old could work it. Funny thing is, when she's remembering the old days, what she's got up to, she's totally with it, sharp as a tack. She yabbers on, doing the voices, acting it out an' everything. Good as some of them radio plays what she loves. Seems like it's crystal in her mind. But when it comes to what's happening today, the fog rolls in. Have you brushed your teeth? Where have you left your glasses? How many sugars do you take? – Stuff like that and she's proper flummoxed.

Faded, that's her. Patchy, like the old rug in the hall. Some places you can see the colour coming through, others it's wearing into holes. Sometimes when I come into the room, she has a look on her face, like she's looking right through me into the past.

Don't never want to get old.

10.

ELOISE

Is it on? You sure? What light? Well, if you say so.

Ahem. Jolyon. Jolyon Slaughter.

Shouting, who's shouting? I am merely articulating clearly into this little silver machine. You young people would do well to follow my example. Tits and teeth. No mumbling. Come on. Bugger. I had it clear in my head until you butted in. If you are to remain as my aman… my helpmeet, Boy, you'll have to learn to shut your trap when the muse is upon me. Now…

Jolyon Slaughter. The very name drips class. Jo-ly-on. Those round, overfed vowels. Slaughter. Those brutish… erm… *What are those other things that aren't vowels? Never mind.*

I was making my way along the guest house's threadbare carpet to the shared bathroom, preparing to soak off the tedium of the typing pool, when suddenly – booof! – I bumped into him. Jolyon. Forsaking his normal West One haunts, he was slumming it, he told me later, paying a visit to an old school chum who, having fallen on hard times, had taken up residence in the bedsit at the top of the Brompton.

It was a soft landing. Even back then Jolyon was well padded, though not unattractive in a cuddly, teddy bear sort of way. Back then, I wasn't sophisticated enough to appreciate that his suit was Savile Row and his tie real silk, or that the heady scent that filled the air as I bounced off him was a mixture of Parisian cologne and Cuban cigars. But I recognised the whiff of money all right.

'Hel-lo, gorgeous,' he purred. 'I'm Jolyon. Jolyon Slaughter.' And he gave a little bow. 'Whom do I have the pleasure…?'

'My name is El—' I remembered just in time, 'El-oise,' I said coolly, noting that impressive 'whom'. No one had ever whom-ed me before.

'Well, well, well. What do we have here?' Jolyon walked round me, smiling, showing small, yellow teeth. 'A working-class one? A Brummie, if I'm not mistaken.'

'I am *not* a Brummie,' I protested, my accent, I fear, slipping in the heat of the moment. 'I'm from the West Midlands, I'll have yow know.'

Jolyon doubled up with laughter. In my consternation, I dropped my washbag. Bending to retrieve it, our heads almost touched. I heard him gasp. When we straightened up, his pale eyes were wide and his mouth open. I glanced down. My dressing gown was gaping. In that moment, I realised Jolyon had been treated to a front-row view of my pert little puppies.

He rubbed his soft hands. 'Oh, how I love a naughty filly. Would you care to accompany me to a local hostelry for a little drinkie?'

I was in a dilemma. This man was a complete stranger. Urse always warned me never to accept drinks from strangers.

'What is it that you do for a living?' I asked, taking care with my pronunciation.

'I'm a chartered accountant,' he boomed. 'I look after other people's money. And I'm bloody good at it.'

That settled it. Five minutes later we were in the pub downing brandy and Bénédictines. After closing time, I gave him another peek at my puppies and that was it. I never went back to that engineering company.

Did I mean to flash him or did my robe come undone by some unseen force of its own? Or maybe it was one of those 'accidentally-on-purpose' Clement Freud moments? To this day, dear reader, I don't know. What I do know is, three months later Jolyon and I were man and wife.

Note to Boy: I may still have that robe somewhere. It would make a wonderful centre-piece for the Eloise Slaughter Museum of Fashion History. You know, in a glass case? Along the lines of Kate Middleclass's wedding gown. I can see it now. It may have been just a shapeless M&S quilted nylon thing but it played a pivotal role in my story.

11.

BRADLEY

What have I done? Let loose the Godzilla of Lanky Gate, that's what. I've had some bad ideas in my time but buying her that digital recorder is probably the most worst yet. She never stops. And the filth what comes out her gob.

I try to leave her to it, get on with the housework, but she won't have it. Wants me there, pressing the buttons, cocking an ear to her goings-on. I reckon half the time she only says what she says 'cause she knows it makes me feel uncomfortable. I try to hide it but it's not easy when your face has gone bright pillar box.

Still, apart from the mucky stuff, one thing is coming over loud and clear. Miss E used to be rolling in it. Can't help but wonder where it's all gone.

Got one. A mouse. In the new CatchEm Mousetrap. Humane, see? Don't much like the dirty little things with their pink wormy tails but that don't mean I want to off them. Let it go down by the wheelie bins.

Miss E laughs at me. 'You do realise, don't you, Boy, that the little buggers just wait until your back is turned, then scurry up the fire escape and back into my kitchen?'

'What do you think? I had a fancy for a change of style.'

Nearly jump out my skin. It's the first time, I seen her without the scarf thing wound round her head, though sometimes it slips to one side while she's dozing. When it does that, I tiptoe over and pull it straight.

She's took it off and stands, proud as punch, pink scalp showing through strands of grey. It don't help that she's tied back what's left of her hair with a ribbon. Pale blue it is. Or was. Honest, she looks like a gift-wrapped skull.

Her scalp ain't too healthy neither. Dom had a mate with a lurcher once. Rex he was called. The dog. Not the mate. This Rex got some sort of skin thing. They tried everything, even shampooed him with Ma's Head and Shoulders. Didn't do no good. Poor mutt's skin was peeling off in pieces big as cornflakes. One night, Dom and this mate took Rex and tied him up outside the vet's. Just left him there, tied to a drainpipe. Never heard what happened to the dog. Anyhow, that's what Miss E's head reminds me of. Mangy old Rex.

'Can't tie you up outside the vet's, though, can I?' I mutter. She sees from my face I don't like what she's done.

'You disapprove?'

'It's not that. You need your scarf thing,' I go, dodging the question, 'to keep out the cold. You lose half your body heat through your head, you know.'

She sticks out her bottom lip. 'It itches,' she says, raking her nails through her hair, leaving red tracks. 'And it's called a toque, ignoramus.'

'If you say so. And when was the last time it saw soap and water?'

She looks up at me from under her lashes, her naughty girl look. I take her toque to the bathroom to introduce it to soap and water. I rinse it through by hand. She trots after.

'Have you done something to the interior design in here?' she goes, peering round. 'You know I don't like people messing with my things.'

All I done is throw out her old towels. Thin, prickly, grey things they was. Got her half a dozen fluffy white ones. And a wooden towel rail to hang them over, so's they don't get baked rock hard on the radiator.

'Tidied it up a bit,' I say, rinsing out the toque. The water turns cloudy.

'Hmm. Next time check with me first,' she goes, but in the mirror I catch her giving the new towels a pat.

While her scarf thing dries, I sit her by the gas fire and make some grub. When I go looking for her with her bowl of leek and potato on a tray, she ain't in the sitting room no more. She's moved to the bedroom, sitting at her dressing table, staring at herself, pulling at her hair.

'What's happened to me, Boy?' she sighs. 'I used to have such lovely golden curls.'

'We could get you a wig.' The words is out of my mouth before I even think. Then I make it worse. 'Or them hair extensions, like all the girls have.'

Truth is, the only thing I know about girls' hair is what I seen in them shampoo ads, where it says on the screen, 'So-and-so is wearing natural hair extensions.'

But there's no going back now. Her eyes is lit up and she's away.

'All the girls, you say? Oh, yes! Why then we must have them. Absolutely. Never let it be said that Miss Eloise Slaughter is behind the times. One must keep *à la* mods and rockers?'

I must be getting carried away along with her, 'cause then I say, 'While I'm at it, why don't we get you some new make-up? How long you had this stuff anyhow?'

She runs her hands over the pots and jars, knocking over a few more. Then she has to tell me the ins and outs, don't she? How they was made specially for her delicate skin in Paris. How they was hand-mixed to her own recipe. How much they cost and how exclusive they are. I unscrew the top of one. Green goo lies on the bottom with a puddle of yellow liquid on top. Looks like a gob on the pavement. I take a sniff. It's rank.

'You can't put this on your face,' I tell her. 'Not with your skin being so delicate an' all. Tomorrow after I done your cleaning, I'll go on a shopping spree. Hair extensions and some new war paint.'

'That will be something to look forward to. Talking of which...' A sly look comes over her. 'You think I've forgotten, don't you? With all this talk of toques and Parisienne cosmetics? Well, I haven't. It's time, Boy, ready or not. Digi-whatsit at the ready? Right. The wedding night. The cherry popping. Lovely!'

12.

BRADLEY

Course, I ain't got the foggiest about extensions and make-up. That's girls' stuff. All I know is what I seen on them TV ads. But I know someone who does, someone with greeny-brown eyes and lips what smile even when she ain't smiling.

Molly's surprised when I turn up, I can tell. But in a good way. I've come back for my free drink, I tell her, giving her a flash of the pearlies. She says it don't work like that. All the time smiling.

'I'll bring it over,' she calls out, as I take my seat. 'The usual?'

Ain't never had a 'usual' before. Makes me feel good.

It's quiet. Only one other customer. Bloke on his laptop. After a few minutes he packs up and leaves.

'This is nice,' I call over the racket of the machine. 'Got the place to ourselves.'

Molly comes over with my drink. When she puts it down, she's got this funny look in her eye, like she's half excited, half embarrassed. Soon as I look into the cup, I get why. She's drawed something different in the foam. A heart.

I don't know what to say. She stands there, hands on hips, waiting, redness spreading up her neck to her cheeks.

Then I find the words. 'If I asked you out on a date, would you say yes?'

'Yes,' she says, no hesitation.

'OK,' I go. 'How about right now?'

'*This* is not a date,' Molly says. 'This is me helping you do your shopping. I didn't blag time off work for this.'

We're in Boots, the big one, and she's not so smiley now.

'It's not for me. It's for my boss,' I tell her. 'She's getting on a bit. Can't get out. Please. You gotta. You'd be doing me a real favour.'

She twists her mouth, not convinced. 'What you looking for exactly?'

'Make-up. And a wig. Or extensions. I ain't sure. Something to make her look better at any rate. That's why I need your help.'

That smile is back. 'Why didn't you say? If it's fashion and beauty, I'm in. I'm crazy about it. Why else do you think I'm slaving away in Manky Mazzies?' She gives a giggle. 'That's what we call it when Mr Argyros isn't around. Saving up, aren't I? I already paid for an FE course in the history of fashion but that was only in the evenings and the woman who taught us was a right frump. What I really want to do is go to uni. Fashion and textile design, that's my absolute dream.'

She hugs herself and I pull a face, like I'm impressed.

'Not sure extensions are such a good idea though,' she goes, chewing on the inside of her cheek. 'Not for the older woman. You need plenty of hair to anchor them. And they're tricky to fix.' Her eyes brightens. 'Unless you want me to come round and give you a hand.'

'No,' I go quickly. 'No. The old lady, she's... she's the shy type. Don't take to strangers.'

'OK then. Let's see what they've got.'

She wanders up and down under a sign what says 'hair products', taking packets off of the displays and reading the labels. I do the same, though I ain't got a clue what we're after.

Molly comes up to me, dead pleased with herself. 'How about this?'

She tosses me a packet. I go to catch it, then see what's inside. Something hairy, like what I seen in the trap. The packet skids across the shiny floor. Molly gives me an 'are-you-mental?' look.

'Thought it was a mouse,' I go.

'A blonde mouse? Honestly, Brad. It's a hairpiece, you wally.'

I pick it up and read the label: Miss Lustrous Instant Ponytail. Though it's flattened under the cellophane, I see it's blonde curls attached to a plastic comb.

'You'll need this as well. Golden Summer Glints. You use it like shampoo. Covers all grey – or so it says here.' She holds out the box and I take it. But she don't let go. Seems like she's expecting me to say something.

So I go, 'Do you wanna go on a date sometime? A proper one? With me, I mean?'

'That'd be cool,' she says.

'And this?' I push back my beanie there in the middle of Boots, so's she can get a proper dekko at my face. 'You sure *this* don't creep you out?'

She tilts her head like she's making up her mind. 'No,' she says. 'It makes you different, that's all. Like Harry Potter. You know, with his…' And she zigzags her finger across her forehead, drawing his lightning bolt scar.

'Oh,' I say, 'is that why the girls scream when they see me? They mistake me for Daniel Radcliffe.'

We laugh so loud, the shop assistants' heads snap round like a bunch of meerkats. Outside on the pavement, we're still giggling. I'm having a good time. I don't want it to end so I tell her I need to get some new threads. Does she know anywhere cheap?

'If we're quick, we've just about got time to get to Camden Lock market,' she says, taking my hand.

13.

ELOISE

You sure you're ready for this? It's pretty racy stuff. My goodness. Blushing already and I haven't even started. Red as a pineapple.

But there is no place for prudes and shrinking violins here. We have to face facts, Boy. Sex sells. If I'm going to shift enough copies of this bloody book to make my fortune, there has to be sex. And plenty of it.

So, the wedding night. I'll do my best, dear reader, to paint you a vivid picture. My new husband, Jolyon and I are installed in the Kim Novak Suite of the Hotel Royale. Soft lamplight is catching the crystals of the chandelier, sending rainbows flickering across the ceiling. A champagne bottle melts down into the ice bucket with a sigh, like that of a satisfied lover.

You sure that thing's on? I don't want you missing this stuff. It's dynamite.

So, chandelier, champers, satisfied lover, blah, blah, blah. The scene is set for the wedding night. Or rather the half-night, as it's already gone four in the morning. But what's this? Jolyon and I are lying chastely apart on the coverlet; he in his monogrammed cream silk pyjamas, I in my almost-too-short-to-be-decent pink chiffon baby-doll negligée.

What's going on?

I am making him wait. That's what.

While piling on his agony, I am replaying in my head moments from my wonderful day. The sensual swish of ivory brocade against my legs. The giddying perfume of the ice-white roses in my bouquet. The gratifying gasps of Jolyon's friends as I swept into the registry office, looking exquisitely delicious. And last but not least, the unexpected break in Terry's voice as he handed me to Jolyon, whispering, 'She can be a little madam sometimes but tek good care of 'er – or I'll chop off yower todger with me meat cleaver.'

So many poignant memories.

Of Terry and Urse, as out of place in the Hotel Royale as two aquatic animals on a tandem. Of Terry forever tugging at his starched collar and Urse pulling at her skirt. Of the mercifully short speech I wrote for Terry which he read, haltingly, to a silent room, in his broadest West Midlands.

Thank sod, they left soon after we cut the cake, so the remaining guests could take to the dance floor. Jolyon's father, the Major, showed off a surprisingly energetic jitterbug, I remember. There was one awkward moment when an old goat, who I later found out was Jolyon's godfather, got over-friendly with me during a smoochy number. A quick kick to the shins soon sorted him out. That apart, I had such a glorious time that, despite Jolyon's pleas, I didn't want to leave.

So that's why it's 4am before the happy couple – that's Jolyon and me, in case I've lost you – find themselves stretched out on the bed, marriage still unconsummated. From time to time, Jolyon's hand twitches towards my thigh, but I slap him down. I'm waiting to hear the magic words that will unlock my passion.

'All right,' Jolyon sighs at last. 'I'll get you the apartment in Holland Park.'

'The one with the balcony? And the second bathroom?'

He nods. With a squeal of delight, I fling myself on him, covering his face in kisses. Thirty seconds later he's on top and inside, silk PJs round his ankles, hammering away like a plump mongrel on a particularly alluring trouser leg. Doggy snuffles turn to piggy grunts, piggy grunts climax in a little squeak, like a baby dormouse.

Five seconds later, we are back to lying side by side. Only this time, both of us have grins of satisfaction across our faces. He's thinking, no doubt, about his brief sexual sprint. I'm thinking about the four-bed, two-bath apartment near Holland Park that Jolyon has just promised to buy me.

'This is just the start, my darling,' he goes on, hopping out of bed to pour us two foaming glasses. 'I've got ideas, big ideas for the practice. Nineteen fifty-six was our best year yet but I have an idea that will make us even richer. It's a corker.'

And he goes on about his plan. I don't pay much attention. When he pauses for breath, I stop his accountancy lecture with a kiss. 'What a clever Joly I've bagged.'

For a moment, he looks unsmilingly into my eyes. Then he does a surprising thing. Wrapping the silk coverlet round his waist, like a Roman emperor, he skips to the window, pulls up the sash, sticks his head out and yodels the chorus from *Oklahoma* in a loud but not un-tuneful baritone.

I lie back on the pillows. My husband is happy. I am happy. I am happy to have made him happy. Because – have you guessed, dear reader? – it was not my cherry that was popped that wedding night. That deed had been most efficiently taken care of in the store-room of Terry's pie factory, over a sack of flour, by a butcher boy called… dammit, I had his name a second ago.

No, it was Jolyon whose virginity was surrendered. Jolyon, with his suggestive winks, rolling eyes and spittled lips, had never 'been' with anyone before our wedding night. 'Not even a prozzie,' he confessed tearfully, early on in our courtship. 'Not even a pretty boy at school.'

As he begins 'Oh-oh-OK-lahoma-ing' for a joyful third time, I interrupt. 'Joly,' I coo from the bed, curling my finger. 'Do you think you could do that again, only slower this time?'

'Crikey. Twice in one night,' he growls, advancing towards the bed. 'What a naughty little sexpot you are.'

Colin. That was his name. The butcher boy. Jolyon was right. I was a sexpot. A naughty little sexpot.

Note to Boy: Wasn't that fun? I wonder if I should go into more detail. You know, be more explicit. Sex up the sex. That's what people want, isn't it? What do you think? More grunt and grind? You've gone very quiet. You're not going to be sick, are you?

Jolyon's idea did indeed turn out to be a corker. He styled himself 'accountant to the stars', dispensing financial advice to showbiz types. 'They're the perfect clients,' he liked to say. 'Lots of money. Bugger all common sense.'

They were all on his books, the big names of the day. Kay and Alec, Anthony and Dirk. Joan and Jean. Richard and Diana. Michael and Larry. And later, from the world of pop, Helen, Nina and Frederick. A Kink and two Shadows.

Money poured in faster than I could spend it. And let me tell you, I knew how to spend. Clothes, holidays, cars and, my greatest passion, interior design. I found I had a natural flair for it, a flair which was to stand me in such good stead later, as my fashion career burgeoned.

I totally transformed the Holland Park apartment, several times. Whether the style was Victoriana, Arts and Crafts Nouveau, or the scrubbed pine and cheesecloth of the mermaid look, I had to be first. Then I saw a house in an estate agent's window. Nearer the park and with a garden and five bedrooms. Much nicer than our poky little apartment. Jolyon bought it and I transformed that one too. By this time we were back to Victoriana and the decorating cycle, I must confess, was growing a trifle tedious.

I was bored. Jolyon was always busy. My only so-called friends were his clients or their equally bored wives. True, my days were filled with lunches, private viewings, first nights, premieres and book launches, but they meant nothing to me.

Applying lipstick one day before lunch at Wheeler's with the latest Cadbury's Flake girl, I paused, tube of Carmine Kick in mid air, and looked deep into the mirror. What did I see? Emptiness. Pointlessness. Worthlessness. I needed something to give meaning to my existence.

I know, I thought, *I'll pop a sprog*.

14.

ELOISE

Me, a mother? No one was more surprised than me at this change of direction. I'd never had the 'earth goddess' urge before. Hardly surprising, when my own mother was more concerned with polishing taps than playing peekaboo.

Once the thought was lodged in my head, I couldn't concentrate on anything else. I just *had* to have a baby. Indeed, I wondered why I hadn't thought of it before. A baby would make my life complete. Nine months of putting my feet up, eating what I liked and being fussed over, a few years of dressing the offsprog up in adorable mini garments, then, before it got too irritating, it would be time for boarding school.

There was one hurdle: the conception. Jolyon and I hadn't had regular 'relations' for ages. I wasn't even sure if he was capable of impregnation. For the whole nine years of our marriage, he'd been using rubber johnnies. What if he wasn't up to the task? All that turkey bolster business hadn't been thought of back then; as for inner-tube babies and MDF clinics, they were far into the future. Not to worry, I consoled myself, if Joly wasn't up to the job, I would subcontract; i.e.

make use of the services of a third-party lover. I had plenty to choose from.

Note to Boy: Do some digging. Try the gossip columns. In those days my name was linked with many a dashing young star. But – and this is paramount – only include the names of the dead ones. Dead men can't sue.

As it turned out, third-party intervention wasn't required. All it took was a red and black basque from a Soho sex shop and a bottle of single malt, and I got what I wanted: preggerhood.

Months of intense preparation followed. There was my maternity wardrobe to plan, layettes to buy, a nursery to design and a string of nannies to interview. Meanwhile, I grew the size of the Albert Hall – with two small St Paul's cathedrals balanced on my chest.

At last, I was ready. Except I wasn't, as I discovered the day my waters broke. During all my activity, there was something I had completely forgotten about: the actual birth. So when things started to happen, baby-wise, I hadn't a clue what was going on. Except I didn't like it. Not one bit.

By the time a tight-lipped Jolyon had fitted me into his blessed Porsche – not an easy matter – and got me to St Mary's, Paddington, I was hysterical, sobbing and begging everyone, including the car park attendant, for drugs.

I recommend it, a Caesarean. Well, after I made the midwife cry and decked the pompous little twerp of a consultant who dared to suggest – while sporting, if you please, a ridiculous spotty bow tie – that I was making a lot of fuss about nothing, they had little choice. It was either a general anaesthetic or general mayhem.

As they were about to wheel me down, Jolyon popped his head round the door.

'Everything tickety-boo?' he asked, nervously.

'Don't you come in here with your stupid prep-school slang, you useless lump of lard,' I yelled, grabbing a metal bedpan. 'As soon as I get out of here,' I said, drawing back my arm, 'I want a divorce.'

The bedpan hit the wall. Jolyon retreated. His baby daughter was two days old before he dared show his face again.

What a blissful time that was. Tucked up in my private room, off my head on painkillers, my little bundle of joy safely swaddled in a plastic cot down the end of the corridor, I held court, bossing the staff and shouting abuse at Jolyon. If only I could have stayed in that hospital forever, but, outrageously, after four weeks, they kicked me out.

That's when things began to go wrong. Though I love and adore my darling Tabitha now, she was quite honestly an impossible infant. Screaming to be fed at all hours, even – get this – *in the middle of the night.* Doing disgusting and extraordinarily colourful things in her nappy, absolutely ruining her Harrods layette. Refusing to play pat-a-cake, when I'd cancelled a hair appointment specially. Don't tell me *that's* normal behaviour for a newborn. Exasperated, I did the only sensible thing and left her to the nannies' professional care until she learned to behave.

Why the name Tabitha, you may be wondering, dear reader? It was Jolyon who came up with it. And thank sod he did, as it turned out.

'What do you think?' he asked tentatively, cuddling the baby and kissing her head. Unaccountably, he didn't seem to mind if his daughter puked and shat over him. Indeed, he seemed to gain pleasure from it. 'Great Aunt Tabby was always awfully decent to us boys. She might even remember me with a little something when the time comes.'

'Yes, fine. Do what you like. It's not as though I'm ever going to speak to the brat, is it?' I said, stomping off to my room.

I did a lot of stomping at that time. Motherhood had turned out to be another big, fat disappointment. The sound of the constantly mewling infant set my teeth on edge, and whenever my hopeless husband opened his trap, I had the urge to bludgeon him repeatedly over the head with a blunt object until his face resembled a bloody blancmange.

I think they call it the baby blues.

Do you ever get depressed, Boy? No? That's surprising, when you have so much to be depressed about. Little or no education. An accent you could open tin cans with and a family who don't give a damn what you get up to.

Stand up. Let me look at you. Hmmm, not entirely beyond hope. You do have a modicum of style, I'll give you that. Clean and polished like a pebble on the beach – and about as interesting.

A bite of lunch, did you say? Oh, you didn't? Well, do it anyway. Two soft boiled eggs and a nice piece of ham. Not the packet stuff. Off the bone. Cut fine. And don't get that walnut bread again. I've been picking bits out of my teeth ever since. White sliced that I can chew into a nice mush. My tastes are very plain, as you know. Oh and a Black Forest gateau. Fresh cream, mind. None of your frozen muck.

After that we'll tackle another momentous moment in this, my poignant tale. The day I met the two women who were to change my life. Don't hover. Off you go. Lunch won't buy itself.

I was resting, I remember, following a stressful morning watching the day nanny bathe the offspring. My, what a mess the child made, kicking her ridiculous little limbs, squealing and squawking the whole time. The bathroom sheepskin was soggy and my head was throbbing by the time she'd finished. I left the nanny to mop up while I had a much needed lie-down.

My eyelids were closing, when the bedroom door burst open and in walked two of the most extraordinary creatures I had ever seen. This was, remember, at the beginning of the sixties when matching hat, shoes and handbags were still the rage, and girls thought they were being daring if they didn't wear gloves, and secretaries were sent home from work in disgrace for wearing 'American tan' stockings.

All I could do was stare. Tall and thin, they couldn't have been more contrasted. One was all in black, save for a blood-red scarf at her throat, matching her lips. A black beret sat on blue-black hair so oil-slick sleek, I wondered it didn't slide off. Dark glasses hid her eyes. She held a long cigarette holder, which smouldered.

Her companion was in white. Starched white blouse, collar up, tucked into high-waisted cream Capri pants. A bird's nest of wiry, blonde hair tangled high on her head. Mascara-clotted blue eyes blinked from a tanned face. She held a miniscule white dog, which snarled.

Think a more extreme Audrey Hepburn and Brigitte Bardot's beatnik sister and you've got the picture.

Striking a pose, the two gazed at me in horror, as if *I* were the one got up like a pig's breakfast. As one they rushed at me, a torrent of words tumbling from their lips, overlapping and interrupting each other, like a pair of chattering monkeys. So I wasn't sure – I was *never* really sure – which one was which.

'My, hasn't she—?' 'Let herself go—? I should say so…' 'I

know she's dropped a tot but really…?' 'Do you think she moisturises?' 'How old is she again?' 'My God, I do believe she's wearing chainstore.' This last they chorused together, somehow ending in unison.

And that, dear reader, was my introduction to the bizarre world of Trip Pinkerton and Dazzle O'Grady.

There. They're here at last. Now the fun will begin… but tomorrow. I am totally drained for today. You are dismissed, Boy. Give me strength! No, I do not mean you've got the sack. I mean you can go home. No. Leave dear old Sapphie within reach. Quite, quite drained.

15.

BRADLEY

She don't take to it. The ponytail. Not at first. 'Specially not when I tell her how much it cost. Fifty, I say. Well, I got my new threads to take into account.

Got the snazziest jacket you ever seen – blue Puffa. Electric blue, Molly calls it. In the market. Nice and warm. At first the bloke won't budge. Molly says to walk off like we ain't bothered. Bloke comes out from behind his stall, calls after us, grinning like a fool and waving. We go back. End up getting a forty-quid jacket for twenty-five. Molly high-fives me. Got some jeans and a coupla tees an' all. Well set up I am now.

Anyhow, Miss E has a right mare. Going on about me spending her money like water, leaving her on her own for hours. So when I tip the ponytail into her hand, she curls her lip. She ain't impressed and, to be fair, it don't look much.

'Give it a chance,' I tell her. 'Wait till you see it after Madame's shampoo and set.'

She giggles at that but it's still a struggle getting her to lean over the bowl so's I can lather her up. That's easy-peasy compared to what comes next. You has to leave the colour on, only for twenty minutes, but do you think I can get her to sit still? She's wandering about the place, dripping dye everywhere. I'm running along behind with a cloth, doing my best to keep it off of the rugs and the furniture. Get it all over my hands. Wet wipes to the rescue again!

She's in front of her dressing table mirror, wet hair plastered to her head, and my heart's in my mouth, I can tell you. I get out her big old hairdryer and her silver brush. Brush in one hand, dryer in the other, I work on her hair, blowing it, brushing it – like I seen Ma doing.

She's getting excited. I'm getting edgy. What if it's gone wrong? What if her hair turns green? Or falls out? I blow and brush, blow and brush, all the time praying, *Please God, let it be OK.* I stand back, holding my breath. Her hair catches the light. It's still thin, mind, but now it's like a golden halo.

'Wisps of sunshine,' Miss E coos to herself.

I tell her to hold on, we ain't finished. I give the ponytail a brush while she puts on her specs and reads me the instructions: 'Section hair into squares, then backcomb to provide a cushion to secure the hair piece in place.'

I catch Miss E's eye in the mirror and have to ask, 'What's backcombing when it's at home?'

She takes the comb from me. 'In the sixties, I was the queen of the beehive,' she goes. Her knobbly old hands reach up and sort of whisk the hair with the comb. Then she gives it to me to take over. Takes some juggling and I drop the comb a time or two but I manage a pretty good job, if I say so meself. All the while she's giving me instructions. 'Right down to the roots. That's the style. Careful. Don't yank it.'

I backcomb her hair up, smooth it down, like she shows me, then scrape it together. Next comes the ponytail. I clip it in place, tidy up a few stray hairs, give it a spray and finish the whole thing off with a blue ribbon – a new one, bought special. She stares at herself in the mirror and shakes her head so the ponytail flies.

'Now for your face,' I go, unpacking the bag of tubes and jars what Molly chose. 'Do you want me to have a go?'

She looks at me like I said something really dumb. 'I think after all these years I can manage to put on my own face, thank you very much.'

I'm that relieved, though, of course, she makes a right hash of it. Even with the new stuff, even though Molly ain't picked nothing too garish, she goes over the top. Squirts cream from the tubes, smears gobs of stuff out the jars, and tops the lot off with clouds of powder. We cough our lungs up.

'There,' she goes, the dust settling. 'That's much better.'

I take it all in. Big Angelina Jolie lips over her thin ones. Thick layer of shiny gold eyeshadow. Pink circles on her cheeks. A clown's face.

I'm digging my nails into my hands, trying not to laugh but she's happy. That's the main thing.

I busy meself clearing everything away. Half hour later, when I come to ask what she wants to eat, she's still there, touching her face, turning her head this way and that, swishing and sighing.

'You are *so* rocking that ponytail, Miss E,' I go.

She pulls the fake hair forward and rubs it against her cheek, eyes half closed. 'I am rather, aren't I?'

Rest of the day, she's in a brilliant mood. Following morning, it's another story.

'You keep your half-caste hands off my things,' she's shouting, white as a ghost and trembling. 'Do you hear?'

All I done was ask her about that locked room, testing the water. I could give it a spring clean, I say. Flick a duster round. No bother. If she was to give me the key, I say. She goes ballistic.

'That's private!' she yells. 'Private. You're not to go in there. Do I make myself clear? No one's allowed in there.'

'Keep your hair…' I clock the ponytail that's by a miracle survived the night. Squashed and skewwhiff but still hanging on in there. *Good work, Miss Lustrous,* I think. So what I say is, 'Crystal, Miss E. Sorry.'

I mean, no sense riling the old girl. More easier to find the key for meself.

'So, you was famous, was you, Miss E, back in the day?'

It's a little while later and I'm doing some hard-core buttering up. We're in her bedroom. She's in the busted armchair by the window, still sulking, pretending to read her magazine. I'm changing her bed. She looks up from the mag and glares at me.

'Famous like Cheryl Tweedy?' I whip off the dirty sheeting, turning away so I don't have to see the stains. She never cleans herself properly, see, after she's been. And I ain't gonna wipe her bum. That's a step a million miles too far.

One mention of Cheryl and a smile creeps across her face. She can't help it. Loves her Cheryl and her *X Factor*, Miss E. Always on at me to show her how to vote. I've give up trying to explain. It don't go in.

She puts down her mag. 'You've heard of Alma Cogan and Diana Dors, of course?' She don't wait for me to answer. 'Well, I was more famous than the two of them put together. Imagine that! Such a life. Such a life I had. Right up until… Oh, Howie!' she whispers, filling up.

She's gone. Gazing into space, thinking about this Howie. Knowing better than to ask, I go on quietly making the bed, fitting the new plastic cover, unfolding the clean sheets still warm from her rattling old tumble drier, putting them to my nose to grab a lungful. How do they do that, cram all the smells of sunshine and summer into a little plastic bottle? I tuck the corners in, all neat an' that.

'Wish you'd let me get you a quilt,' I go, breaking the silence. 'A duvet would keep you nice and cosy these chilly nights.'

She comes to. 'What did you say? I was years away.'

I explain again about the duvet but she won't hear of it.

'I like a good thick Witney blanket and an eiderdown,' she says. 'Look at that eiderdown. I bought it in Sloane Square – must be forty years old and it's still serviceable.'

Don't look too clever to me, to be honest with you, shedding feathers everywhere. But now she's on to another story about what a trial it was for her to go shopping back in the day. 'One could hardly buy a kaftan in Granny Takes a Trip or grab a quick gin and it in the Markham without hordes of photographers and reporters chasing one.'

'Was you, like, a supermodel?' I go. The point being, to keep her talking so's she forgets she's supposed to be teed off.

'Haven't you been listening to a thing I've said?' she goes, pulling herself up in the chair. 'Me? A model? Do I look like the sort of person who parades about like a brainless coat hanger? Not sodding likely.'

I look over. Her big old bum fills the seat. Under her nightie, the fat falls into folds on her lap. Her short, meaty legs dangle in mid air – and I have to agree. 'Fair point,' I go.

Lucky for me she's back onto her favourite subject: herself. 'I, Boy, single-handedly inspired a fashion revolution. Several revolutions in fact. Others have claimed the honours but I'm telling you, without Eloise Slaughter there'd have been no swinging sixties, no Carnaby Street, no "I'm Backing Britain". You know, the Freddie Forsyth song? Surely to goodness you've heard of the swinging sixties? Well, take it from me, I was the one who grabbed the sixties by their big hairy balls and made them swing.'

To make sure I'm getting the picture, she does the mime. Disgusting.

'I was the toast of the catwalks,' she says, eyes sparkling. 'The darling of Fleet Street, with acquaintances by the hundred, lovers by the dozen, a social life that was the envy of Holland Park. Why that look? Don't you believe me?'

All the while she's been telling me how popular she was, how everyone knew her, I been thinking: where are they now, all these pals of hers? I have to say my piece.

'Don't take this the wrong way, but I been working for you a while now and in all that time, you ain't had one single visitor,' I go. 'No one knocks, unless they're looking for that long-haired OAP rocker on the top floor. No one rings, unless it's to ask if you're thinking of getting double glazing or to tell you you've won a villa on the Costa in a competition.' I take a deep breath. 'You might have been popular once, Miss E, but seems to me – apart from your girl, Tabitha, and she ain't put in an appearance – you ain't got no one.'

I stand by for the explosion. It don't come.

Instead, she speaks quiet. 'It's rather ungracious of you,' she goes, 'but out of the mouths of sucking pigs… It's true.' She lets out a long, bumpy sigh. 'I'm not as sought-after as I once was.'

I stop what I'm doing and squat down to take her freckled hand in mine. Dry as leaves, her skin is. Thin as tissue. You could tear it, just like that, if you wasn't careful. Ain't never been that close to her before. I notice little lines between her wrinkles, dividing her face into squares. Her face looks old, but not her eyes. When I stare into them, funny thing is, I don't see an old lady. I see all the lives she's lived before, the people she used to be. The chubby little girl spoilt rotten by her mum and dad. The stroppy teen giving the local lads the run-around. The crafty woman who come from nowhere and made good.

She looks back at me and I wonder if she sees in my eyes all the people I could be. It's not an easy thought to have. I hold her look for a beat, before dropping her hand. 'Let me,' I go, reaching up to gently pull the dangling ponytail free.

She don't flinch. She don't move. She smiles.

'Perhaps we have more in common than I first appreciated,' she goes. 'We're both hiding away from an uncaring world, Boy, licking our wounds. Unloved. Unnoticed. Underestimated. Both of us running away. You from your present. Me from my past.'

I give a shiver. It's gone cold. She feels it too. She pulls the purple thing closer.

'Enough of this gloomy talk,' she says, shaking off the mood with a toss of her head. 'Now,' she goes, 'tell me about this villa on the Costa I've won.'

16.

ELOISE

So it was that in my darkest hour, Trip and Dazzle saved me. Friends of one of Jolyon's more colourful showbiz clients, they'd been sent on a mercy mission. I'd been moaning to someone – Sarah or Susanna, probably; it could even have been Vanessa – about the many disillusionments of motherhood. Taking pity, she'd sent me something to cheer me up.

I'd expected champers, theatre tickets or perhaps a sexy young man. Instead, wise woman, she'd sent me Trip and Dazzle. With Jolyon at his workaholic worst and Tabby, quite frankly, a snivelling, puking advert for contraception, I think I'd have gone round the bend if that luminescent pair hadn't burst into my life like an explosion of fireworks.

I began living at last.

Trip and Dazzle spent so much time together, they had evolved an extraordinary way of speaking over each other, their voices weaving in and out hypnotically or – more usually – hysterically, as I discovered on that first encounter.

'Emergency, emergency…' 'Ditch the beige chainstore…' 'Get her something groovy…' 'Sloane Square or High Street Ken?' 'What do you think…?' 'No, what do *you* think…?' 'I asked first…' 'No, I did.'

My, what an afternoon we had the first time they took me shopping. I came back laden with bags and boxes. Back at the house, we cracked open a bottle of Joly's finest champers and held an impromptu fashion parade, taking it in turns to march up and down wearing the new purchases.

It was the first of many West End expeditions, as my new companions turned my ideas of fashion and style upside down. No more dressing like a forty-year-old matron. No more striving for sophistication and elegance. And definitely no more matching shoes, gloves and handbags.

What Trip and Dazzle had realised, before anyone else, was something was stirring on the London fashion scene. A style revolution was in the making. Though I didn't know it then, I was about to take my place on its front line.

Right on cue came fantastic news. Great Aunt Tabitha had kicked the bucket. You remember? We named Tabby after her? And Jolyon was right. So chuffed had she been by our touching gesture, when she snuffed it, she did indeed leave him a tidy sum. Though the D word hung unspoken in the air and Jolyon and I were hardly on speaking terms, I didn't hesitate to call a truce.

'Please, please, please, Joly,' I begged, 'please, let me have some of the old trout's money. After all, it was me who went through the trauma of childbirth to produce your darling daughter.'

'But a *shop*, Ellie,' Jolyon sneered. 'That's trade.'

'Not a shop, Joly. A *boutique*. There is a difference.'

'Either way, you don't have retail experience.'

'How can you say that?' I sniffed. 'I go shopping almost every day. In any case, I will be more management. Others will do the actual work.'

Jolyon looked unconvinced.

'Boutiques are the in thing. All my friends are getting them,' I went on. 'It doesn't have to be a big one. A teeny, weeny one will do. I've found just the place.'

Jolyon rubbed his chin. 'I'm really not sure it would be a sound investment.'

'You can lick my lallies.'

Jolyon's objections collapsed as his manhood rose.

'Where is this... boutique?' he slurped from between my bosoms.

'You won't have heard of it. It's in a back alley somewhere near Oxford Circus. Carlaby Road or something.'

I know what you're thinking, dear reader. People – so-called fashion historians mostly – will tell you it was others who first began trading in the funny, little Soho street that set London swinging and the whole world talking. Lies, all lies. It was me, this little miss from the Midlands. Eloise Slaughter. Me. *I* discovered Carnaby Street. Without me, there'd have been no John Stephen, no Lord Kitchener's Valet, no Kleptomania and no Kristina sodding Krabtree... but I'm jumping ahead.

You know me, once I get an idea in my head, I don't hang about. As soon as Jolyon's cheque had cleared, I got spending. I signed the lease on the Carnaby Street shop and took Trip and Dazzle to view. Unusually, their enthusiasm was slow to ignite.

'Too far from Selfridge's... Smells of cabbage,' they grumbled, wrinkling their noses.

N° 8 Carnaby Street had indeed until then been a greengrocer's. Boxes still lay scattered on the damp floor and the blackened corpses of fruit and veg rotted in corners and hung from hooks.

'Only a week till we open,' I told them, shoving a broom in Trip's hand and a mop into Dazzle's. 'Less moaning, more cleaning.'

Already, you see, I was showing signs of the firm but fair management technique that was to make me such a success in the bitch-eat-bitch world of fashion.

'But we've just had our nails done,' they complained. 'We can't do it…' 'We won't…' 'Where are the workers?'

'Sisters, we're on a tight budget,' I explained. 'You *are* the workers.'

'I thought you said Jolyon had coughed up a thousand…' 'No, it was two…' 'Wasn't…' 'Was.'

It was actually four thousand – a fortune in those days – but I didn't correct them.

'That's all earmarked,' I told them.

'Ear what?' my dim friends squeaked in panic, hands flying to their earlobes.

'How many times?' I sighed. 'I've set aside a certain amount for expenses. You know, cars, clothes, travel and—'

'We remember… parties!' they trilled in unison.

'You're learning fast, my potty protégées. Now get to work.'

Outwardly I was confident. Inside I had my doubts. Jolyon's cheque was generous but it was almost all spent. For a start, there was my new flat. I couldn't bear to be under the same roof as Jolyon for another day. I'd gone straight from the bank to the estate agents. And Lowndes Street was so handy for Harrods.

'A trial separation,' I'd told him and Tabby, taking my leave as they wept on the doorstep. In reality the marriage was over. The rest had gone on essentials. A red Mini, a fresh wardrobe of clothes for me and, of course, vintage champers for the launch party.

'I doubt, my dense darlings,' I told Trip and Dazzle, 'if there's more than fifty quid left to do up the shop and buy stock. We'll have to do the best we can with the meagre resources to hand. Keep sweeping.'

As the girls fussed and brushed, I wandered round, kicking at rotting cabbage leaves and seeking inspiration. My eyes lighted on the hooks in the ceiling.

'What if we hang the clothes from those?' I said, an idea beginning to dawn. 'Don't throw those wooden crates out either. We can use them. And the potato sacks. Trust me, it'll look gear,' I said, fingers crossed behind my back.

So it was that I discovered my gift for improvisation, for thinking on my feet, for creating a gorgeous something out of a shitty nothing.

Fuelled by ciggies, espressos and fine red wine, we worked for several days. I say 'we'; I took a more supervisory role. Like Alan Sugar in *The Appendix*.

Note to Boy: The more I think of it, the more I'm coming to the conclusion that Lord S's gruff, 'don't come 'ere with that load of old bollocks' management style was a steal from yours truly. Is it worth a court case, I wonder?

Trip and Dazzle daubed rainbows and sunrises over the damp brick walls, sprayed the wooden crates gold, splashed glitter-paint over the sacks and draped everything else in blue-black velvet – curtains left over from my Victoriana period. As I predicted, it did look gear. In fact, better than gear.

'It's sensational. It'll knock everyone out,' I told them. 'Especially if we keep the lights down low,' I added, noticing drips in the paint and glitter shedding onto the floor.

Still the dim duo weren't happy. 'But Ellie… what are we going to sell?' they whined, wringing their hands. 'We can't open… not with an empty shop.'

'Boutique,' I corrected, though the same thought had been worrying me. Only days to go and we lacked two important elements: stock to sell and a name to go over the door. That was when I had another one of my fantastic strokes of luck.

The evening was wet and I was hurrying home from a hard day supervising at the boutique. Taking a shortcut through Soho on the lookout for a cab, I turned a corner and found myself in a dark cul-de-sac round the back of Regent Street. I was about to retrace my steps when I spied a pile of plastic bags, stacked against a pair of scruffy double doors.

What instinct drew me to those bags I'll never know – but thank sod it did. I pulled them open and peered inside. They were stuffed with off-cuts, fabrics in all shapes and colours, scraps and ends of rolls. Looking up, I saw a brass plate on the wall. Liberty's. The fabric was left over from Liberty's – the famous West End department store, for those of you, dear readers, who have the misfortune to inhabit the provinces.

The cab driver wasn't too happy about cramming so many bags into the backseat beside me but, after I'd flashed a leg and tipped him extravagantly, he agreed to take me to Notting Hill Gate where I found my droopy-eyed friends at home, smoking and looking miserable.

'What are we going to do, Ellie? No stock, no shop… it's a disaster,' they sniffed as I swept in.

'Courage, my bemused buddies,' I told them, grinning. 'I've had another of my inspired ideas. I know how we'll get stock. We'll make our own. Or rather, you will. Put the bags there, my man,' I instructed the scowling cabbie.

On the short drive from Regent Street, I'd come up with a plan involving Trip and Dazzle and the old manual sewing machine they used for bespoking their clothes. It wouldn't be *that* much of a stretch, I assured them. All they had to do was to transform the scrag ends of material into a range of desirable, must-have fashionwear in forty-eight hours. And what exactly would they make? I had an idea about that too; an audacious idea, but, with the confidence of youth, one that I felt sure would work.

Trip and Dazzle weren't so sure. They scuttled around, flapping their hands, wailing, 'It's impossible... You can't make us... We're going on strike.'

'Listen, you won't have to make many. We'll spread the stock around,' I soothed. 'We'll call it...' I searched for the right phrase. 'The Less is More look. Light up a ciggie, pour yourselves a strong coffee and get that Singer whirring.'

How easily those strokes of genius came to me in those days, dear reader. 'Less is more', the mantra stolen by so many over the years. Damn you, Mary Porterhouse!

As for the name over the shop, that was my idea too. At least, mine and Bruno's. Oh yes, Bruno. I almost forgot to mention him. An irresistibly good-looking bundle of long-haired, blue-eyed Northern charm, Bruno Cartwright had ambled into the boutique and my life during those frantic days before the opening.

He was a budding entrepreneur, he told me, looking for his first break. His instinct for business had brought him first to London and then to Carnaby Street. 'London fashion is going to be big,' he said. 'I can taste it in the air.'

He didn't mind what he did, or, more importantly as far as I was concerned, if he was paid; he just wanted to be part of what we were doing. What could I do, dear reader? We did indeed need someone with business know-how – and did I already mention how irresistibly good-looking he was?

I gave him a job. Then, dear reader, I took him home and bedded him. A smart move, as it turned out, on both counts. For Bruno, as well as being blessed with freckle-faced good looks and a healthy sexual appetite, had an unfailing instinct for fashion retail, an instinct that was apparent from our very first night together.

'What an arse, you've got, Ellie,' he murmured, in the throes of passion. 'I love it. Plenty to get to grips with. You've got the most heavenly body I've ever seen.'

I pulled away from his embrace, libido temporarily on hold. 'Heavenly Bodies? Wouldn't that make a great name for the boutique?'

'Cracking,' he said, propping himself up on one elbow, catching his breath. 'Tell you what. What about this for a logo?' He traced a curvy outline in the air. 'Dramatic silhouette of a female body. You could model for it.'

'What? Starkers?' I said, hands to my cheeks in mock horror.

'Of course not. You'd be wearing a banner with "Heavenly Bodies" on it to cover up your naughty bits. Talking of that… come here, lass!' he growled, making a grab for me. I responded, my libido very much back in action.

Hence the famous Heavenly Bodies logo was born. What a team we were back then.

Note to Boy: All this talk of passion action is making me hungry. It must be lunchtime. Or teatime. Grubtime of some ilk. Just feed me, will you?

17.

BRADLEY

It's after three when Dom comes in, reeking of weed. I turn over, away from the smell of rotting leaves. I feel my bed dip as he sits down.

'Come on, man. Don't be like that,' he goes, fingers jabbing into my back. 'Open up them peepers and talk to me.'

I stay face to the wall. Chatty Dom can be worse than crabby Dom. Either way, I'm likely to end up on the wrong side of his temper. Already he's losing his rag. 'Wake up, you strawberry-faced freak.' He thumps me on the back. 'Anyone can see you're faking. Wake up!'

I'm worried he's gonna rouse Ma and then I'll have the two of them on at me. I give in and sit up. 'What was that for?' I go, rubbing my back.

'That's for nothing,' he goes. 'Think what you'll get when you *do* do something.' He sniggers like it's the most wittiest thing anyone's ever said. I cross my arms.

'What you been up to then, eh?' he says, lighting up another spliff.

'Working.'

'Oh yeah. Forgot. My baby brother's a working boy now.

Where was her place again? Must pop in for tea and buns next time I'm passing.'

'Up West,' I mumble. 'Hyde Park.'

Oh my days! Must of been half asleep. I could of said anywhere. I could of said Hammersmith or Fulham, Ealing or Brent. He wouldn't have knowed the difference. But no, I gotta go and come out with Hyde Park.

'You had a proper shufti yet?'

'Told you, didn't I, there's nothing you'd be interested in.'

'Is that right?' he says, mouth twisting into a smirk. I know what's coming. 'Bollocks!' he hollers into my face. 'Don't give me that, you poofy loser. She's gotta have something. Posh place up West.' He grabs me, twisting the neck of my tee till it half strangles me. Got the grip of a Rottie my brother, 'specially when he's been blazing all night. 'You better not be holding out on me, you bender.'

'OK, there is something,' I go, pulling at his hands. I feel his grip relax. 'A room she keeps locked. Might be something in there.'

'That's more like it,' he says, opening his fingers. I fall back on the pillow, gasping for air. 'That weren't so hard now, were it? You let me know what's what when you've been in there. *Capish?*'

He weaves across to the window and opens it. I catch the earthy smell of his warm piss as he relieves himself onto God knows what – or who – down below. Five seconds later he's toppled onto his bed and is snoring.

I lay awake, worrying I've messed up. Had to give him something though, didn't I, otherwise I'd have been mincemeat. He still don't have the actual address and Hyde Park's a big place. I'm safe for now, but how long will it last? Dom and his fists is bound to get it out of me in the end. It's just a matter of time.

'What are those marks on your neck?'

We're in the kitchen and I'm making her what she calls 'a spot of light luncheon'. That's a plate of sarnies to you and me. She's standing behind me, watching, interfering.

'Love bites,' I go, quick as.

'Really?' she says. 'Seems unlikely.' She reaches up to have a better look. 'They look more like—'

'That's personal,' I go, pushing her hand away. Straight off, I regret it.

But all she says is, 'Hmmm.' Then her mind's back on her belly. 'More tomato,' she goes, getting in the way. 'Plenty of salt. That's right. Two slices of ham. And mustard. English. Don't slop it on. A smear will suffice or you'll take my head off. No, no, no. Into triangles, nice and dainty, like they do at the Ritz.'

I do my best but I ain't much good at dainty. Doorsteps is more my style. She don't seem to notice. I arrange the chunky triangles on a plate and put it on the kitchen table.

She sits and nods to a chair. 'Aren't you going to join me?'

I take a seat. She grabs a sarnie. I pick one up. She chomps. I nibble.

Then out the blue: 'You share a bedroom with this brother of yours, do you?' she asks. 'That must be difficult. I could never have shared with the Carthorse.'

Already she's lost me but I humour her with a bit of conversation. 'Ain't never knowed nothing different.'

'Just how many mistakes can a person make in one small sentence? Are you out to beat some sort of record, Boy?'

I keep quiet. *Don't rise*, I say to meself.

'I expect you have lots of fun together, you boys?' she goes, through a mouthful of bread. 'Pillow fights, midnight feasts and so on.'

I lick my finger and dab at the crumbs on my plate. 'Yeah, lots of fun,' I go, my voice flat. 'Laugh a minute it is.'

'And a few arguments I bet. All that testosterone.' She fixes me with a look. 'Tell me, do you get on with your brother?'

'Dom's all right most of the time. Long as he hasn't had too many bevvies or been on the weed. Then he can get bit...' I stop. I'm letting my mouth run away with me. That ain't like me. I ain't usually one for gabbing, see, not unless I got something particular to say. But I can turn it on when I have to. Like when the Old Bill comes calling or one of Ma's boyfriends turns up unexpected while she's entertaining another fella upstairs with a White Ace or six. But mostly I prefer to keep my thoughts inside my head. Less trouble that way.

She leans forward. 'He can get a bit what? Unpredictable? Violent?'

I roll the crumbs into a little ball. 'Wound up, I was gonna say.'

'So wound up that he might, for instance, grab you round the throat so hard it leaves marks?'

I stay silent, concentrating hard on rolling them breadcrumbs.

'I see,' she says, reaching for another fat triangle. She chews, then she says, 'Have you ever thought about moving out? Getting a place of your own.'

I just about choke. 'How am I ever gonna be able to do that?'

'Well,' she says, a sneaky look coming over her, 'I've been thinking about taking in a lodger. But it's a question of finding the right person. At my age, one doesn't relish the thought of sharing living space with a complete stranger. What if *you* were to become my lodger? What do you think about that?' Plate empty, she folds her hands in her lap.

'Me? Move in? With you? Here?' I go, still coughing. I get up and fetch meself a glass of water.

She turns to watch. 'You seem to have grasped the essential elements of the proposal. Why so shocked? Is that such a horrible prospect?'

I don't know what to say. So I take a big gulp of water and say, 'I don't know what to say.'

'You won't get a better offer. An elegant apartment in the West End. Sophisticated conversation. Fine dining.' There's a judder from the ancient old fridge. It hums, like it's wanting to join in the conversation.

'It's a nice idea,' I go, glancing round at the cooker with its door wedged shut with a stub of folded Radio Times, the chipped worktops and the cracked tiles. 'But I don't reckon I could stretch to a West End rent.'

Even while I'm saying this, I'm thinking what it would be like. No Ma and her boyfriends cackling through the thin walls. No Dom waking me up, off of his face, pissing out the window, slapping me about whenever he feels like it. Just me, behind my own door. Doing what I want to do in peace and quiet.

'Silly Boy! I wouldn't charge you!' she goes. 'Not if you were live-in staff, working on an expenses only basis. That's the usual form I believe. You can take the guest room by the front door, the one to the right. Would that suit?' She pauses. A thought has struck her. 'Don't go getting any ideas about the book, mind,' she goes, wagging her finger. 'I can only offer you a small percentage. Your contribution is, when all is said and done, very minor. Not that you'll be out of pocket. Mark my words, royalties on a celebrity memoir like mine can run into millions. When word gets out that I, Eloise Slaughter, high priestess of fashion, am penning a tome, a bidding war will break out. Just you wait and see.'

'Board and lodging's fine by me. I don't want nothing from your book.'

'Nothing?' She wrinkles her brow. 'No, no, no. We can't have that. Remind me to talk to you some day about your poor negotiating skills. How do you expect to get on in the world if you don't drive a hard bargain? One per cent, and that's my last word.'

'OK,' I shrug, thinking, *What does it matter? I ain't never gonna see a penny anyhow.*

She gobs into her hand and holds it out. I hold up mine and she high fives me with her wet palm. 'Done,' she goes, adding under her breath, 'you certainly have been.' She picks up her empty plate. 'Right, for your first duty as my in-house, personal private secretary, another round of the same, if you please, Boy. More mustard this time.'

She's happy. She's got me at her beck and call day and night. I'm happy. I got my own room in the West End rent-free. Not to mention access to her bank card whenever I need a top-up. Not bad for a poofy loser, eh Dom?

I'm grinning like a loon when I join the queue at the caff. It's busy. Molly ain't so happy.

'Before you ask, I'm working through my lunchbreak *and* doing an evening shift,' she goes, blowing upwards so her fringe flies out. 'I'm shattered. Been rushed off my feet all morning. I won't have time to be running any errands for you today.'

'That's a pity,' I say, ''cause I was gonna take you for a bite at the Macky D's down the road later. My treat. To say thanks.'

That little lie does the trick. Can't seem to go more than two minutes, that girl, without a smile.

'Why're you so full of the joys, anyway?' she goes.

'Nothing special. It's going well with me and my boss. That's all.'

'The old lady? The one with the ponytail?' she giggles. 'How'd it go with the makeover?'

I tell her about the hair dye and Miss Lustrous, exaggerating a bit, making her laugh. 'Funny old bat she is,' I go. 'Reckons she was a big celeb back in the day. Miss Eloise Slaughter, star of Swinging London, if you can believe a word.'

Molly's eyes bulge. She don't look tired no more. '*The* Eloise Slaughter?' she goes, a bit too loud. Blank faces turn our way, then back again, when they see there ain't nothing interesting going down. 'Oh my God, I've got to hear this. Go and sit down. I'll bring your drink over.'

I go for a flat white this time.

'You heard of her, then?' I go when she comes over.

'Are you joking me?' She takes a seat, even though she ain't supposed to sit with the customers. She's heard about Miss E, she tells me, at her evening class.

'My teacher was a real fan – although she did sort of give us the impression she'd died. You still hear about Quant, Hulanicki, Krabtree and the rest, you see, but Eloise Slaughter sort of disappeared off the radar.' Molly's pretty excited to start with but as she goes on she gets super-hyped. 'A heroine, my teacher called her. A trailblazer. As important to the women's struggle as the invention of the bicycle. You know, when Victorian women threw away their corsets and biked off down the country lanes. Oh my God, Brad.' She flaps her hands, like they's on fire or something. 'She's a legend. And you work for her.'

I don't get the half of what she's on about, to be honest with you. But I do get one thing: Miss E really *was* someone back in the day.

Molly don't need no encouragement to fill me in some more.

While she's chattering on, I find meself hypnotised by them eyes. Are they green or are they brown? The more I look, the more I can't decide. You'd think green and brown mixed together would come out muddy. Hers don't. They're like sunlight on a green sea. Not that I ever seen the sea. Not for real. Not unless you count the Thames other side of the Barrier. Been there a few times.

'… nearly twenty thousand pounds,' she goes.

That gets my attention all right. 'Twenty thousand quid? For what?'

'Cloth ears,' she goes, giving my arm a little push. 'For a vintage Krabtree original. The other week. Don't you watch the news?'

'Wildlife documentaries is more my style.'

'There was this sale on in New York. An auction. The biddings went mental because the dress had a mark on it. Yeah, a dirty mark. A handprint. Could have been done by some famous old pop singer they reckoned. The dress belonged to one of his girlfriends, at any rate. That's what sent the bids up. Crazy, isn't it?'

'Straight up bonkers,' I go.

Twenty K for a dirty dress. These people mad or what?

18.

ELOISE

My jaw hits the parquet. What *have* they done?

From the scraps Trip and Dazzle, working through the night, have stitched and scrunched together any-old-how a series of the tiniest of tiny skirts. Slung low on the hips, they barely cover the fundamentals.

I swallow hard. 'They're very…'

'Original? Stunning?' the duo suggest, hopeful eyebrows raised.

'Short, I was going to say.'

Their faces fall. 'She hates them…'

'Told you she would.'

I hold up my hand. 'They're shockingly indecent.' I pause for effect. 'Exactly what I was looking for.'

The girls' squeals threaten the window panes.

Novelty: that's what the fashion world craves more than anything. Something fresh to tickle the punters' fancy, grab their attention and make them empty out their purses. Something to make women say, 'I don't need it, I can't afford it but I *have* to have it.' And novelty is what our creations provided.

The shortiskirt – for so I christened it – was my first must-have triumph.

I know what you're thinking, dear reader, but bear with me.

Though we enjoyed ourselves, spraying vintage champers over everything, the opening of the Heavenly Bodies boutique wasn't exactly a riot. One or two press turned up to ooh and aah over our 'groovy' vegetable-themed décor and 'artisan' displays, but no one showed much interest in our skimpy skirts, although five got nicked.

We spent a gloomy first week in the boutique playing 'spot the customer'. I was beginning to think Jolyon had been right. Then Trip – or was it Dazzle? – ran in all of a do-dah, waving a copy of the *Daily Herald.*

Once more my gob was smacked. 'Get your pins out, girls!' screamed the headline. It was a double-page spread, splattered with pictures of long-legged models prancing and romping in our shortiskirts – the five pieces the *Herald's* fashion reporter had 'borrowed'.

Next morning when we arrived to open up, we found a queue of excited shoppers stretching almost as far as Beak Street. Pow! We had a hit on our hands.

Before long, the celeberati started slipping 'quietly' into the boutique, tinted-windowed Rollers purring at the kerb. Mentioning no names – discretion, as you may have noticed, is my catchword – Sandie, Marianne and Kathy were almost never out of the place!

Note to Boy: There must be cuttings somewhere. I wonder where the sod I put them?

Success brought its own problems, of course. The shortiskirt begat the shortidress and then the shortishort. Sales increased and Trip and Dazzle couldn't keep up with demand. We needed to step up a gear. It was Bruno who came up with the solution.

'We'll move into mass production, lass,' he said, puffing on a post-coital cigarette. 'Lease cheap factory space in Soho, hire some dolly birds and set up a production line.'

And that's what I did. Rented a run-down warehouse and filled it full of young former office skivvies. With Trip and Dazzle's help – though they mostly ran up and down between the machines, squawking out contradictory instructions – a plentiful supply of shorti items was soon rolling out.

It was the summer of 1964, a warm one as I recall, and Heavenly Bodies was as hot as the weather. A steady procession of wheeled rails trundled between the Soho sweatshop and Carnaby Street. Long queues outside the boutique became a daily occurrence. Fights frequently broke out. We doubled the prices, and still they came. So we doubled them again. We were making silly money. Life couldn't have been better.

Until *she* turned up. Kristina Krabtree. Don't you loathe the pretension of those two Ks? Today, as I'm sure you are sick to death of hearing, Kristina Krabtree is an international celebrity, a NATO ambassador and best buddy of that irritating Irish do-gooding warbler. What is his name? O2, is it? Back then she was just another young hopeful from the back of beyond – Leicester in her case – out to make it in the big city.

She looked then much as she does now, give or take the odd nip, tuck and lift. Dressed in demure black, she wore her hair in a severe blonde bob with a heavy fringe like a slab of white chocolate. These days, of course, it's a wig. At least, that was my conclusion after pressing my nose to the jellybox screen during some *Stand Up To Comic Children's Relief* programme she was on. Definitely a syrup.

Anyway, there she was, young, wig-free and nosing about in my boutique. I didn't know then who she was, of course, but immediately I smelled a kipper. There was something about the way she was examining the clothes, turning them inside out and squinting at the seams, pulling at the buttons. Normally I left the vulgar business of selling to others. On this occasion, I approached her in person.

'Exquisite aren't they?' I said, narrow-eyed.

'Still flogging yer shortiskirts, I see?' she said in the flat Leicestershire accent she had in those days, before she perfected her Radio 1 transatlantic drawl.

'Such a popular range,' I said, taking the skirt from her and hanging it back on the banana hook from where it had come.

'Last season maybe, pikelet. But face it, the shortiskirt's had its day. Girls are after something more radical.'

'Like what?'

'That'd be telling,' she laughed and, with a flick of her blonde locks, was gone.

I soon found out. Within weeks, those white-blonde locks were all over the fashion pages. No queues lined up outside Heavenly Bodies, no celebrities swanned in, no fights broke out.

Meanwhile, over in the King's Road, the newly opened KK boutique was bursting with punters, frantic to snap up the new craze: tubes of cheap jersey, cut even shorter than my shortis. For reasons I could never fathom, Kristina Krabtree's buttock-skimming fanny warmers were all the rage. The shorti was out. The mini was in.

Quant and Courrèges and Uncle Tom's Cabin soon waded in with their versions, all claiming to be the first. Heavenly Bodies was forgotten in the rush. Fashion writers and popstars I'd been on first-name terms with were 'in meetings' when I called. At Les A they were *désolé*, but no table was available.

I drank my Veuve Click at home with Bruno. Things were bleak for this little miss from the Midlands.

Four times. Four times that bony-arsed blonde bitch stuck it to me. Four times. She didn't leave it at the miniskirt. Oh no, she had to go on sticking it to me. Time after time after time after… until… until… Oh no. This is too much. I can't.

Note to Boy: Going for a lie down. No, don't fuss. Bring me two aspros and my little blue friend.

19.

BRADLEY

I'm in there. The little bedroom. Not the locked one. The one she says I can have. The one she calls her guest room, though there ain't been no guests for a while, you ask me. I'm clearing a space, not that I need much. Nice little crib. 'Cept for the wallpaper. That's horrible. Red splodges like bloodstains, supposed to be flowers – roses or poppies maybe? – come out at you, making your eyes go funny. All except for that, like I say, nice.

I'm rummaging through the stuff lying about in there. Sticking it in a box. Dusty old junk it is. All of a sudden, she's at the door. 'What in the name of sod?' She's done her silent creeping up thing again. Can see by her face she's forgot already.

'I'm moving in, Miss E. Remember? Gonna be your live-in staff?'

She gives me such a glare. 'The cheek of it. Put those things back where you found them.'

'Doing a bit of tidying up. Was gonna chuck this junk in the dustbin.'

She draws herself up to her full five foot nothing. I've

offended her. 'You will do no such thing. There could be valuable treasures in there.'

'Don't think so.' I hold out the cardboard box for her to check. Like I say, it's just junk. Dried-up biros and felt-tips, a chipped glass bowl with blobs of sugar in it set like concrete, a coupla greasy cookbooks with the pages falling out, a brown electric plug, a screwdriver with the handle broke off, a load of scrunched-up plastic bags, a ball of pink rubber bands what falls to dust when I touch it, and a pair of broken John Lennon sunnies. She rakes it over, picks out the shades and puts them on. She don't half look daft, one eye hid behind the yellow glass, the other blinking at me. I know better than to laugh.

'Live-in staff? And I agreed to this nonsense, you say? I must have been off my head. Very well, if you're now part of the household,' she goes, accepting it just like that, 'I'd appreciate a pot of tea and a plate of cakes. One really shouldn't have to keep asking for these things, you know. They should appear as a matter of course.' She counts them off on her fingers. 'Breakfast at eight. Elevenses at eleven – obviously. A spot of light luncheon at one. High tea at four. Dinner at eight and a nightcap and snacks just whenever the hell I feel like it. Got that?' She looks at her wrist, though she don't wear a watch. 'It is now well past teatime. Chop chop.' She claps her hands.

I check my phone. It's all of twenty-five past one.

'I only just this minute cleared up your dinner… luncheon, I mean,' I go. 'It's hours till tea.'

She holds up a hand like she's stopping traffic. 'Silence,' she goes. 'Tea in the drawing room. Immediately.' She turns on her heel and goes out.

I'm standing there, still holding the box, wondering what the heck to do with her junk, when…

'What in the name of sod are you doing?'

I jump a mile. She's back, still with them one-eyed sunglasses on her beak. She's forgot again. I start to go through it all, about me moving in an' that.

'Never mind about that,' she goes, butting in. 'What happened to my teatime snack? These things should appear as a matter of course, you know, without me having to constantly remind you.' She counts them again, like she's on rewind. 'Breakfast at Tiffany's. Tea at elevenses – or coffee. And high luncheon at erm...' She tosses her head, like it's me what's getting mixed up. 'I really shouldn't have to spell it out. Chop chop.'

'What about these things?' I go, holding out the box. 'What do you want me to do with them?'

She peers over the top. 'That load of old junk? Chuck it in the bin.'

Getting more weirder by the day.

Talk about jammy! A few days later, she has a fancy for 'real tea'. Gets me to buy some loose stuff, with leaves and flowers in it. More like compost than tea, you ask me. What's wrong with a nice tidy teabag? But no, that won't do, not for Miss E. Has to be leaves.

I'm in the kitchen and, as usual, she's bossing me long distance from the sitting room. 'Mind you use the best cups and a teapot,' she shouts. 'Let's have some class for once.'

I seen the good tea set when I was doing out her cupboards. All packed away. No visitors, no call to use it, see. Cups is so thin, when you hold them up to the light, you can see shadows of the painted flowers through them. Each flower is different, like someone's bent over with a tiny brush, doing each one by hand, taking their time, doing it proper, then finishing off each cup with a thin line of gold round the rim. Like she says, classy.

No telling how long they been stuck away, mind. Need a

good wash before we use them. Don't want to catch bubonic plague nor nothing. I run the hot tap and start washing them. When I lift out the teapot, something rattles inside. I take off the lid and tip it up. What falls out is one dead fly and one door key.

'Get a move on with my jasmine tea,' she shouts. 'I'm thirsty.'

'Coming,' I yell back, and slip the key into my back pocket.

Later, while she's full of tea and macaroons – the right ones this time – head tipped back, doing her impression of an old sow, I go down the corridor and try it. The lock turns sweet as. But I don't go in, not yet. Don't even open the door. Lock it up and put the key in the teapot where I found it. Gotta give this some thought.

I'm at the gym on the treadmill, hypnotised by my own reflection. That scraggy kid, thin arms pumping, that can't be me, can it?

It come to me as I was moving in. There's a big old mirror on the back of the door in my room, see? *My room!* I'm stripped to my boxers washing down the paintwork an' everything. As I work, I keep seeing meself in the mirror. It ain't a good look. *You need to muscle up, Bradley,* I tell meself. *Do some exercise. Get some protein supplements down your neck. Make a man of yourself. No excuse, now you don't have Dom and Ma taking the Mick of you.* Then I think, *Why not join a gym?* There's one upstairs over the Chinese massage parlour. Thirty-five quid a month, it says on the board on the pavement. She'll never notice that.

I'm having a free try-out. The gym instructor watches me, while I work up a sweat. Big black bloke. About Dom's age. Only proper hench and he knows it. Making out like he's some bigshot – clicking his stopwatch, sucking on his biro and writing on his clipboard – even though he's only working in a crappy little gym over a Chinky knocking shop in Praed Street.

'You'll need to get some kit, if you're gonna join,' he goes, giving my navy tee and skinnies a disapproving once-over. 'And you can't train in that hat, man.'

'If you insist,' I go and take it off. I see his eyes widen. Can't help hisself. He recovers quick, probably thinking I don't notice. But I do. I always do. Funny thing is, these days it don't get to me half as much as it used to when people gawp.

Once I get the hang, I'm enjoying meself. I press the buttons, running faster and faster up a steep hill, then back down the other side. Only trouble is, without the beanie my hair is annoying me. Bouncing up and down. Up in the air, down in my eyes. With every jog, covering and uncovering the thing on my face. Fringe. Thing. Fringe. Thing.

I keep my finger pressed down on the button till I'm going full pelt. Then I punch the big red *stop* button with my fist and slow to a walk, then a stop. I bend over, sucking in oxygen and laughing.

'You OK?' the instructor calls over.

'Where do I sign?' I say, when I can speak.

I'm back at Miss E's in front of the mirror in my room. Take her big scissors and chop off my fringe. Real short. Hack at it, like it's a hedge. Check it out. Don't like it. Looks dorky. Get to scissoring again. Get another mirror out the bathroom and hack some more till I've give meself what amounts to an all-over number two. I'll need to get it tidied up at the barber's but I reckon it looks pretty good.

That is more like it, I say to the skinhead hard nut grinning back from the mirror. *That is much more like it.*

Next day, after the barber's, I go to the coffee shop. The hissing of the shiny machine behind the counter – like a steam train it is – drowns out just about everything but I don't have to hear the words to know what Molly's saying.

'My God,' she mouths. 'What's happened?'

'Haircut,' I go, running my hand over the stubble. 'Don't you like it?'

She moves away from the machine so we can hear each other. 'I never realised… I mean, I've never seen it properly before. Your…' Her voice drops away.

'Birthmark. It's a birthmark. You can say the word. It ain't seven years' bad luck nor nothing.'

'Why'd you do it? Cut off your hair?'

'Been hiding behind that fringe for far too long.'

She thinks about that one for a sec, then goes, 'Long fringes are *sooo* last season anyway.' And her mouth spreads into one of them smiles. I smile back.

When her shift is over we go for a walk in the park. It's only early afternoon but it's already getting dark. Even though I ain't sorry I chopped my hair, I'm thankful for the gloom. We walk for a while, keeping well apart, until we come to a bench. We sit. She picks at her cuff. No one speaks.

'Haemangioma,' I go, my voice too loud. I put my hand to my face, feeling the roughness and say more quieter, 'That's what the doctors called it anyhow. Come when I was a few months old. Think about it. You pop out this cute little nipper, then after a coupla weeks you notice this thing crawling across its skull. A little red mark at first on my forehead. Tiny. No bigger than your little fingernail. Like the stork had pecked me, my nan used to say. Why do they do that, nans, trot out them stupid stories? As if anyone's ever gonna believe them.'

Like I said before, I ain't usually one to run off at the mouth but somehow as the darkness falls, I feel like letting it out.

'It don't stay small,' I go on. 'Oh no. Day by day it grows, creeping down my forehead like some horrible fungus. Lucky for me it stops when it gets to my eye. Thank God it does, 'cause Dom told me that if it goes across your eyelid, you go blind.' I give a half-laugh. 'But then, what does he know?'

'What did the doctors say?' she says, looking down at her hands.

'Ma was always up the hospital with me when I was a nipper. They said best leave it alone, on account of how close it is to my eye. That in time it would vanish of its own accord.' I half-laugh again. 'Still waiting on that one.'

'How awful for you. Poor Bradley.'

She puts her hand on mine. My chest tightens and it's all I can do not to push her away. She's feeling sorry for me. I hear it in every word and it's starting to give me agg. But I swallow it down and carry on.

'Got used to it. Had to. Even got used to the stares and the people what talk to this,' I point to the thing, 'not to me.'

She blinks and a tear runs down. She smears it away with a finger. 'And your mum? Must have been bad for her too.'

Know what, till she says that, I ain't give no thought to how it must have been for Ma, trailing round the hospitals, hearing the same old BS from the docs, pushing me round the shops, squaring up to the raised eyebrows and the mean whispers. We never talked about it, her and me. Not once. Maybe that's why I'm so keen to spill my guts now.

'Be honest,' I go. 'I really don't creep you out? You're cool with the way I look?'

Her hand's still on mine. 'I've told you.' She gives it a squeeze. 'You look fine. You know, handsome.'

Maybe she don't just feel sorry for me. Maybe she really

does like me after all. The tightness in my chest eases. Then the words come gushing out, words I didn't even know I was gonna say till I say them.

'I really like you, Molly. Ain't met no one like you before. I can talk to you. About everything. You're safe, you are. Safe.'

I lean forward. Her black hair brushes against the thing. She don't pull back. Everything is quiet. No traffic. No dogs. No lairy lads in boombox motors. Time stops. Is this how it is? Is this the moment? One second I'm sure it is, the next, I don't know. I freeze. Then she reaches over and lightly, so lightly, like she's stroking me with a feather, runs her fingertip from the stubble of my hair, across my forehead and down to my eyelid.

I close my eyes and breathe out. I feel good. I feel normal. Don't never want this moment, this exact moment of time, to end. I run my tongue over my lips. This has gotta be the moment. I bend my head. Then she comes out with it.

'Know what?' she goes. 'A dab or two of concealer and you wouldn't hardly notice that. I could have a go for you now, if you like. I've got some in my bag.'

My stomach feels like it's dropped off of a cliff.

She ducks down. A dog yaps. Brakes squeal. A passing motor thumps out hip-hop. The world – the noisy, stinking, rubbish world – crashes in. Worst of it is, she don't even know what she's said. When she straightens up, she's holding out a tube of something and she's got one of them stupid smiles across her face.

I'm out that park and away before you can say 'two-faced bitch'. Stop to chuck up in a bush.

So much for her not being creeped out. So much for me being normal.

I'm back in my room, freaking out.

Miss E's in the Land of Nod. Good. Don't have to explain to her all over again who I am. I fling meself on my bed. Punch seven bells out the pillow. Curl meself into a ball. Roar silently at the wall. All the time saying to meself, *Don't you cry. Don't you dare cry.*

What was I thinking? How could I have been taken in by them smiles and them soft words, them eyes with the flecks of gold sunlight in them. She ain't no different from the rest. They're all the same. Only interested in theirselves. Not in some freak with red paint splashed across his mug.

By now I'm working meself up into a right state. Miss E's as bad, I'm thinking. Who does she think she is telling me where I can and cannot go? I live here, don't I? All fired up, I pad to the kitchen and get that key out the teapot.

Teeth clenched, breathing fast and shallow, I step quickly down the hall, unlock the door and push. The door sticks. I put my shoulder to it and hear something slide across the bare boards. Can't get the door open wide enough to get in. So I reach round with my hand, feeling for the switch. I click it on. Blinking in the sudden light, I poke my head round the door. What a sight!

20.

ELOISE

Heavenly Bodies was sinking fast. Fortunately, Jolyon Slaughter Associates wasn't. In fact, it was surfing along atop the crest of a towering wave made entirely of crisp fivers and fat cheques. The solution was obvious. Divorce Jolyon as I'd threatened and grab my share of his money. Did I feel guilty about fleecing him so roundly? Did I buggery.

When I told Jolyon over the phone I wanted a divorce, first he cried, then he begged and finally he turned nasty. 'You're not getting your grubby little Brummie hands on a penny. I earned it and I intend to keep it,' he bellowed.

On the other end of the line, I was coolness personified. 'You don't scare me, you dickless windbag. I have right on my side – not to mention the brightest, most fashionable divorce lawyer in town.' I slammed the phone down.

For you see, dear reader, I had Mr Featherstone-Leigh. 'Don't get angry. Don't get even. Get everything.' That was Mr Featherstone-Leigh's motto.

How well I remember the first time I went to his office – sorry, chambers – off the Embankment. My entrance in a Heavenly

Bodies bell-bottomed jumpsuit in shades of lime and orange, a feather boa round my neck, caused quite a stir. As one, the charcoal- and navy-clad secretaries and typists halted in their tracks, eyes swivelling.

'Miss Eloise Slaughter to see Mr Featherstone-Leigh,' I announced with a self-assured swish of my elephant trousers.

A timid secretary led me up creaking stairs and down wood-panelled corridors to his office, leaving me at his door. I turned the handle and went in.

'Halt!' The voice was so deep, I felt it vibrate through the little hairs in my ears. 'Out and knock.'

Backing out as if the man were royalty, I pulled the wooden doors shut behind me with a clunk, waited then knocked three times. Nothing. I knocked again, louder this time. For the love of sod, what was the man playing at?

'Come!' he bellowed, so loudly I staggered back. Recovering myself, I stepped inside.

Before me stretched a maroon carpet approximately the size of a tennis court and, over in the distance, silhouetted against the window, sat a figure at a vast desk. Deafened by his voice and blinded by the light from the window, I tottered forward on my three-inch platforms. This was not the impressive entrance I'd planned.

Mr Featherstone-Leigh made no move to rise and greet me. He sat at his desk, in his hands a pistol, which he was stroking.

Lord, what had I got myself into?

'Sit!' he barked, pointing to a single chair set before the desk. I sank onto it. 'Identify yourself.'

I cleared my throat. 'Erm… Eloise Ssslaughter,' I stuttered. No man had ever made me stutter before.

'Louder!'

'Eloise Slaughter,' I repeated with all the confidence I could muster. 'May I say, what lovely offices, I mean chambers—'

'State your business.'

I shifted uneasily in my seat. 'I want to get rid of my useless lump of a husband but keep as much of his money as possible.'

'Hmm, brutal but honest,' he said. Was that a faint smile on his lips? Picking up the pistol, he strode to my side of the desk and perched on the edge. I gave a gasp. The material of his suit – finest cashmere and Italian wool, if I'm any judge – stretched tautly across his perfect buttock. The weapon nestled in his groin, like a baby in its crib.

'Phew.' I waved a hand in front of my face. 'It's hot in here.'

Lifting the gun, he aimed it at my forehead. I stared deep into those unblinking, unreadable eyes. His finger tightened and, as he pulled the trigger, I felt a surge, not of fear, but of excitement. A small yellow flame sprang from its barrel.

He slid the silver cigarette box towards me. 'Do you?' he rumbled.

'All the time,' I purred, taking a cigarette.

Instantly, I was in lust.

There was mention of lunch but we never made it to the restaurant. We only just made it past the front door of his Chelsea bachelor pad before falling upon each other like starving wolves. An apt description since, stripped of his bespoke trappings, the flawless Mr Featherstone-Leigh – we never felt the need to progress to first-name terms – was an animal. Within minutes he'd given me the most nerve-jangling, teeth-tingling orgasm of my life. Five minutes later, he did it again.

I'd had quite a lot of sex in my life before Mr Featherstone-Leigh, but he was in a class of his own. Meticulous, energetic and relentless in everything he did, he had me yelping and squeaking with passion.

Afterwards Mr Featherstone-Leigh would shower, dress with care and head off to the court to put in another sombre performance. In the evenings, after more luscious leg-over action, we'd discuss my case. How he was going to take Jolyon for half of every penny he'd ever earned. How I was going to be very rich indeed.

Jolyon, of course, was contesting the financial arrangements with all the tenacity and cunning of a first-rate accountant. I wasn't worried. Not with the peerless Mr Featherstone-Leigh on my side.

The week before the case was due to be heard found me supremely confident. More fool me. I'd underestimated the well-connected Jolyon. Mr Featherstone-Leigh, whose sources were impeccable, broke the bad news.

'His QC. His godfather,' he told me in his clipped tones. 'The judge. At school with his father, the Major. The three of them. Members of the same golf club.'

This was not good. 'Worse than that,' I said, recalling an incident at our wedding reception, 'his godfather tried to tongue me once and I kicked him on the shin. He's bound to bear a grudge – and a scar probably.'

That was bad enough but Jolyon's trump card left me speechless. We were pressing for a fifty–fifty settlement. That would mean, his lawyer gleefully informed Mr Featherstone-Leigh over an informal brandy at their club, that I would get precisely nothing. Why? I hear you wail, dear reader. Because fifty per cent of nothing is – *better double check the maths on this, Boy* – nothing. Jolyon claimed he was skint.

I know. I was flabbergasted too. Then mad. Then sodding mad. The news was so surprising that, when it leaked out – thanks to the cunning Mr Featherstone-Leigh – it made the financial pages under the headline 'Millionaire moneyman loses fortune overnight'.

How could this be? Jolyon, as you'll know if you've been paying attention, was a showbiz accountant, a highly successful one. His client list was more star-studded than a Frank Ifield yodelling party. How could he be broke?

'He's shitting us,' I told the gorgeous Mr Featherstone-Leigh, snuggled up in his cosy king size. 'He must be.'

Together, we hatched a plan to foil the lying toad. We knew we couldn't get him on the paperwork. Jolyon was far too crafty at booking cooks. We had to play it sneaky.

Luckily for me, Mr Featherstone-Leigh had connections of his own. His second cousin was an expensively educated, very intelligent girl who had broken her parents' hearts by chucking school to become the lead singer in an all-girl group, Dolly and the Delights. Don't bother looking them up. They were one-hit wonders. Their one and only record was dreadful but, to everyone's surprise, a big hit. 'Kissy-wissy, Flirty-wirty', or something along those lines.

Dolly – real name Delilah Cavendish – adored Mr Featherstone-Leigh. Indeed, what woman could not? He had a word in Dolly's shell-like and persuaded her in his reverberating monosyllables to pay a visit to the City offices of Jolyon Slaughter Associates. Jolyon, of course, positively drooled at the prospect of handling her and her popstar fortune. He was in the middle of his sales spiel when Dolly interrupted.

'But didn't I read in the papers only a few days ago that your business – this business,' she said, no doubt fluttering her eyelashes, 'has gone bust? Something about a messy divorce? I could never trust my money to a bankrupt—'

'Ah, that,' laughed Jolyon. 'That's just a technicality for the benefit of the court. I would explain, my dear, but it's rather complicated and I doubt you'd understand.'

'Try me,' Dolly, who was something of a maths genius, said brightly. 'I'll do my best to keep up.'

Flattered, Jolyon spilled his entire can of worms. How his City accountancy practice was now based in Nassau. How he'd parked his cash in accounts so far offshore you'd need a very long telescope indeed to spot them. How his fortune was hidden under more corporate umbrellas than a wet Ladies' Day at Ascot. In short, how, though he was one of the wealthiest men in London, he hadn't a dime – on paper, at least.

'It's fool-proof. I'll still be raking it in, while the little wifey – the *ex* little wifey – won't see a penny,' he boasted. 'That woman will be lucky to get her cab fare home from court.'

'That is so utterly devious.'

'Thank you, my dear,' he preened.

Later that evening, Dolly played us the tape. Did I mention she'd hidden a Dictaphone in her oversize handbag and recorded the lot? She really was a very resourceful young woman. Much later, she went to live in some godforsaken part of Latin America. In fact, didn't I read somewhere she'd been voted president for life there? I wonder if she makes her ministers listen to 'Kissy-wissy, Flirty-wirty'? I would.

Mr Featherstone-Leigh didn't even have to confront Jolyon in court. All it took was a call to his lawyer. Mr Featherstone-Leigh played the tape to him over the phone and, after hearing only a few seconds of Jolyon's bragging, the lawyer simply hung up. He knew the game was up and so did his client. When the case came up, the judge, mauve with indignation, was forced to find in my favour. I got everything I asked for. Exactly half of Jolyon's entire fortune. One and a half million lovely, lovely quid.

We'd won a glorious victory but my celebrations were muted. With the end of the case, I knew, would come the end of my affair with Mr Featherstone-Leigh. It was the thrill of the chase that had brought us together. With our quarry cornered and brought down, the liaison lost its thrill. We had one last bonk for old times' sake and parted forever. He became a High Court judge.

How I missed Mr Featherstone-Leigh, but there were compensations: one and a half million of them. At last I was what I knew I deserved to be – filthy rich. There was one spanner in the ointment: Bruno. Oh yes, dear reader, Bruno was still on the scene. When he wasn't working away in the office at Heavenly Bodies he was sulking in my apartment, waiting for me to stagger home from Mr Featherstone-Leigh's Chelsea pad for a change of knickers.

It came to a head one night. He wasn't into 'open relationships' he told me angrily. He was a one-man woman. That was fine by me, I told him. As long as I wasn't that woman. In any case, the delicacy of Mr Featherstone-Leigh's exquisite technique had spoiled me for Bruno's rough and ready 'Come here, lass' Northern style of rogering.

Which left me with a problem. Though relationship-wise I was more than ready to move on, I still needed Bruno's business brain.

Heavenly Bodies, you see, was still in the… ditherings, is it? You know, up the whatsit without a doodah. After the whole shortiskirt debacle. Remember? KK, on the other hand, was riding high. The cash injection from the divorce couldn't have come at a better time. It was just what was needed to finance a comeback. For that I needed my whole team solidly behind me, including Bruno. I was in a dilemma. How could I chuck Bruno out of the bedroom but keep him in the boardroom?

My, my, wasn't that fun? Not as much fun as doing it. Oh, Mr Featherstone–Leigh, what a wonder you were. What is wrong with you, Boy? You've had a face like a wet Wednesday in Clacton for days. Fix me a drink. A good long one. After a hard morning's memoir-ing – it is still morning, isn't it? – I'm in dire need of something to thench my quirst. Sod me, was that a smile? Whatever next?

21.

BRADLEY

I'm back at the low rise, bricking it. Can't seem to get it out my head, what that Molly said. Every time I think about it, I feel sick to my stomach. One good thing come out of it. It made me realise, in this life you gotta look after Number One. 'Cause no one else is gonna, no matter what they say. That's my priority from now on. Looking out for what's best for Mr Bradley McCreedy.

That's how come I end up back at Ma's. There's things there I want, see? I want them and I'm gonna have them. It's risky but I plan it careful. I go on a Tuesday, middle of the afternoon, when I'm fairly certain no one's at home. Ma will be at the bingo, then down her local, either drinking her winnings or drowning her sorrows. Dom has to go to Offender Behaviour, half past two, or Nick, his probation officer, is on the phone giving him earache. That's why he's always in a bad mood of a Monday. Knows he's gotta get up next day.

Can't tell from down in the street if anyone's in or not. I go on up the steps and along the walkway to the front door. Put my head to the kitchen window. All I see is the usual shambles. All I hear is nothing. Let meself in, quiet as.

'Ma? Dom? It's me. You there?'

Nothing. Coast is clear. Got the place to meself. Stand in the kitchen. First thing I clock is the radio. It's Ma's. She has it on the whole time. Radio 2. When she's in a good mood, she shimmies about to it, fag hanging off of her lip. When she's having words with one of her blokes, she turns it up, probably thinking we can't hear what's going down. She'd be lost without it. *Could have that*, I think. Just take it. I pick it up but it's only a tinny little thing. I put it back where I found it, giving its sticky case a pat.

Forcing meself not to look at the tea slops I know is staining the sink and the lime crust building up round the hot tap, I head for the stairs, hopping up, light on my feet, two at a time. What I see at the top takes the wind out my sails. Draped over the banisters to dry is a load of men's' clothes. Underpants, vests and a coupla them check lumberjack shirts. Way too old-style and gynormous to be Dom's.

Only explanation is, while I been away Ma's latest has got his feet under the table. I rack my brains for a name. Stan, that's it. Rougher than her usual and that's saying something. Chavvy sort of a bloke with a beer belly what hangs over his beer belly. Like all of them, he stinks of fags, cider and violence.

Eyeing the pants like they might rear up and grab me, I edge past and into the room what I used to share with my dear brother. It's a mess. No surprise there. Don't look like he's put nothing away since I left. It's all piled up on my bed. Socks, boxers, tees, denims and damp towels mixed in with snotty tissues, packets of Rizla, three or four of them throwaway ciggie lighters, empty tinnies, cans of Lynx – what Dom calls 'ho juice'. And, of course, a stack of porn. Disgusting.

My lucky QPR kit should be somewhere in the bottom of the wardrobe, where I used to keep my clothes. Have to ferret about among Dom's stinking Cats and Addidases to find it. The next thing I'm after, the book, I find under his bed, tangled up in console cables. 'Hello, Mr Sherlock Holmes,' I go under my breath, brushing the fluff off of its cover. 'Been missing you.'

Amazingly, the photo frame is where I left it, under my pillow. I run my thumb over the crack in the corner. When I was a little 'un, Dom used to find it funny to keep snatching it off of me. Chucked it out the window one time. Lucky for me we're only two floors up and it landed on grass. Still got cracked. Jealous, see. On account of how he never had no picture of his dad.

I'm staring at the photo when I hear something. Someone's letting theirselves in, walking down the hall, clomping up the stairs. I figure it's better to know what you're gonna have to face. I sing out, 'That you, Dom?' All I get is a grunt. I try again. 'Stan?'

Ain't chicken nor nothing but with Stan we're talking big. Real big. Used to wrestle – or so he told Ma and Ma told me.

'Hope you don't mind, Stan,' I go. 'Just getting a few things.' I'm hating the way my voice is sounding, all wobbly and tight. 'That's cool, ain't it, mate?' *Mate! What am I saying?*

The only sound is the footsteps. By now they has reached the landing. They stop. A deep voice snarls, 'What the fuck do you think you're doing?' Next thing, the door bursts open, a figure forward-rolls in, commando-style, and lands on the mat.

'Hiya, Dom,' I go, offhand as I can.

'That give you a start, didn't it, little bruv?' he goes, lying on his back, laughing. 'You really thought it was Stan, didn't you, you loser?' He clocks my number two for the first time. 'Bloody hell, Brad. You was an ugly little fucker before, but with no hair... fuck me.' He covers his eyes, like he can't bear the sight.

'Very funny,' I go.

He springs to his feet. 'Tell you what *is* funny. You going...'

and he puts on that whiney voice, '"That all right, Stan? My bestest friend, my gayest bumchum?"' He smacks his lips together, making smooching noises.

'Thought you'd be out at your course,' I go.

'Bet you did. Sadly, it was not to be.' He pulls his mouth down. Like he cares. 'Today was the day some pissed-off pusher hit the red mist and twatted the soft waste-of what calls hisself our offender manager. Lip split right up to his nose. Blood everywhere. Prick had it coming, mind. Only wish it was me what had smacked him. Then it was *weeaaah weeaaah,* here come the copper-nobs and the para-morons, and "Maybe you could come back next week, Dominic, if it ain't too much trouble?" Funniest part was, guess what we was supposed to be doing today? Anger management.' He laughs again. 'Ain't that something?'

'I'll be off then,' I go.

'Off where though?' he goes, turning snidey. 'That's the question. Where's my little bruv laying his stubbly little bonce?' He goes to rub my head but I sidestep. That's when he spots I've got something behind my back. 'What you hiding there?'

I show him the kit and he gives a snort. 'Don't tell me you're having a go at footie. You was always rubbish at it. What position you playing? Left back in the changing room?' Loves his little jokes, our Dom, even if no one else does.

'You know,' I mumble. 'Keeping fit an' that.'

'Fit for the knacker's yard more like. Look at you.' He pokes me. 'Arms like a girl. Legs like knotted string. Seen more meat on a kebab stick. Get a load of these.' He prats round the room, flexing his guns. Though he ain't exactly no Arnie, I gotta admit, he's got more beef on him than me. I fumble with the kit and there's a clatter and a thump. Before I can stop him, Dom's grabbed the book.

'What's this load of old toss?' he goes, flicking open the pages. '*Have I the honour sir, of addressing Mister…?*' Only he reads out 'honour' with a haitch and has several goes at 'addressing'. I'm having trouble holding it in. '*Mister…*' he tries again, then. '*Sh… Sh… Sh…*' he stutters.

'It's Sherlock Holmes, you plank. Even a numpty like you must have heard of Mr Sherlock Holmes, the famous detective?'

'Who're you calling a numpty?' Dom tosses the book and makes a lunge. There's a crunch. He's trod on the photo.

He bends to pick up the smashed photo frame. 'Thought you'd have give up slobbering over this years ago.' A look comes in his eyes, a mean look. 'Well, well, well. What do we have here?'

'Give us it, Dom,' I go, holding out my hand.

He turns away. 'Ain't that sweet? Bradley and his daddykins enjoying theirselves in the park.'

Every centimetre of that picture is branded on my brain. The sky is so blue, the trees look greeny-black against it. The man smiling into the camera is tanned and fit, with kind eyes screwed up against the sun. He's wearing a red shirt, sleeves rolled up. His arms is up above his head, holding onto the chubby thighs of the baby on his shoulders. The baby is laughing, digging its fingers into his dark hair and kicking its bare little legs, making that bit of the photo blurry. Me and my dad. The only picture I got of him.

'How do you account for this then, eh?' Dom pulls the photo out its broken frame and flaps it in my face. Only it ain't a photo. I see that now. It's a piece of paper with printing on the back. A picture cut out a magazine.

Dom's killing hisself. 'Ain't that the mutt's nuts?' he splutters. 'The bloke whose picture you been cuddling up to all these years ain't your dad, he's some gayboy from a catalogue advert. And, if that ain't your dad – you get where I'm going with this, Bradley? – that means this,' he jabs at the paper, 'this little nipper on his shoulders ain't you. I mean, now I come to think about it, how could it be? This is a beautiful little baby. Not a *Monsters Inc* freak with a fucking great red stripe down its mush.'

With a roar, I launch meself at him but Dom is ready for me. He ducks out the way, dancing on his toes, going, 'Come on, you fairy, show us what you got.' I try to land a punch but he's too quick. He weaves about, slapping and tapping, waiting for his moment to finish it. It can only end one way, I know that.

Though Dom gives me a running commentary, I still don't see it coming. 'This is how you do it, Bradley, see? Come up on his blind side, quick jab to the face, in out and away, before he knows what's hit him.' My head snaps back, there's a stinging on my cheek. I stagger and the back of my head connects with the wall. My knees go soft.

'You ain't no fun,' Dom goes, skipping from foot to foot like a boxer, breathing hard. He wipes his nose on the back of his hand. 'Know what, Ma and me, we just about got used to the idea that we wasn't gonna have to put up with your wet, noncey ways any more. Now here you are, creeping back like a bad smell. Get out my sight,' he goes, grabbing a magazine and flopping down on his bed. 'Go on. Get lost.'

I go to collect my stuff.

'Leave that,' he shouts. 'I brung you that kit for your birthday.'

No way am I gonna leave that kit. This is the new Bradley we're talking about. Any case, I know full well he never bought it, he lifted it. I look at the mess, at Dom, lolling on his bed, turning the page this way and that, so's he can get a better ogle of this tart's arse. I pick up the picture of my so-called dad and scrunch it into a ball.

First time, the lighter don't spark. Dom looks up. I click

again. This time, there's a yellow flame. I touch it to the crumpled picture. It catches. I throw it on my bed and watch as the flames spread. A charred circle appears and grows, like a mini forest fire. Smoke curls up and pools at the ceiling. All this takes about two and a half seconds. Two and a half seconds when Dom just sits there, mouth open. Then he screams.

'What the fuck is wrong with you?' he goes, diving from his bed, flapping with a towel. He only makes it worse. 'You crazy little freak.'

I take a moment to enjoy the white panic in his eyes, then, real cool, wrap the kit round my book and tuck the bundle under my arm. As I let meself out, I hear his can of 'ho juice' explode.

22.

ELOISE

'Whose is that?' Bruno asked with more enthusiasm than I'd seen him muster for many a long week. 'She's a beauty.'

Heavenly Bodies had grown over the decade we'd been in business. By now, in the mid 1970s, we occupied a whole row of Soho premises. Bruno was peering down from them into Carnaby Street at the sleek, electric blue flanks of a sports car parked at the kerbside.

'Oh, the Triumph Stag,' I said airily. 'Didn't I say? It belongs to our new operations director. I decided to make some changes.'

Bruno's teeth clenched. 'No, you didn't mention it, Ellie. I'd have thought—'

'That's you, you chump,' I interrupted, bursting into laughter. 'You're the new operations director.'

His face went through a whole dammit of expressions, ending up in pure delight. 'Me? A bloody director? Oh, come here, lass,' he said, hugging me tight, the first time we'd been in physical contact since before Mr Featherstone-Leigh came on the scene. Then his grip loosened and a note of suspicion entered his voice 'But why? After all, you and I aren't—'

'For the label, of course. It needs you. And sod it, I need you,

Bruno. And you're no use to me if you're moping. Look,' I said gently, 'just because we're no longer… you know, doesn't mean we have to… you know.'

He seemed to understand.

'You're right,' he beamed. 'We're still a good team.'

'The best. With your brains and my… whatever it is I have, the sky's the limit. Now,' I said, dangling the Stag's keys under his nose, 'are you going to take me for a spin or what?'

With Heavenly Bodies back on track, I had time to enjoy my new single status. I say, enjoy. I mean, revel in, relish, lap it up like a Persian cat who hasn't had a bowl of cream in months.

Oh yes, dear reader, life was a crazy, thrilling merry-go-round. I was rich. I was single. I knew how to party. Round and round the carousel I spun, whirling off to a different junket every evening and into bed with a new man whenever the opportunity arose. It was as if until then I had been living in black and white. Now I was in a Technicolor dream.

In the end, I discarded all my lovers. Once my needs had been met, why would I want them around, getting under my feet, demanding time and attention? No, I was having a good time, but my real focus was my only true love, Heavenly Bodies.

Having almost come a cropper because of that damned miniskirt fad, I was determined to build a more secure empire. No one would ever catch me napping again. What I needed was a new fashion sensation. I called a crisis meeting with Bruno, Trip and Dazzle. This is what we came up with.

The longitube. Fashion, as I've mentioned before, dear reader, is all about novelty. What would women find novel, after flashing their legs up to their knickers? Why, something that covered them from neck to ankle, of course.

I must admit to having a wobble of confidence when I saw Trip and Dazzle's prototypes. With their trademark wonky seams and uneven hems, the new line made wearers look like badly squeezed toothpaste tubes – hence the name, longitube. The public, I'm happy to say, had no such qualms; they loved the longitube from the start.

Once more the Carnaby Street boutique echoed to the happy sounds of ringing tills and brawling customers. Once more we were the talk of the fashion world. Then it happened again. One Monday – nothing. No customers. No sales. A glance at the *Evening Standard* early edition told me all I needed to know. Kristina Krabtree had launched a 'revolutionary new look'. The maxi. That's right. Another blatant rip-off.

Again, incredible though it may seem, people preferred her tailored, mud-coloured skirts to our more eccentrically cut ones. Her collection took off into the stratosphere, while ours ploughed into the runway and burst into flames, scattering debris far and wide. That is to say, we were paddleless up Manure Gorge. Heavenly Bodies was lucky to survive that one.

You'd have thought I'd have learned my lesson, wouldn't you? As quickly as I produced a new fashion sensation, Kristina sodding Krabtree, the bitch, would first copy and then eclipse it. Wherever I went, it seemed she was two steps behind me, waiting to trip me up. Not – as she has claimed over the years – the other way round. Undeterred, I went for the hat-trick.

What did I come up with? It mostly consisted of fishnets that were more holes than tights, torn shirts with provocative messages scrawled across them – the 'You Make Me Vomit' range was especially popular, I recall – rubber trousers held together with safety pins, and lots of chains and studded dog collars. We called it the Rag Bag look.

'Copy this, Kristina Krabtree, if you dare,' I muttered.

She did, of course. Within weeks her boutique was full

of blasphemous t-shirts, designer-shredded jeans and paint-besplattered leathers. And that, dear reader, is the true story of how punk was spawned. Not Viv, not Malc, not Jean Paul Goatie Beard and certainly not whatsisname… Sid sodding Clash Pistol. Nicked, the whole damned lot of it, from my Rag Bag look. Yes, dear reader, once again I'd been done over.

Oh God, this is hard. I don't know if I can… Perhaps if I wet my whistle. No, for sod's sake! I mean a drink. Get me a drink. Courage, Eloise. You can do this.

23.

BRADLEY

Done it now, ain't I? Burned my bridges. Or my bed. Ha, ha! Can't never go back to Kilburn. If Dom or Stan don't kill me, Ma will do the job. And guess what? I don't even care. Got a room. Got means in my jeans. I'm free. This calls for a celebration. This calls for a spending spree.

I take a detour to Oxford Street, swinging along, grin on me wider than a double-decker. For the first time since I was a nipper, I ain't even noticing if people is gawking.

First on my list is a top-of-the-range laptop, some DVDs to play on it, and a smartphone. Won't even have to hide the electronics from the old girl. Tell her it's for the book and she's cool. Anything for the book is OK by her. A sleeping bag and some more threads. Got a fancy for some coloured tees.

I'm on a high right up until I'm back at Miss E's front door. Then I get cold feet. She has enough trouble remembering who I am at the best of times. How's she gonna react when she sees my scalped head? I let meself in quiet as, but her bat ears is twitching.

'Good. You're back,' she sings out, coming into the hall. She pauses then, not even giving me a second glance, sails on into the sitting room, calling over her shoulder, 'You sort out supper. I'll see what's on the jolly old jellybox?'

Can't last, I think. Sure enough, I catch her giving me sideways looks as we tuck into our M&S spag bol on trays in front of *Come Dine with Me,* one of her favourites. She loves it when the people get hammered and slag each other off. Keep expecting her to come out with some outrageous comment about my barnet. 'Cause she ain't never gonna be diplomatic, is she? Not Miss E. She don't say a word. The suspense is killing me. When the adverts come on, I have to ask her what she thinks.

'About what?' she goes, winding spaghetti onto her fork.

'My hair an' that.'

'Better,' she says, concentrating on her plate. 'I can see your eyes now. Your eyes are your best feature. Did you know that? Some might say, your *only* feature.' She looks up. 'I've always had a soft spot for deep, dark eyes. They're so… unknowable.' I realise it ain't my eyes she's talking about.

'Nothing else?' *Brace yourself,* I think.

'Now you come to mention it,' she goes, waving a forkful of spaghetti thick as a baby's arm in my face. 'There is something. You've introduced some colour into your wardrobe. What would you call that? Aubergine? Maroon? Burgundy? It suits you, at any rate. Makes a nice change from black. One of the many benefits of living with a fashion icon I suppose. Style, you see, is catching.'

With that, she posts the gynormous load into her mouth, sucks up its dripping tails and sits there chewing happily, not giving a flying fig there's juice spilling down her chin in a red river onto her clothes. Never so much as mentions the thing on my face.

Oh my days, but she is random.

What's the first thing I do when I get the laptop set up? Google her, of course. Miss E. Bit of a disappointment, to be honest with you. Molly was right. She's fallen off of the radar. There's plenty of Wikis on fashion way back when but 'Eloise Slaughter fashion designer' brings up a big fat zero. Then I remember something. Heavenly Bodies. That's what her business was called. I try that. Underneath the gyms, beauty shops and star-gazing stuff, there's a link to a Wiki on Swinging London. I click through and, sure enough, come across this:

'As well as more famous names, several maverick fashion houses began to emerge from Carnaby Street and King's Road, Chelsea at this time, including KK and Heavenly Bodies.'

Now we're getting somewhere. I click on Heavenly Bodies. It comes up 'page does not exist'. What a let-down. I click on KK. A Wiki about a mile long appears.

I'm in my room. This is the life.

It's turned out mint. I love it. I ask Miss E if it's all right to do it up a bit. She don't seem bothered either way. 'Whatever makes you happy, as long as I'm not inconvenienced,' she goes. She's in her own little world. If it ain't about her book or food, she ain't interested.

First off, I drag the bed under the window. So's I get the light, see? I can lay in bed first thing, after the sun comes up and before Miss E stirs. Proper luxury it is, curled up in my super-warm sleeping bag, snug as, in my own room.

Get meself down to the DIY shop and buy paint, rollers, brush cleaner, rolls of plastic to cover everything and a paper suit to wear, so's I don't mess up my threads. Feel a plonker wearing it, mind, but no one's gonna see and it does the job.

One Coat, Pure Brilliant White I go for. It's cheaper. Twelve pounds ninety-nine for a big tin. Work on it for two whole days but when I stand back, I can still see them poppies or whatever bleeding through, even though I follow the instructions to the letter.

Go back and have it out with the manager. 'One Coat,' I go. 'It's called One Coat. It should do what it says.'

Smirking, he explains – to the thing, of course – that it ain't meant for going over wallpaper. Seems like a con to me but he just walks off, shaking his head. What can I do except buy another tin? Another layer does the trick. No more bloodstains on the wall. I'm happy.

One thing I'm missing is books. She ain't got much I'm interested in, Miss E. You'd think there'd be something worth reading in all that clutter, wouldn't you? But it's mostly old newspapers and women's mags. I do the rounds of the charity shops, picking up paperbacks.

Always loved reading, me, but, as I've found out, it can be bad for you. 'Specially at school. When you go to a dump like ours where most of the teachers, let alone the kids, acts like they got ADHD, it spells trouble to let on you like reading, even admitting you *can* read.

All a quiet kid can do is try to become invisible. Ain't that hard. You sit at the back, eyes down. Don't say nothing to no one. Don't raise your eyes. Don't never, ever, *ever* put your hand up. Gradually they stop noticing you, the other kids and the teachers. You become more fainter and more fainter until – poof! – one day you ain't there at all. Nobody bothers you after that.

Remember one time, this new kid made the mistake of bringing a book in to read in his dinner hour. *Harry Potter*, it was. Like throwing fresh meat to a pack of pit bulls. They was on to him soon as he cracked the pages. Even the girls piled in.

Playground supers couldn't break it up. Had to send for Mr Whiteley, the PE teacher. Though he let the first eleven footie team call him Philip on match days, everyone knew never to mess with Mr Whiteley. One look from him was enough. You could just tell he could handle hisself. Anyhow, they soon quieted down when Mr Whiteley come on the scene. By then it was too late; poor Harry P was in shreds.

New kid got moved on. Never saw him after that. Lucky him.

Still, now I got my own room, I can read what I like, for as long as I like with no one to wind me up. Got three books already. My *Sherlock Holmes: the Complete Stories* what I brung from Ma's. *Angels and Demons*, 'cause it sounds like a computer game, and *Middlemarch* which I'm guessing is about the war. I'll be coming at you soon, Mr G. Eliot.

Caught another little critter today. Take a closer look this time. Shiny black eyes stare back. I put my finger in to touch its twitching whiskers. Then its worm of a tail squirms into sight and I drop the trap. Mouse jumps for it. As it's darting under the wheelies, I see it's only got three legs.

She prowls at night. I hear her tip-tapping up and down the hallway. Mostly I reckon she gets up to fiddle with her puzzles – loves her jigsaws, Miss E – but sometimes she trots down the corridor in my direction. First time she done that, it got my heart pumping, I can tell you. Lying there, thinking, *What if she comes in here and starts acting all weird an' that?*

But she don't. She toddles on past and stops at the room

opposite mine, the locked one. I hear the floorboards creak and I wait for the sound of the key turning. It don't come. Boards creak again. I hear a murmur. I slip out my warm sleeping bag, creep over and put my head to my door to listen.

'You in there?' she whispers.

I'm about to answer, thinking she's talking to me, when she says, 'Of course you are. Where else would you be but locked inside? Where you can't hurt me.'

She's only talking to whatever it is she's got in there. How bats is that?

After that I hear her loads of times. In the middle of the night, outside the closed door, whispering. About time I took a look, I reckon.

I been shopping. 'Ain't got none of your macaroons in Waitrose today,' I shout, as I'm unpacking in the kitchen. 'Have to get some next time.'

'Ain't, ain't, ain't. It's all "ain't" with you, isn't it?' She's done her favourite trick again, creeping up behind me, making me jump out my skin. 'The words "aren't", "isn't" and "haven't" are strangers to you. Really, Boy, how do you expect anyone to take you seriously if you speak like a retarded barrow boy?'

'Sorry, Miss E,' I go, eyes down. 'I am trying.'

'I shall have to take your education in hand. Repeat after me: *As they don't have any Cameroons in Waitrose.* Say it.'

'As they don't have no… any macaroons in Waitrose,' I go.

'*I shall have to shift my skinny arse.*'

Can't help but crack my face at this. Miss E's playing it serious.

'Go on,' she says. 'Repeat.'

'I shall have to shift my skinny arse.'

'*And go and get some from Sainsbury's.*'

Now we're both grinning.

'OK. You got me,' I go, firing imaginary pistols with my fingers at her. 'I'll get my coat.'

She beams back. Don't hurt to humour the old girl.

24.

ELOISE

It began with a rumour, a whisper really. There was a problem at KK's Hackney warehouse: fleas. They'd opened up a box of imported scarves, so the story went, and found it infested. So, not just fleas, foreign fleas.

The warehouse was inspected. No sign was found of the insects. Still the gossip persisted. Orders were cancelled, buildings were fumigated. KK sales began to slide. Then the final straw. Following an anonymous tip-off, the press gathered outside the KK flagship store in High Street Ken, anticipating an announcement.

Instead they found a tearful young woman – Penny was her name, I happen to remember. Mystified, they thrust their microphones and cameras in her face as, chin wobbling, she sniffed her way through her shocking tale. She'd been bitten half to death after buying a pair of trousers from KKs, she told them.

'Show us!' someone from the back called out. I wonder who that could have been? Coyly rolling up a trouser leg, the girl revealed an ankle red raw with bites. As the cameras flashed, it was clear, KK was in big trouble.

Kristina Krabtree was powerless. No matter how many times

she denied the flea story, people had seen the evidence for themselves on that poor girl's leg. She struggled on for a few weeks, but in the end she had to close the High Street Ken store, then the one in King's Road. Within months, she'd slunk away overseas. Launching a new label in the States, she said, but we knew the truth: she was running away.

You could say, she had to 'flea' the country.

Note to Boy: I say, that's rather good.

I snapped up the Kensington lease at a rock-bottom price and reopened it as the first HB Superstore. Business boomed. I was on top of the fashion world. Kristina Krabtree was down and out. I had won. Hah!

If there was any justice in the world that would have been the last any of us would have heard of Kristina Krabtree. OK, we get it. She does good works. But does she have to bore us with them all the time?

It's not fair. I gave the fashion world so much. It should be me playing Lady Bountiful and posing with photogenic African babies. Me getting the damehood and the invites to Palace dinners. Me. Me. Me. If there was any justice in the world. And people wonder why I'm bitter.

Note to Boy: This is important. Get the lawyers to scrutinise this chapter with a fine toothbrush. The best Tabby can afford. I think I'm pretty safe after all these years but just in case. That make-up artist is long dead, thank sod. Lovely job he did. Made me itch just to look at that ankle. And the actress won't talk. Not now she's a national treasure and up for a part in Corrie. *In any case, I haven't actually admitted anything… have I? Don't want my arse sued by Dame High-And-Mighty-Look-At-Me- I'm-A-Bloody-UN-Goodwill-Ambassador-Who-Takes-Tea-With-Archbishop-Nelson-Tutu.*

25.

BRADLEY

I'm in there. The locked room. The one she calls her box room. The one I'm not supposed to go anywhere near, ever.

Should be all right. She's in her bedroom, spark out. Not so much asleep as passed out. Been working on her book all day, see? That means chatting and tippling, and tippling some more. Gotta give it to the old girl, she's got some stamina. Gone midnight before she crashes. I creep in and, to the usual soundtrack of guffs and snores, take the recorder out of one hand, the glass out the other, and pull the covers up to her chin.

I'm knackered meself, to be honest with you, but I'm just about bursting to stick my beak in. Time I investigated what's in that room. Get the key from the teapot, creep down the hall, unlock the door and slip my body through the gap.

It's worse than what I remembered.

Everywhere there's stuff, scattered across the floor or stacked up in piles. Handbags, plastic bags, paper bags, carrier bags, bin bags, shoe boxes, cardboard boxes and a coupla suitcases. Everything dead old, split and busted. Everything gross.

I shake my head. Miss E's one of them crazy hoarders, like them nutters on TV. A woman's boot lays at my feet. Silver with laces. I pick it up and put it to my nose. Cheesey.

Well, Bradley, I say to meself, *this is one big job and no mistake. Needs a proper sort out and you're the man to do it. How else you gonna find out if there's anything worth anything among the grot?*

Even though it's late and even though I'm cream crackered, there's no time like the present. It ain't easy. I pull a bag from the pile and it sets off a mini avalanche, making a noise like a crackling log fire – not that I've heard one of them, mind. Saw a car on fire once, by the lock-ups. But that don't count.

Anyway, one thing I do not want for definite is to be buried alive under a pile of Miss E's old rubbish, so I turn my attention to the two suitcases. Gotta be something interesting in them. At first I'm naffed off they're locked but soon as I show them the kitchen knife, them rusty old locks snap straight off.

Nothing but more let-downs, though, when I lift the lids. Rags. Bits of material, sewed together like one of them patchwork bedspreads from the olden days. Only these ain't done neat and tidy. They're higgledy-piggledy. Pins and chains and zips stuck on some of them. Marker pen scribbling on others. What *is* this junk? Why's she keeping it under lock and key, like it's the crown jewels or something?

Tripping over a heap of weird shoes, I find a stack of yellowing newspapers. 'Mr Wilson moves into N° 10', it says on the top one. I pick up a magazine. *Vogue*, it's called. The date on the front is April 1977 when Ma was just a nipper. The cover shows this model, dead glam, only round her neck like a necklace, she's got this bike chain. '*It's Rag Bag Time!*' the writing says.

I come across a box of records. Old-style LPs, like what they flog down The Vinyl Countdown off of the High Road. But when I flick through, I see the edges of the record sleeves is worn right down to the cardboard and the records theirselves are a mass of scratches.

It's not even as though they're rare. Just the usual boring stuff that oldsters go for: Beatles, Stones, Abba, Bob Dylan, Rod Stewart, Elton John and some others I ain't heard of. All looking dead young and hairy. And the get-ups some of them prance around in! They look like someone's just taken a load of...

Ping! A lightbulb goes on in my head. *God, but you are slow sometimes, Bradley.*

The old rags. The bike chain. The weird shoes. The LP covers. Suddenly it all makes sense. This ain't some random rubbish she's hoarding. It's her clothes. Miss E's. The clobber she and her mates done back in the day. The stuff she's always going on about.

Yesss! I sit back on my heels, my brain in overdrive. A good night's work, Bradley my son.

All of a sudden, I'm bushed. Gotta get some kip. I'm making to leave when I spot something. A carrier. Dark green. *Harrods* wrote on the outside in swirly gold writing. So heavy, I almost rip the plastic handles off when I drag it out. Tip it up and catch my breath. Necklaces and bracelets slither out, dozens of them. Coloured stones glint, like red, green and blue eggs in a gold and silver nest.

I hold two big old stones up to the light, thinking they'll make nice coloured patterns, like in a church. Been to plenty of them with Ma, I can tell you, when I was a little nipper. Only instead of beautiful lights, dark shadow monsters rear up the walls, giving me the willies. I pick up the bag to put them back and something glints at the bottom. I reach in. It's a little heart on a chain.

Classy, not like the rest of her bling. Could even be real gold. I spot a tiny catch. Inside, two faded photos. I snap it shut and let it dangle from my fingers. It twists in the air. The chain's so thin it almost looks like it's suspended. As it flashes in the light, I think to meself, *This just gets better and better.*

It's next morning and I'm well narked. Not only am I missing half a night's sleep but them mice is taking the pee.

What happens is, I've just set mouse number three free, when I've noticed he's only got three legs an' all, just like the last one. That's too much of a coincidence. Seems like Miss E's right. I been catching the same little bugger over and over again. So, what shall I do about little Stumpy? Let him carry on living in the back of the fridge, or get a proper trap, one that will snap his cheeky little neck, just like *that*?

This laptop's so cool. Done a whole load of research while she's hooked on one of her favourites, *Silent Witness.* The more gorier it gets, the more happier she is. I sit with her, MacBook on my knee, looking up stuff.

That Molly might have been a bitch but she did get one thing right: the stupid prices people pay for second-hand clothes. Vintage, they call them. Unbelievable. When I read what they're trousering, my eyebrows nearly hit the roof.

Miss E flicks a look my way. 'That's not porn, is it?' she goes. 'Something's got you excited.' Her eyes dart back to the TV, not wanting to miss a second. A doctor dressed in white is about to stick this great long blade into the chest of a dead body on the slab.

'Checking out how the Hoops got on, that's all,' I go. 'You know? QPR?'

The doc lifts his arm.

'Kewpie arse?' she goes, still distracted.

'Queens Park Rangers? My team?'

She drags her eyes away. 'Judging by your face, they won.'

'Yep. Four–nil,' I smile. 'Golden.' We ain't even playing.

Out the corner of my eye, on the telly I see the knife plunge down.

26.

ELOISE

It all worked out splendidly. That's why you could have knocked me down with the proverbial when Bruno tore a strip off me over what he called 'the KK nonsense'.

'I don't hold with it, Ellie,' he lectured. 'Up North, where we call a spade a bloody shovel, people wouldn't let you get away with the half of it. But down here, anything seems to go. I see the shenanigans and I turn a blind eye, but that doesn't mean I like it. Spying on each other, nicking each other's ideas, you're all at it. But hounding a woman to the point where she has to leave the country,' he shook his head, 'that's taking things too far.'

'I don't know what you mean,' I said, nose in the air.

'You can deny it all you want, I know you were behind that flea business, somehow or other. Do you know what's the saddest part? You think you've won. You think you've got one over on Kristina Krabtree. You haven't. All you've done is ratchet up the stakes. She'll come back at you, harder and stronger than before, probably when you least expect it. Don't come crying to me when she does. Seriously, Ellie, from now on, watch your back.'

I brushed his warning aside with a wave of the hand,

thinking, *Silly, paranoid old Bruno.* If only I hadn't been so cocksure.

Things were never the same between Bruno and me after that. He remained loyal, of course, throwing himself heart and soul into the label, but the closeness we'd enjoyed – first as lovers, then as colleagues – had gone.

Heavenly Bodies wasn't the fun it used to be in the sixties and seventies, either. OK, so financially, things were looking up. With no KK to compete with, whatever we came up with sold like hot tarts. But success brought its own problems. Everyone was so busy and so stressed out, meeting deadlines, acting like grown-ups. Even Trip and Dazzle. No one had any time to enjoy themselves. No one had any time for me. The eighties rave scene was just beginning. Shoulder pads were huge. Hair was enormous. Yet, here I was, a highly successful, still desirable, businesswoman and I had no one with which to share the exuberance of the times.

Belatedly, I realised a great truth: money isn't everything. Having some beats the hell out of having none, but, let me tell you, it is possible to be rich and miserable. Look at the Queen; she never looks exactly chuffed with her lot, does she? Like her Maj, I was flush but fed up. Ripe, in other words, for adventure.

Right on cue, through the melancholy mists of mind-numbing monotony, the smothering smog of… something beginning with 'sm'… there galloped a knight in shining white satin: Howard Arthur Haggarty. Dreamy, swoony, sexy Howard. Except, of course, he wasn't riding a horse and white satin would have been a tad conspicuous for a snapperazzi.

Normally I wouldn't have given the time of day to a lowly freelance snapper on the prowl, but I was without a man. And I never like to be without a man.

Howard wasn't just any man. There was something different about him. An air of mystery I could never quite put my finger on. So what if he was barely half my age? I'd earned myself a toy boy. In any case, from the top of his artfully quiffed shoulder-length mullet to the tips of his beautifully put-together toes – which, by the way, he could wiggle independently – he was delicious. And deliciousness trumps everything in my books.

I seized the moment – and him. Within six hours of our first encounter, gyrating on the cramped dance floor at Annabel's, he was in my bed. Within six days, he'd moved into Lowndes Street. Within six months he was got up in a pastel pink *Miami Vice* suit and marched, looking as lickable as a strawberry ice cream, down the aisle of Chelsea Registry Office.

The honeymoon in a beach hut on Barbados lasted three months. With handsome Howard by my side, showering me with compliments, covering my suntanned body with kisses, and dependable old Bruno at home, taking care of the business, I'd never been so happy.

Only one little grey cloud marred my blue horizon. Bruno and Howard hated each other on sight. Bruno blew his top when I called a meeting on my return and announced I was going to make Howard a partner in Heavenly Bodies.

'My partner in the business, as well as in life,' I said.

'But Ellie, he's a photographer,' Bruno objected. 'And not a very good one at that.'

I wasn't going to be dictated to by Bruno. True, he was something of a business genius and could spot a dodgy deal a mile off, but I was too full of myself to listen. Oh, the overconfidence of youth! Or middle-age at least. I thought I knew everything. I know better now.

'Anyway, it's too late,' I told Bruno curtly. 'Howard's already got his lawyer pal, Fergus Machin, to draw up the papers.'

'That creep!' Bruno said. 'Never trust a lawyer with the smile of a crocodile.' Harsh words, coming from him, who wasn't usually one to sound off about people.

Howard, on the other hand, never missed an opportunity to poke fun at Bruno. 'Old Stick-in-the-Mud' he called him to his face.

But they mostly managed to rub along without too much aggravation until the day I overheard an angry Howard on the phone.

'I'm her husband, Bruno,' he yelled. 'You'll do as I damn well tell you, or else. I'm in charge now. Not her.' And he slammed the phone down.

'So, you're in charge, are you?' I said, scarcely able to contain my fury. 'That's news to me.'

'Plumpkin!' Bruno crossed the room and made to kiss me. I avoided his embrace. 'You know how it is. You have to lay it on the line with Bruno's sort or they run rings round you.'

I was as cold as a marble statue.

'What I meant was, now we're married, I can take some of the burden from your adorable shoulders.' He nuzzled my neck. 'It must have been so lonely for you, all those years at the top. But you have me now to take the pressure off.' Gently, he turned me round and reached inside my jumper, his voice dropping to an almost inaudible murmur. 'I'm your right-hand man.'

I could never stay cross with him for long. Howard always was my weakness.

'Can I have a word?' Howard said, looking unusually serious. This was some weeks later.

'Uh-uh,' I laughed, 'sounds ominous.'

Howard remained unsmiling. 'You know, Plumpkin, don't

you, that you are perfection in my eyes?' he said. 'That there is not one single inch of you that I would change in any way?'

I preened, dear reader, as any woman would.

'That's why it's so difficult for me to say this.' He put a hand to his troubled forehead. 'You're in the public eye as never before, the inspirational figurehead of a thriving company, the adored wife of a new, young husband.' I preened some more. 'And that makes people jealous. It kills me to say this but some people, some horrible, spiteful people, have been saying – forgive me, Plumpkin – they've been saying you've put on weight.'

I stopped mid-preen. 'Put on weight?'

'Not only that. They say you're out of condition, your hairstyle's stuck in the seventies, your skin's leathery and—'

'Who are these people?' I screamed. 'I demand you tell me their names.'

He wouldn't. 'I'm no snitch,' he said.

After I'd calmed down, Howard explained the best way to answer my faceless critics was by getting toned and grooming the hell out of myself.

So it was that every morning before breakfast, Stefan from Stockholm would put me – legwarmered- and leotarded-up – through a workout that would have had Jane Fondle sweating like a pig; while at mealtimes, Pauline from Potter's Bar would serve me meals consisting of vegetables so miniscule, I had to put on my glasses to locate them on the patterned plates.

In addition, Howard booked me into spas and treatment centres, skin clinics and wellness retreats. Every part of my body was cleansed and creamed, pummelled and peeled, scrubbed and scraped. Any hair that wasn't plucked, waxed or zapped was seaweed-treated, permed, tinted and caramel-highlighted.

'Making perfection even more perfect' is how Howard described it.

Achieving perfection was sodding hard work, though, and took up most of every day. I was hardly ever to be seen at Heavenly Bodies. Time went fast and before I knew it, it was our first anniversary. We'd planned a big celebration party at Robin Scott's.

Note to Boy: Robin Scott's Jazz Club? You must have heard of it. It was legendary. No? It was this groovy little Soho basement dive, seedy but fashionable. Everybody went there, even people like me who can't stand jazz. It won't have lasted. Long gone, I expect. Or maybe it was Johnny Scott's? Or Tommy. I don't know. You're the researcher, Boy. Research away!

'Thought I might pop into the office tomorrow afternoon, Howie,' I said lightly, teasing my curls into ever greater heights with a giant comb. 'It's been ages. Don't want them forgetting who I am.'

Howard was lying on the bed in an open-necked shirt and check cotton slacks, his feet bare and adorable toes wriggling. He was watching me from under heavy lids, silently smoking. Leaning over to the ashtray, he lazily tapped the ash from his cigarette.

'No need, Tiny Toes. Everything is running like clockwork. Me and your superannuated bean counter' – he meant Bruno – 'have got it covered.'

'Still,' I said, irritated by the brush-off. 'I thought I'd go in.'

'I've told you. You don't need to. It's all fine.' He stubbed his cigarette out in the ashtray, grinding it in until it disintegrated.

I swivelled to face him, big comb in hand. 'Howie, is there something you're not telling me?'

He sighed. 'If you must know, I've been thinking about

making a few changes. I wasn't going to trouble you with them, not until it's decided. But I should have known. I can't hide anything from you, can I? You know me too well. Sit down, Plumpkin, and I'll explain.'

Do you know what I was thinking at that precise moment, dear reader? Not about the business. Not about Howard going over my head. I was thinking, *Arrrrrgh! I wish he wouldn't call me that.* Of the many pet names Howard had for me, Plumpkin was by far my least favourite. In any case, I wasn't his Plumpkin anymore. I'd lost almost half a stone.

So shallow! So blind! Life has taught me a few lessons since then. I like to think I am less self-obsessed and superficial as a result.

I settled myself on the foot of the bed and, somewhat distracted by those animated toes, tried to concentrate on what he was saying. They really were extraordinarily long and dexterous, his toes.

Then I heard him say 'takeover'.

'Hold on a sec,' I said. 'Did you say takeover, Howie? Who are we buying out?'

Howard gave a dry, little laugh. 'Other way round. Don't you remember? The big meeting in Leicester I went to, while you were at the aromatherapy place in darkest Wales?'

I had no recollection of Howard going to Leicester.

'I'm sure I mentioned it. Anyway, the upshot was, I had a meeting with this company – Fashion Inc, a new outfit, very go-ahead – and they're interested in acquiring HB. It looked promising, so I set the wheels in motion.'

'You did what?' I yelled, springing up.

Howard flushed. 'I exercised my right as your husband and equal business partner,' he snapped, swinging his legs down and reaching for another cigarette, 'to investigate the approach further. It seemed to have quite a few positives – Fergus thought so too.'

'I might have known he'd be at the bottom of this. I don't trust him, Howie. He smiles too much.'

'I'll have you know, Fergie, as well as being one of my oldest pals, is one of the country's top legal brains.'

By now I was pacing. 'I still don't like him. And I don't like the sound of this takeover deal either. It would change everything.'

Howard puffed on his ciggie. 'That's the beauty of it. Nothing will change. You and me will stay at the head, running the business, no doubt with some fancy new titles. Trip and Dazzle will still take care of creative, and that old fart Bruno will whinge on as usual about profits and losses.'

'If nothing's going to change, what's the point of the takeover?'

'Tax,' Howard said darkly. 'Being part of a bigger concern would make us more tax efficient.'

'You have the figures to support that statement, I assume?' I said, my brain now fizzing. 'Hit me with some numbers.'

'Well...' Howard seemed stuck for words. 'Actually, Fergie has them.'

Anniversary or not, it was time to give Howard some home truths.

'Until you can show me hard proof, Howard, there will be no more talk of a takeover. Got it? This is my business. I'm not about to hand it over on the basis of some tax fiddle cooked up by Fergus sodding Machin.'

'*Our* business, Plumpkin,' Howard said quietly. 'HB is our business now, yours and mine.'

'Yes, OK. Our joint business. Joint – that means we *both* have to agree to any changes. You can't do anything without my signature. You have to understand, Howie, Heavenly

Bodies isn't what I *do,'* I told him. 'It's what I *am*. I will never, not in a million years, agree to a takeover – and certainly not for the sake of saving a few quid in tax.'

I'd never seen Howard so incensed. 'You're as bad as him, Old Stick-In-The-Mud,' he said, throwing his hands in the air. 'Set in your ways. Scared to take a risk. You know why? Because you're afraid you're past it.'

Feeling strangely calm, I lifted my chin and said, 'I will never agree to this deal, Howie. That's my final word.'

'And this,' he said, pulling on his jacket, 'is mine.'

A few seconds later I heard the front door slam.

Heavenly Bodies isn't what I do, it's what I am. That's what I'd said to Howard. Sounded pretentious but it was true. Later, alone in bed, red-eyed and wretched, I heard a small, frightened voice inside my head whisper, *And without it, what would you be?*

What indeed?

27.

BRADLEY

Thought everything was sweet but she's not right. Not shouting orders. Not slagging me off. Not the bossy Miss E what I got accustomed to. You'd think it would be a relief. To my surprise, I find I'm missing her mouthing off at me all day.

Instead she lays in bed cuddled up to that recorder, hour after hour, whispering into it. When I pop in to ask if she's all right, 'Everything's tickety-boo,' she goes, sounding like she's about to top herself. Don't want me there. Don't want me pressing buttons. Don't want me listening in.

So I'm at the gym most days. Might as well. Really getting into it. Go in the daytime when the drones is at work, when I can get up a good sweat without worrying about people looking. Not that they upset me. Not anymore. Not since I give up hiding behind my hair. Now when people gawp, I gawp right back. Eyeball to eyeball. They always look away first.

Half hour, forty minutes on the treadmill is nothing. I'm lifting pretty decent weights too. What with the gym and the protein shakes I'm having in the mornings, well, the upshot is, when I catch meself in the mirror these days, the lad what looks back seems like he can take care of hisself.

Gets me running stupid errands, she does. Sends me out to get rid of me, you ask me. Washing blue, that was one. 'Adds brightness to your whiteness,' she goes, not sounding that bright herself. Then it's an old-fashioned bulb for her lamp. 'The light's so much kinder to one's skin tones.' Or Five Boys chocolate. That was another one. 'My childhood in a chocolate bar. If only the rest of life had been as sweet, eh Boy?'

I go, even though I know I ain't got a cat's. While I'm at it, I keep a lookout for her Gypsy Creams. Still no luck. In the end I don't even bother asking for the weird stuff. People only look at you like you're a spaz. Don't matter anyhow 'cause when I get back, she never asks if I got it. Like I say, seems like it's just an excuse to get shot of me.

Usually she's still in bed, either kipping, muttering into the recorder, or going through her pictures. 'My research,' she calls it, when I try to help. 'Hands off,' she says. 'That's my research.'

Her room's a right old mess. Reminds me of a hamster Dom had once, until he forgot to fill up poor little critter's water bottle. Anyhow, before he got bored of it, Dom used to give this hamster the *Sun* to chew up. That's her bed. Miss E's. Like some giant hamster's been building a nest. When she rolls over, it all goes flying, streaming off of the bed onto the floor. No prizes for guessing who has to pick it up?

Tidied up my room. My gaff's nearly as full as hers, 'cepting my stuff's neat. Kicks in a line at the bottom of the built-in wardrobe, jeans hanging at one end, tees in the middle, hoodies at the end. All in colour order. Line up my books and music and stuff on the shelves. I like lying on the bed, looking it over, knowing where everything is.

Went a bit mad with DVDs. Got a twenty-minute workout, so's I can keep them muscles pumping. And – my pride and joy – a Lord David box set. Play them at night on the laptop, earbuds in, when she thinks I'm typing up her book. Twenty-four of his shows I got for forty quid. Kaning. That'll keep me happy for weeks.

Careful always to pay cash, mind. Take it out with her card in the hole-in-the-wall a few hundred at a time. Her daughter bungs in a nice wedge regular as clockwork, so why should I worry? No need to keep a check. Letters come from the bank every now and then. Statement, it says at the top. I don't pay them no mind nor does Miss E. After that first one, don't even bother to open them. Stuff them in the drawer of the little table in the hall and forget all about them.

Things is sweet. Until for some reason I do. Check her account, that is, when I'm getting out some money. Statement rolls out the machine, like a mini toilet roll. Take a look and nearly pass out. *It can't be. Machine must be busted.* But when I dash back to hers and open the latest statement from the bank, it tells the same story. 'Balance: £307.12.'

Go hot and cold. How can there only be three hundred quid? The rate I'm spending, it won't last the month. *No need to go headless,* I tell meself. All that's happened is the old girl's daughter's forgot to make a payment or two. Or the bank's cocked up. One word from Miss E and it'll be sorted.

She's out of her room for once. That's good. Not dressed, mind, just in them old grey trackie bottoms under her nightie. But up, on the settee, sitting quiet, jigsaw in front of her.

I give her the blow-by-blow on the hole-in-the-wall situation – without letting on I been creaming off, of course. She goes on staring at the table, listening to me or not, I can't tell. I finish with, 'So, you need to have a serious chat with your girl, Tabitha, Miss E. You need to give her a call.'

She sighs like she's tired to her bones. 'Tabby?' she goes. 'She called me yesterday. Such a treat. Or was it last week? I get the days beflummoxed.' She picks up a green piece of field and hovers it over the jigsaw. 'At any rate, you were out shopping.'

'What did she say?' I go, trying not to sound bothered.

'Something about a tribunal. Some silly nonsense about bullying.' She turns the piece, presses it down, trying to make it fit. 'In consequence, she's taking a break from her work until the dust settles.'

So her daughter's got the heave-ho for throwing her weight about. Wonder who she takes after?

'Did she mention your allowance?' I ask. Miss E looks up and frowns. 'Did she say… is she gonna be able to pay you while she's on the dole, I mean, taking a break?'

'My allowance? Cancelled,' she goes, not sounding that upset. She picks up the puzzle piece and gives it a hard glare, like it's the bit of cardboard's fault it won't fit. 'That's no problem. There should be more than enough in my account. My needs, as you know, are modest.'

'But Miss E…' I start up.

She ain't hearing me. She's staring at the piece. Next thing, her mouth opens and – snap! – she's only gone and bitten off one of the sticking-out tabs. Spitting out gobs of cardboard, she shoves it into place. 'There,' she goes, 'that's the sky done.'

I look over. A green chewed-up piece of field is stuck in the middle of a grey, fluffy cloud.

She stands. 'And now, I shall retire to my boudoir. Fill the hot water bottle, Boy. I've got a big day ahead. Tomorrow I'm at the Hot Spot.'

With Miss E safely tucked up, I sit and worry. What am I gonna do with her daughter out of work and no money coming in? And even more stressy, what if her girl starts sniffing about? How long before she joins the dots and comes looking for me? There's some hard thinking to be done.

28.

ELOISE

You can go, Boy. Yes, I do know how to work it, thank you very much. No, I don't want anything. All I need from you is your absence. For sod's sake, go and find something to dust, will you?

Has he gone? Good. Time to face it. I've been putting it off for too long. Time to tell you how my fortune was lost, my heart broken and my life ruined. Because, be honest, dear callous reader, that's why you're going to buy the book, isn't it? To read the gory details. To bask in Scheissenfreunde, or whatever it's called.

A week, he stayed away. Howie. I was dozing on the bed when I heard the sound of a key in the lock. It was him, I knew it. Then there he was in the doorway, dark curls falling across his brow, brown eyes burning.

'Come to collect your things?' I asked, the mistress of cool.

'How do you do that?' he said. 'Unwashed, greasy-haired and stinking of booze, yet still so desirable.'

Be honest, dear reader, would you have been able to resist? I certainly didn't. He ran towards me, arms raised, and I threw myself into them.

Though I was ecstatic at his return, I needed to clear the air.

'I haven't changed my mind,' I said post-coitally, pulling the sheet up over my breasts. 'I'm not going to sell Heavenly Bodies, Howie. Either you accept that or…' I took a deep breath, 'we go our separate ways.'

'Don't look so serious,' Howard said. 'The takeover's yesterday's news. We won't talk about it anymore.' He put an arm round me and I snuggled down. 'I've had a much better idea,' he said. 'Wait till you get a load of this.'

Always my weakness, Howie. If only one could bend back the fingers of time, like in that song. You know? If only.

It began with the designs.

'Who did these?' I said, pouring over an unfamiliar portfolio of sketches. 'They don't look like Trip and Dazzle's work.'

'They're not,' Howard said. 'Those two are getting stale. I got someone else in.'

'I don't know, Howie. Everyone's crazy for New Romantic this season. It's eyeliner and epaulettes as far as the eye can see.' I pointed to a particularly outrageous drawing. 'No one's showing anything remotely like this.'

'Aren't you always telling me,' Howard said, 'what the punters crave is novelty. So let's give it to them. While the rest of the sheep follow the flock, we strike out on our own, gambolling through the buttercups in pastures new.'

It wasn't like Howard to wax so whatsical. What had come over him? He'd seemed different since our big row. He'd always been excitable – that was one of things I loved about him – but now he had the light of a fanatic in his eye. Not wanting a repeat of our bust-up, I did my best to be tactful about the sketches.

'They're certainly novel,' I said, leafing through them again, 'but are they commercial, that's what troubles me?'

Howard laughed. 'Did you worry whether the Rag Bag look, the shortiskirt and the longitube would be commercial? Of course you didn't. You just went for it and hoped the punters would follow. Come on, Chunky Chicken, where's your spirit of adventure? It's cut-throat out there, you know that. Take your foot off the accelerator and you're left eating dust. Play it safe and you're dead. We have to be bold.'

'There's bold and there's downright reckless.'

A frown of irritation creased his brow. 'You're supposed to be a shock frock designer, aren't you?'

'*The* shock frock designer,' I corrected.

'So, show them you've still got it. Shock the shit out of them.'

I bit my lip. All my instincts told me Howard's designs wouldn't sell. I'd never gone against my instincts before, but he seemed so sure. There was only one other person whose opinion I valued: Bruno's. Right on cue, he slouched past the boardroom, face as long as a seaside donkey, as usual. I called him in and he sat, the sketches in front of him, grating his nails into the salt-and-vinegar stubble of his chin. How long had he been growing a beard? I hadn't noticed it before.

'Hmmm,' he said, annoyingly non-committal, taking his time, examining each drawing before laying it to one side. 'They're different. I'll say that for them. Nothing like the rest of the market.'

'That's just what I said.' I folded my arms, pleased to have my opinion vindicated.

'Different but… I don't know… there might be something there.' Bruno said, a hint of excitement creeping into his voice. 'Let's face it, our collections haven't exactly been setting the world alight lately. This might be the kick up the backside we need. A reinvention of the label.' Then he smiled. Bruno actually smiled. 'A redefinition of womanhood. An end to body fascism. A sort of anti-fashion fashion. Yeah, it might work. I say we go ahead.'

The die was cast.

The Anti-Fashion Fashion collection – that name stuck – was to be launched at our autumn/winter show, which Howard insisted on calling HB88. The date was set for March. The venue, London's famous Hot Spot.

I should explain. Bruno and I had set up the Hot Spot as a private club ages past, soon after leasing the High Street Ken premises. Perched on the top floor above the store, it was exotic and decadent – in décor and in clientele. What had started as a bit of fun, a place where we and our friends could meet and let our hair down without fear of prying eyes, ears and cameras, had quickly mushroomed into something far bigger. Soon, our weekly, invitation-only soirées were filled with the hippest of the hip. It became *the* place to be.

We'd really gone to town on the decor. It was sumptuously decked out. You couldn't move for tassels and fringes, Indian rugs and Tiffany lamps, *chaise longues* and silk cushions, and, towering above it all, the famous jungle-size pot plants. As if that weren't enough, everything was reflected to infinity in dozens of mirrors. It looked like an Amazonian brothel.

Allow me to paint you a picture, dear reader, of a typical evening. In one corner, a hollow-chested performance poet flirts with a long-limbed hoofer from *Top of the Pops;* on the dance floor, a Bond girl sways in the arms of Scandinavian sculptor obsessed with making casts of celebrity penises; on stage, rock-and-roll royalty jam with a wide-eyed busker they'd plucked off the street; while observing the scene from beneath the giant palm fronds, hot off the red-eye from New York, are a trio of grotesques from the Warhol factory.

Sadly, the Hot Spot had cooled somewhat since those heady, early days and eventually I'd been forced to close it down. But, sentimental old thing that I am, I'd never disposed of it. Even dust-sheeted and silent, its palm trees long shrivelled, it had a magical atmosphere. Howard and I went to check it out.

A beaded lamp tinkled. A dusty ostrich feather fluttered. A crispy brown leaf whispered to the floor. What was that? The echo of ghostly laughter? And that? The shadow of a figure bopping past?

'So many memories,' I breathed, my voice thickening.

Howard squeezed my hand. 'It'll be perfect,' he said.

'Just as soon as we get shot of all this seventies shit,' I replied.

The show was beginning to take shape. To mark twenty-five years of Heavenly Bodies, Howard suggested we combine the launch of Anti-Fashion Fashion with a major retrospective.

'It'll be mega,' he said. 'And who will be the star of this swanky show?' He circled my belly button with his index finger. 'You, my wifey wonder, you.'

Those months before the show were the happiest I'd ever known. I had the show of a lifetime to look forward to. I had Heavenly Bodies. I had Howard.

Oh sod. Now we're getting close, I don't know if I have the strength. Sapphie! Where are you, Sapphie?

29.

ELOISE

That's better. A glass or three always loosens me up. Thanks, Sapphie, old girl.

Right. The night everything changed forever. Here goes… or I could sing you a song, little digi-whatsit? How about 'Oh-oh-oklahoma'? Or recite 'The Lion and Albert'? Terry knew all seventeen verses off by heart. I would, only I fear my memory isn't as faultless as his. Words keep slipping from my grasp.

To tell you the truth, I'd rather do almost anything except what I know I must do. Tell you about the day my faith in humanity was shattered. The day my dream of happiness came to an end. The day the shit bomb exploded.

So confident, so sure of himself, Howard took complete control of the Hot Spot show. I pressed him for details, of course I did. I was used to being the boss – plus I had no desire to make a prat of myself in front of the *glitterscenti* of the fashion world. Though he was reassuring, he gave nothing away.

'Relax, Sugar Lump,' he said, the day before. 'You'll be fine. We wouldn't want to squash your impulsive, spontaneous nature by over-rehearsing you, would we? Chill. That reminds me, I've got you a present.' Out of his pocket he took a little plastic bag. 'A toot of magic snuff to calm the nerves.'

I didn't want Howie to think of me as another old stick-in-the-mud, so I bent over the coffee table and...

Next thing I remember, I was underwater, or so it seemed. Everything was a blur. Occasionally I'd drift to the surface and things came fleetingly into focus: the coldness of tiles against my cheek; the shattering ringing of a bell; the rise and fall of voices.

Then, butterflies. Suddenly the air was full of them, big, white butterflies. I soared upwards to join them, bumping against the ceiling. Looking down I saw Howard and another figure, kneeling in front of someone, talking earnestly. That someone was me.

'Time for a top-up toot, Plumpers,' I heard Howard say, his voice echoing. Handing me a rolled-up fiver, he pushed my head down, down and down until once more I was underwater.

A stripe of sunlight slicing across my bed woke me. I lay, feeling as though I'd been beaten to death, buried, left to putrefy, dug up, and beaten to death all over again. Gradually I became aware of sounds and smells from the kitchen. I followed the sounds.

'Morning, Eloise.' A beaming Howard was stirring a saucepan, as I staggered in, groaning. 'Sit yourself down. Big day ahead. You'll need a decent breakfast inside you. Scrambled do you?'

I should have known something was up. Howard never called me Eloise.

All day long misgivings about the new look, as well as a ferocious, scrambled-egg laced hangover, gnawed at my guts. Would Anti-Fashion Fashion be the brilliant success Howard and Bruno thought it would be? So much depended on it. To add to my unease, word came late in the afternoon that Trip and Dazzle were boycotting the show.

'Boycotting?' I said. 'Do they even know what the word means?'

'What do you expect?' Bruno said. 'You didn't use a single one of their designs.'

Nine o'clock that evening found me sitting in the dressing room backstage of the Hot Spot, nervously patting panstick over the bags under my eyes, the sounds of the HB88 show, already well underway, filtering through.

Howard had disappeared to deal with something. He didn't say what or where. Bruno, as ever, was on hand. Thank sod for Bruno. He'd had a new spring in his step since we'd hit upon Anti-Fashion Fashion.

'The old frocks raised a few eyebrows,' Bruno said, bustling in during the interval, quite like the Bruno of old. 'It doesn't hurt to remind people how revolutionary we used to be.' He rubbed his hands. 'And will be again. Wait till they cop a load of this new collection. It'll knock their socks off.'

'Have you seen Howard?' I said, distracted.

Bruno shook his head. 'Not to worry. We managed without him before. We'll manage today.' He looked at his watch. 'Right. Five more minutes till the interval's over, then you're on.'

Suddenly I couldn't breathe. 'I can't do it, Bruno. Not without Howard.'

'You don't need him, lass,' Bruno said, grasping my shoulders and giving them a reassuring shake. 'You don't need anyone. You just have to believe in yourself, like you used to. All right?'

'I don't know,' I said, with a wan smile. 'I've got a bad feeling.'

Boy. Boy. Where the hell are you? I need a bowl or a bucket or… too late. Get the mop.

30.

BRADLEY

Getting careless. Stupid of me. Can't sleep, see? Had one of them nightmares where Dom's got his hands round my throat. Can't shake him off. My chest is bursting. I'm panicking. I know I can't black out, else he'll finish me off for certain. My hands drop away. Darkness closes in like a black swamp. That's when I wake up, gasping, armpits dripping. I throw the covers off and lay there, sucking in the cool air and thanking God I ain't living with Dom no more.

Go for a wazz. On the way to the khazi, I check on her. On her back, mouth flapping. She's been in a funny mood lately. Spends all day in bed, muttering to herself. Tells me to leave her 'the sod alone' when I ask if I can get her anything. Dry toast and tea, that's all she wants. Not even any gin. Not a drop. Funny thing is, though she's off the booze, she threw up the other day. Still, she looks well away now. *While I'm up,* I think to meself, *could get some more done.*

It's been going well, see, sorting out of her stuff. Been at it a coupla weeks, on and off. Frocks and coats I been hanging up to get rid of the creases. Got some rails from Argos. Not cheap stuff – £14.99 each. Smaller stuff I been putting in clear plastic boxes. Smuggled it all in without her noticing. Everything takes ages, 'cause I'm having to do it on the sly.

Getting somewhere, though. Can see the floorboards. That gives me a good feeling. Each time I leave, I take a moment. Look over what I done. Neat and tidy, just how I like it. *Looking good, Bradley,* I say to meself. *Looking real good.*

So here I am, 6:30 in the morning, earpods in, The Script going at it full blast. I'm in my element, only half noticing the sky's beginning to lighten outside the little window. Few more sessions, two or three weeks at most, I'm thinking, and I'll be done. And then…

Got plans, see? I'm enjoying having plans. Ain't never had none before. Never thought further than the next morning, the next meal. Now I can think about next week, next month, even next year.

Should of never had them earphones in. I'm sitting on the floor, fixing to pack it in when I remember that Harrods bag. Drag it out for another look at them jewels. Slip a coupla rings onto my fingers and a bunch of bangles on each arm. Don't know why. I bend my wrists this way an' that, liking how they look, how they jangle. I smile to meself. Must be going soft in the head. Then I get this feeling. A prickling at the back of my neck. I know she's there. I turn, yanking out the buds. The din hits me like a punch in the gut.

She's screaming. Miss E's screaming at me. At first it's just a noise, then I make out what she's saying.

'Help. I'm being robbed. Help me, someone.'

One thought in my head. I gotta shut her up. Else there'll be nosey neighbours on the doorstep or, worse still, on the phone to the fuzz. Somehow I'm across the room, into the hall and my hand is over her mouth. Next thing, she's sagging against me.

I take her weight, my arm round her shoulders. 'You've had a shock. Come in and park yourself. It'll be OK.'

I go to guide her to the stool I got in there but she shrinks back.

'No, no,' she goes, 'I can't.' She's pulling away, like there's an invisible beam across the door she daren't cross.

I drag the stool out into the hall. 'Sit yourself down.' I give her a tissue. She has a gynormous blow, big eyes fixed on me. I squat down to her level. 'You do know who I am, don't you, Miss E?'

'Of course I do,' she sniffs into the soggy tissue. 'You're the bastard who just hit me.' She touches her chin. There's a red mark. Did I do that? 'I caught you in here stealing my stuff and you hit me.'

'You ain't… I mean, you aren't thinking straight, Miss E. It's me, Bradley. I wasn't stealing nothing… anything. I wouldn't. I've been sorting it. It was meant to be a surprise, see, my little surprise? Look what I done?' I hold out my arm, pointing to the boxes and the hangers. 'I know you said not to. But I took a chance and done it anyway. Would I go to all that trouble, if I was gonna nick it?'

Her eyes follow where I'm pointing. 'Brad-ley?' she says, slow and suspicious.

'That's me. Moved in to give you a hand, didn't I? Remember?' She's still frowning. Gotta think of something quick.

'This ring a bell? As they don't have any macaroons in Waitrose,' I say in my most poshest voice, 'I shall have to shift my skinny arse and get some from…'

'… Sainsbury's,' she finishes, light dawning. 'Bradley, of course! Nasty council house name. It was the shock. Seeing someone in there after all this time.' She looks towards the open door. 'I thought it was *them*, you see.' She pats her heart. 'Oh yes, quite a shock.'

'Sorry I woke you.'

'No. It wasn't you,' she says, resisting me. 'What was it now?' She frowns, hand to her mouth. 'Oh yes. I remembered something. That's what woke me. I remembered what Tabby told me when she was here the other day. About you. Something rather disturbing.'

'Your girl was here? In the flat?'

'Such a surprise. Yesterday. Or was it last week? I get the days flumfuddled.'

'Never you mind about that now,' I say, trying to shut her down. 'You need your beauty sleep. We can talk in the morning.' I put my hands under her arms and give another heave but it's like her arse is super-glued to the stool.

She stares up into my face, eyes all of a sudden clear, voice steady. 'Have you been helping yourself to my bank account?'

I freeze.

This is what I been dreading. I'm scared but mostly I'm angry. Angry with meself for being caught. Angry with her girl for poking her nose in. Angry this could be the end of my cushy life. I feel it stuck in my chest, the anger, like I've swallowed a big old pebble. Though it's not Miss E I'm angry at, it's her what gets the brunt.

'You what?' I go, towering over her, never sounding more like Dom.

'Tabby informs me you've been making free with my bank card. Is this true?'

'I ain't no thief,' I mutter, teeth welded together.

Thing is, while I'm saying it, I half believe it. Been slaving for her day and night for weeks with no pay. The way I look at it, she kinda owes me.

'Your girl's always had it in for me,' I say, remembering how she disrespected me on the phone that first day. It's like it ain't me speaking. It's like I've been taken over. 'Stuck-up bitch.'

I hear Miss E gasp.

'Go to your room,' she snaps. Like she's Supernanny and I'm a naughty kid.

'Go to hell,' I snarl. 'You can stuff your stinking job an' all.'

I do go to my room but only so's I can start packing.

She tip-taps close behind. 'Going somewhere?'

'Know when I'm not wanted,' I growl, stuffing the laptop and some threads into my backpack. 'I'm outta here.'

'Suit yourself,' she goes with a sniff. 'Plenty more under the stones where I found you.'

I give her a long, cold look. Does she mean it? Does she really want me to go? Does she understand what's going down? I don't even care no more. I shoulder the backpack and brush past without a word.

In the hallway I skid to a halt. It's them bank statements. They ain't stuffed in the drawer no more. They're stacked up on the hall table, all neat an' that, yellow highlighter pen all over them, where her girl's marked the money I took.

'Ain't no thief indeed,' Miss E says, toddling off in the direction of her bedroom. 'Just when I thought his grammar was improving.'

I'm at the front door. 'By the way, for your information,' I shout back, 'no one's ever gonna read that stupid book of yours and no one's ever gonna visit your stupid museum. Know why? 'Cause no one's interested in you, that's why. They've all forgot about you, Miss Eloise Slaughter,' I say her name slow and mean. 'You're nobody.'

I'm wasting my breath.

'Ain't no thief. Ain't no thief,' I hear her warbling from down the corridor.

Outside on the landing, I wait, hoping she'll call me back. Give it ten, then leave.

31.

ELOISE

Alone. Again. I take them under my wing. I nurture them, give them the benefit of my… my… myself, and what do they do? Abandon me. I should be used to it by now, but you never get used to betrayal.

Thank sod, I have you, little digi–whatsit. You and my memories keep me going. Getting the hang of you now. It's not as hard as he made out, the Boy. Such a fusspot. Always interrupting. Asking questions. Proffering snacks. Though no Gypsies, I note. See what I mean? Can't rely on any of them.

They all left me. Trip and Dazzle. Bruno and Howie. All of them. Never thought they would. Never thought they could cope without me. But they did. It was the show that did it. That sodding show ruined everything.

32.

BRADLEY

I'm outside her place, her stupid singing bouncing around my skull. Bad thoughts pile up in my brain like rubbish in the gutter. I get my breathing under control and start to walk. No clue where.

I end up at Tottenham Court Road. Even though it's still early, the traffic's nose to tail. I squat down on a stone step looking across to the dark windows of Aromazz through gaps in the traffic.

I see her boss, the Greek bloke, come striding down the road, rattling his fistful of keys. I see the chubby blonde clip-clop up on her heels. I see the workers juggling their paper cups and breakfast baps, and later their dinner-time toasties and soups. A security bloke in a stupid hat comes out of one of the buildings and moves me on like he's sweeping away litter. I huddle in another doorway nearby, listening to the whoosh of the machine and breathing in its coffee steam every time the door opens. Then I see the streetlights flicker on, one by one, turning the faces of the workers going home into glowing, yellow masks. I see it all. But I don't see her.

I stretch my legs, cross the road and cup my hands against the window. They're wiping the counters, getting ready to shut up shop. Someone knocks on the glass. It's the chubby blonde, waving at me to get off out of it. I push the door and go in.

'Molly is not here,' the chubbster goes in her funny accent before I even say a word. Her eyes is fixed on the place above my eyes, on the thing. 'She is not working today.'

'She on in the morning?'

Her shoulders go up and she turns away.

I walk to the park. To our bench. Sit and stare into the darkness. Pull my old baggies on over my skinnies, and another hoodie under the Puffa. That's better, 'cept for my feet. Root about and pull on an extra pair of socks. My thoughts is tumbling but I try to hold on to them. What are my options? Go back to Miss E? Home to Ma and Dom? No way. No way. What then? Am I gonna sleep in the park? Macky D rubbish on one side, a bin spilling over with dog poo on the other? Not on your flipping life. What, then?

I'm thinking hard, knees up under my chin, arms hugged round me when I see a light dancing along the path. A torch. A bloke bundled up in a knitted navy jumper is heading my way. Longish, dark hair combed forward like he's a geography teacher aiming for the Noel Gallagher look, and missing. He stops in front of me.

'Hello,' he goes, posh but friendly with it. 'Not planning on spending the night there, I hope?'

'What's it to you?' I say into my chest.

'Have you eaten?' He fumbles in a carrier bag and holds out a sandwich. Ham and cheese. I take it. He sits down at the far end of the bench, hands between his knees. 'A day past its sell-by but perfectly edible. The food these supermarkets chuck away, it's criminal.' He gives a little laugh. 'I'm from over there, by the way.' He nods in the direction of a church spire poking up out the trees, the other side of the park. 'Paul.' He takes off his glove and sticks out his mitt.

'Dominic,' I go, not shaking it. *That's all I need, a nosey do-gooder.* Still, I ain't ate all day. I rip open the packet and scarf the sarnie real quick, case he changes his mind.

'New on the streets are you, Dominic?' My mouth's full so I don't answer. 'Only I haven't seen your face before. I like to keep my eye on any newcomers in the locality. It can be… well, let's just say they're not all good guys out there. Seriously, have you got somewhere to kip?'

I go on chewing.

'Because there's a place nearby where you could, you know, bunk up.' He cocks his head again towards the spire. 'Nothing fancy but it's got four walls and a roof. It's going to be a cold one tonight.' He shrugs down into his jumper. 'No pressure. If you want me to leave you alone, I'll understand.'

I swallow. 'Might as well.'

'Excellent. Follow me.'

We're walking across the grass, him in front, pointing the torch on the ground, me following in his damp footsteps. He's talking ten to the dozen. I'm beginning to wonder if this is such a good idea.

'This way,' he goes, heading off along a side path, then across some more grass, muddy this time. 'Not much further. Just along here.' Beams of torchlight bounce off of the trees and bushes, like some slasher film set.

'Hang on a mo,' I go, slowing up. He carries on, then ducks out of sight behind some bushes. 'I thought we was heading for the church.'

'Through here, Dominic,' he calls out. 'As I said, nothing fancy.'

I part the branches. It's a shed. A rough old shed the parkies use. Leaves and logs is stacked up against the wall. The door's half open, a busted padlock hanging.

'You're a vicar then, are you, Paul?' I say, trying to get my head round what's going down. Nothing about this situation feels right.

'Not exactly. Have a peek inside. It's nice and dry. Go on.' He motions with his torch and takes a step back. 'After you.'

Like a div, I go in. It happens so quick. One minute I'm standing at the door. Next he's come up behind me and grabbed me in a bear-hug. We overbalance, falling onto some rough sacking on the floor. He's on top of me and we roll over, him groaning, 'Oh Dominic. My Dominic!' and me struggling.

The stink of his sweat is in my nose, the taste of his spit in my mouth. I try to wriggle out from under but he's pulling at my belt, panting like a dog in a heatwave. I twist my face away and give one mighty shove. He flies off of me and slams into the wall. The whole hut shakes. Sawdust rains down.

'Get away from me,' I yell, staggering up. My hand touches something cold and I grab it. A garden trowel. Only small, but the metal edge glints. I wave it in the air, like a blade. 'Touch me again, I'll cut you.'

Two clean tracks run down his dusty cheeks. 'I thought you… I didn't mean…' He holds out his hands, crying. 'Please. Please, don't hurt me.'

Something about the way he's begging gets to me. I jab out with the trowel towards his cheek. He squeals, even though I miss by a mile. A warm feeling stirs inside me.

'I could have you right now, you perv,' I go. 'The coppers would let me off for sure. Probably give me a medal.'

I jab out and get another rush. I jab again. And again. And again. Each time he squeals. I'm proper buzzing off of it.

He stumbles backwards, falls, and crawls into the corner. His hands cradle the big old bald spot what's showing through his messed-up hair. Cobwebs and splinters is stuck to his jumper. Shoulders heave as he sobs his disgusting heart out. I stand over him, tossing the trowel from hand to hand.

'Get up, you dirty paedo,' I go, when I've listened to his whining long enough. He hauls hisself up, hair everywhere, big eyes on mine. He wipes his snotty face on his sleeve.

'Now, piss off out of it.' My foot follows him through the door.

He's gone and I'm laughing. I'm ecstatic. I'm dancing around the hut. Then all of a sudden I'm crying, choking out big sobs.

33.

ELOISE

Praise sod. A little green light. But does it mean 'on' or 'your flatteries are bat'? Buggered if I know. I'm beginning to wonder if he didn't have his uses after all. He may not have been great shakes as my aman… aman… What is that sodding word? But at least he understood the workings of this damned digi–whatsit and, despite his council house ways, he was getting to grips with a decent G and T too.

Wonder where he's staying?

Not that I care.

What was his name again? I called him Boy. He never seemed to mind. He'll be back. Sod knows, there's nothing for him at home. I'll have to keep a closer eye on him, of course. Sneaking around, telling all and sundry about my museum. What if she gets to hear and pinches the idea?

Have to admit, what he's done in that room is nothing short of a miracle. Of course, under normal circumstances, I would have looked after those pieces myself, given them the benefit of my expert care and attention. But going in there, touching them… You do understand, don't you? I just couldn't bring myself to do it.

Now I don't need to worry. He's doing a brilliant job. Getting everything bagged up, boxed up and labelled. Enterprising. Not that I'd blame him if he were helping himself. That's what this little miss from the Midlands did, after all. Seized the chances presented to me. No one, dear reader, ever made their fortune by playing by the rules. That's the only rule.

It's 4:17 by the glow of the ridiculous little clock he bought, the Boy. Am or pm? Feeling peckish anyhow. Early breakfast or light tea? Never mind. Eggy-weggies will do for both. It's awfully high, this bed. Never really noticed before. Usually there's a handy chair to lean on, but the little sod's tidied that away too. Such a long way down. It's going to be like abseiling down Mont Blanc. I should get something more modern, lower, with one of those built-in jellyboxes that rise up. And a commode. I wonder if they do those? A bed with a built-in commode. With that and a jellybox, one could stay tucked up forever.

Ah, it's so lovely and peaceful without him. Glad he's gone. Glad. Always asking if I wanted anything. Looking at me with those eyes, like a puppy begging for a tummy tickle. What was his name? Oh and David sodding Attenborough. On and on about St David of the Animals. Or was it Dickie? One of the two. I don't care. I don't bollocking care. All I care about is… oh, there must be something.

Sapphie, of course. Sapphie, what would I do without you? You don't skulk away in the fridge, like those naughty eggy weggies. You sit nice and handy at my elbow. Give us a cuddle. Oh, empty! Where are your sisters? Tidied away in the pantry, no doubt. Nothing for it, I'll have to make the trek. After another little nap maybe.

6:43. Grey gloom through the window. Dawn or dusk? Sod knows. Bloody thirsty though. Mouth like a whatsit… a nan's funny, and not even a sip of tonic to thench my… Oh well, nothing for it, here I go, abseiling down the mountainside. Geronimo!

Oops! Bit of a bumpy landing. Not to worry. Put on my party frock to cheer myself up. Found it in the wardrobe and I thought, why not dress for dinner? Or breakfast. Or lunch.

So here I am in the kitchen, all dressed up. I'll say this for whatsisname, he left me well stocked. I have a feast before me. Eggs (a bit runny), beans (a bit burned) and sausages (a bit turned to coal), but it's grub, so who cares? Probably should find a plate. Nah, tastes just the same out of the frying pan.

I located the Sapphie stash, praise be. Five lovely bottles. Well, four and a half now. I needed a few stiff ones to numb the Mont Blanc bruising, you understand. Bit low on tonic and only one lemon. Still I can slum it till he crawls back, thingy between his knees. Can't be long now.

Belly full, G and T to hand, I suppose I have to steel myself. I don't want to. I'd much rather busy myself with something else. Anything else. But I have to, don't I? Or this sodding book will never sell. Come closer little silver digi–whatsit. Let me whisper in your ear.

34.

BRADLEY

She's there. Molly. I walk back to the bench and she's sitting there. Turns out she'd been in Manky Mazzies all along. Boss let her in round the back and she's been hiding. It was her chubby mate's idea. She don't approve of me, see.

'Nearly died when you walked in,' she says. 'They only just got me out the back in time. You looked so angry.'

'You scared of me, then?'

'No,' she goes, a bit too quick. 'Couldn't face you. Not when I knew I was in the wrong. I am *such* a coward.'

'What changed your mind?'

'I thought, well, if he's big enough to make the first move and come looking for me, I should be big enough to say sorry. I tried calling but your phone's off. I couldn't think what else to do. I was gonna give it half an hour. To see if you turned up. It was a long shot.' She tries to smile but her chin trembles. 'Lucky for me, it paid off.'

'Go on then,' I say. 'Get it over with.'

She sucks in air, like she's about to dive underwater. Then the words come rushing out. 'I am so, so sorry,' she goes. 'It was stupid of me. I don't know what I was thinking. I wasn't thinking. I never meant to hurt you.' She stops, running out of puff. When she speaks again, her voice shakes. 'I don't want to change you, Bradley. I like you the way you are. I like everything about you.'

'Even this?' I don't have to point. She knows. 'Be honest with me this time, Molly. Do I weird you out?'

'Well,' she goes, her mouth sort of twisting, 'if we're being totally honest, Bradley, it's a bit of a turn-on.'

'Well, what do you know?' I go. 'Little Molly's got a thing for weirdos.' And I pull my gargoyle face. That throws her for a sec, then we both burst out laughing. When we stop, she says, 'I should be making tracks. Walk me to the bus stop?' The bus comes. She gives me a peck on the cheek and jumps aboard. I swing on after her. 'You nutcase,' she laughs, 'what do you think you're doing?'

'Coming home with you, of course.'

She freaks out. 'You can't. If Mum and Dad ever…'

People are looking. I steer Molly to a seat at the back and explain my situation.

'Thought I could crash at yours,' I go, putting an arm round her shoulder. 'Just for tonight.'

'But Brad—'

'Forget it,' I go, taking my arm away. 'I'll hop off at the next stop. There's plenty of other people I can stay with. No problem.'

I jiggle my foot and gaze through the fugged-up window at the coloured lights and the shadow people.

'We'll have to be quiet,' Molly goes.

It's a proper girl's room with pink fairy lights round the headboard and a pile of fluffy toys on the bed.

'I'm bushed,' I go, falling face down onto the cuteness mountain. It's dead uncomfortable but I stay like that, still in them extra jeans an' that. After a bit I feel her slip in under the covers.

I roll over to make room. We spoon. Me on top of the covers, her underneath. It's nice, her body heat coming through, soft hair tickling my lips. We talk for ages, whispering in each other's ears. Must of slept in the end, 'cause next thing she's shaking my shoulder.

'You better go,' she whispers. 'Dad'll be up.'

'So, you gonna help me?' I say.

'If you do like I said,' she yawns, 'I might think about it.' And falls straight back asleep.

I kiss her on the cheek, watch her breathing for a while, still smiling that smile, then sneak downstairs, head full of the plan I'm hatching.

35.

ELOISE

Right, dear reader, this is it.

This.

Is.

It.

No, I can't. Oh God. But I must. I must. Deep breaths, Eloise…

Alone in the wings, a floating feeling came over me, as if I'd had another blast of blow up my nostrils. Soothing interval music tinkled in the background. Impatient for the finale to begin, the select audience was growing restless.

There was still no sign of Howard. He was supposed to be there. He was supposed to escort me on stage, guide me through. The music struck up in earnest, bursting over the loudspeakers. The interval was over. This was my cue.

It was a Freddie Mercury song. Something about being a great pretender. Something about being left to dream all alone. *Funny,* I remember thinking, *I didn't know Howard was a Queen fan.* That should have been my first inkling. I brushed it aside. My audience was waiting. I glanced round to where Bruno was standing. 'Go on,' he mouthed, as the song faded into silence.

A lone cough rang out. *Come on, Eloise,* I told myself, *do what you've always done: make it up as you go along.*

I'm a trooper, dear reader, always have been. So I had to go on and troop. Looking, I hope, more confident than I felt, I took in a breath and marched onto the stage. Beneath my feet, the boards seemed to rise and fall, like a gently swelling sea. I grabbed the mic stand to steady myself, staggering back as interference shrieked over the speakers. This was not a good start.

Say something for sod's sake, said my inner voice. Don't just stand there like a pillock.

I patted the mike, as if to soothe it and tried again. 'Good evening, fashion slaves!' I said. The words were out of my mouth and echoing round the room before I could stop them. *Why had I said that?* 'Tonight we are here to… to…' *Why the hell are we here*? '… to free you from your shackles with a collection the like of which you have never seen before.'

'That's what they all say,' someone shouted. I shaded my eyes against the lights but all I could see was a shadowy figure at the back.

'This is different,' I went on. 'What you are about to witness is nothing less than…' I thought hard. What was it that Bruno had said? 'Nothing less than a redefinition of womanhood. An end to body fascism. Prepare to have your ideas turned upside down and inside out, as I present to you,' my voice rose, 'a collection that will shock the shit out of you.'

Below me in the front rows, I was aware of jaws dropping. Good. I was having an impact. Exiting stage left, I signalled to Bruno and he made way for the coat hangers to come on. As the first girl hip-swayed past me and onto the catwalk, the audience gave a collective gasp – of appreciation or horror, I couldn't tell. This was it, shit or bust.

36.

ELOISE

After that first gasp from the Hot Spot audience, nothing. Just stunned silence, as coat hanger after coat hanger paraded down the catwalk, each in a piece more extreme than the last. No polite clapping. No cheering. Just a restless murmur, like a breeze lifting dry leaves.

I'd seen this before. It happens every so often when so-called leaders of fashion are faced with something new. Is it appalling? Is it appealing? No one wants to be the first to give an opinion, in case they get it terribly wrong and are made to look fools. So they say nothing. It was like that on that night at the Hot Spot. The audience – literally, in some cases – sat on their beautifully manicured hands, waiting for someone to break ranks and tell them what to think.

What had rendered the audience so reticent? Anti-Fashion Fashion, that's what. Lumps and bumps, that was its essence. In more technical terms, eclectically applied padded augmentations designed to reshape and redefine the silhouette. We're not talking little appliqué patches or twee pads here. We're talking big bulges, humpbacks and pot bellies, lolloping bums and carbuncle-y swellings. That was our big idea. That's what had got Bruno so fired up. That was what the whole future of Heavenly Bodies depended on.

As Bruno had explained to me, the clothes were designed not to disguise imperfections in the body but to exaggerate them. Fat or thin, pear, apple or hourglass shaped, it didn't matter. With Anti-Fashion Fashion body shape was irrelevant. The tyranny of striving for unattainable physical perfection was over.

Unfortunately, nobody had thought to inform the audience of the rationale behind the collection. With no idea what to make of it, they waited for someone to take the lead. Nothing but an ambiguous murmur interspersed with a patter of lukewarm applause greeted the first round of Anti-Fashion Fashion day- and evening-wear.

Slipping backstage, I found Bruno with his head in his hands. 'I don't understand it,' he said, pacing. 'They should be cheering us to the rafters.' Just then an audible groan reached us from the audience. It wasn't sounding good. Bruno stopped pacing and clapped his hands. 'That's it, everyone. I can't stand this anymore. We're cutting to the finale. Get to your places for the wedding tableau. Everyone loves a wedding.'

Not this wedding.

Gasps of disapproval greeted our brave bridesmaids, dear reader, as they flounced, posed and spun. Surely they would warm to our bride? But where had she got to? I found her cowering in a corner, gown hidden under a floor-length purple velvet cloak, hood pulled down low. She seemed reluctant to make her entrance, glancing left and right, as if thinking about making a run for it.

Oh no, you don't, I thought, slipping in behind her. 'Good luck,' I whispered and gave a hefty shove in the small of her back. 'We're depending on you.'

She tumbled on stage, cloak swirling in a dramatic Dracula

fashion round her. Every eye in the room swivelled in her direction. Recovering her poise, she sashayed over to join the rest of the tableau.

'Don't forget the twirl,' I called out.

She glared, then twirled. As she spun, she pushed the hood back from her face and unhooked the clasp at her neck. The purple cloak frisbee-ed away, landing in a heap behind her, revealing the wedding gown in all its audaciousness.

Shall I reveal it to you, dear reader? Though it was a sensation at the time, you may not have seen pictures.

It was purple, very purple. Purple satin, with inserts of leather, lace and I forget what else. One sleeve was short and wide, the other long and narrow and embellished with fake elbows. A stuffed leather hump bulged at the back. One padded bosom overhung the counterbalancing pot belly. Swathes of fabric fanned out into a one-sided bustle that bounced from buttock to buttock as our bride took her place at the centre of the group, blue eyes darting fearfully from side to side.

What would people make of our collection? I held my breath. In the wings Bruno held up crossed fingers.

'Look! It's the Elephant Woman!'

A man's voice, a bubble of laughter in it, rang out from the back of the room, shattering the tension.

It began as a rumble, quickly spreading, surging and gaining power. I felt it vibrate through the soles of my feet. Was it cheering? Was it applause? Was it the stamping of appreciative feet? No, dear reader. It was laughter. The whole audience was laughing at us.

Instinct drove me back on stage to defend our creations. That only seemed to encourage the mirth. The more I remonstrated, the louder they hooted and cackled, until their howls drowned me out. I gave up and, shading my eyes, sought to identify the bastard who'd mocked us, turning the audience against us.

Have you guessed, dear reader? If you have, you're sharper than me. Squinting into the lights, I caught a movement. A man, his hands cupped round his mouth, booing. He dropped his hands and for the first time I saw his face. I saw…

Dear God, this is worse than torture!

Howard. I saw Howard. My Howard. Booing.

Could it get any worse? It could.

I watched, as if hypnotised, as Howard approached the stage and leaped athletically up. 'Enjoying yourself, Plumpkin?' he said, giving my arm a squeeze that made me wince. 'Because I am.'

Fool that I was, I still didn't get it.

'I don't understand, Howie,' I said. 'Is this some sort of joke?'

'You,' he said, poking me hard in the chest, 'you're the joke.'

He turned his back and reached for the mic. 'Ladies and gentlemen,' he began, switching on a thousand-watt smile a gameshow host would be proud of. The audience, no doubt exhausted by their prolonged hilarity, immediately quietened.

'For this, her last ever show… shush, Eloise,' he said, smothering my protest, 'for her last ever show, we gave Eloise a totally free hand. I think you'll agree she's come up with something truly… erm… unforgettable tonight. So, thank you, Eloise, for being such a good sport and giving us such a good laugh.'

Howard patted his hands together. 'But to be serious for a moment,' he said, switching off the smile. 'As you know, for many years Eloise has been the driving force behind Heavenly Bodies, its inspiration and its heartbeat.'

'Hear, hear,' someone shouted. I recognised Bruno's voice.

'But times change,' Howard said. 'Things move on. Tonight it is my sad duty to announce,' he took a breath, 'Eloise has relinquished her position as head of Heavenly Bodies. From today on, the company is in new and exciting hands.'

Fixing my mouth into a rictus smile, like a dog with rabies, I edged up to Howard. 'You can't do this,' I said through gritted teeth. 'I haven't signed anything.'

'I think you'll find you have,' Howard hissed out of the corner of his mouth. Like a magician producing a rabbit, he pulled a wad of papers from the inside pocket of his dinner jacket. 'See?' I just had time to glimpse two signatures. Howard's and mine. 'Fergie brought the papers round last night and you signed them.'

'But last night I was…' I stopped, choking on the words. A sudden, dreadful thought had hit me. *Had* I signed? Was it Fergus I heard talking to Howard? All I remembered clearly was the butterflies. Beautiful, white butterflies. But what if? Oh God. What if they weren't butterflies? What if they were sheets of paper? The takeover papers? I had signed them. I must have. Off my chops on coke, Howard and Fergus had talked me into it.

'Now, if you'll excuse me.' Howard stepped back up to the mic.

'Throughout the sixties, seventies and eighties,' he said, 'Eloise Slaughter was the face of Heavenly Bodies. Tonight, it is my very great pleasure to introduce the woman who will be taking us forward into the nineties.' Howard threw open his arms. 'Fresh off the plane from New York, may I present Fashion Inc's fabulous Miss Kristina Krabtree.'

I died. Dear reader, I swear my poor heart stopped beating and I actually died, right there on that stage, as before my unbelieving eyes, the bitch herself strutted on. Her emaciated frame encased from head to toe in one of her trademark drab sacks, blonde hair glinting under the lights, she waved a regal hand to the audience. And they cheered. Oh how they cheered.

After several minutes, Howard held up his hand for silence.

'And to welcome her on board, tonight we're unveiling our new, re-imagined logo.'

With a nod from Howard, a banner unfurled. The audience ooooh-ed. I gasped, I staggered. If it hadn't been for Bruno's strong arm, I would have crumpled.

It was our logo, all right, but not as I knew it. The central figure was still a woman, naked but for a wide ribbon with the words 'Heavenly Bodies' on it covering her bush and bosoms, but it was no longer the generous example of full-blooded womanhood it used to be. That is to say, me. Oh no. It was a stick woman with xylophone ribs, pointy hip bones and a blonde bob. That is to say, her. Kristina sodding Krabtree.

Needless to say, the audience, now in a cheering mood, gave the new logo a standing ovation. Excruciating though this was, my torment didn't end there.

Almost fainting with horror, I looked on as Howard, my Howard, snaked his arm round Kristina Krabtree's thin waist, pulled her to him and kissed her long and hard on the lips. Then, glancing over at me, he slid his hand down to pinch what little he could grab of her scrawny buttock.

Oh dear God, how shall I bear it?

They were in it together, you see. Howard, the shit and Kristina, the bitch. He was her lover all along. She planted him on me in revenge. After the, you know, the thing with the fleas. Fashion Inc: that was them, set up expressly to fleece me. The meeting in the nightclub, the courtship, even the marriage: all a fix.

Anti-Fashion Fashion was them too. It wasn't enough to

take Heavenly Bodies from me, they wanted my reputation in shreds. They knew those hideous lumps and bumps would be a disaster. I don't suppose they could believe their luck when Bruno went for it hook, whatsit and thingummy.

Why hadn't I followed my instincts? Why had I gone along with it? Because I was too deaf, dumb and blinded by love, that's why. Can you wonder I'm wary of letting people get close to me? Once burned, twice shy.

Stranded on stage, teeth clattering with shock, unable to move, my treacherous husband pawing that woman not six feet away, I was in desperate need of rescue. Suddenly, there he was. My saviour. Bruno. I felt a warmth round my shoulders. I hugged it to me. It was the purple cloak. Bruno had grabbed it and thrown it over me. Clinging to his arm, still numb, I surrendered to its embrace, only one thought in mind: to get away.

Outside, a chill wind hit me in the face like a slap. 'I need a drink,' I croaked. 'Oh, how I need a drink.'

'I'll meet you in the Adam and Eve round the corner,' Bruno said. 'I won't be long.'

'You're not coming?'

'I have things to do first?'

'What things?' But I was talking to myself. Bruno had run off into the night, leaving me, once more, alone.

Where's that sodding bottle? Sometimes, dear reader, the only answer is gin.

37.

BRADLEY

'So yow've crawled back to beg forgiveness, 'ave yow?' she slurs from her bed. 'Just like before.'

Twenty-four hours, that's how long I been away. Only twenty-four hours.

Ain't given much to swearing but, Christ on a bike, how can anyone get into such a mess in twenty-four hours? And what's happened to her posh accent? Don't sound so *Downton* now. Not with the best part of a bottle of gin inside her.

I keep my distance, on account of the pong.

The state of her ain't something I'm gonna forget in a hurry, I can tell you. She's on the bed, tangled up in her old eiderdown. What is she wearing? Holding my nose, I risk a few steps forward. It's a pink party dress and it don't do her no favours. A sort of ballet dress a kid might wear, with sequins and frills an' that. Don't come nowhere near fitting her neither. It's undone down the back and keeps falling off of her shoulders. If it weren't for the old purple thing, it would be all hanging out.

And wet. Everything's wet. The green eiderdown I had dry-cleaned, the sheets I washed and ironed, the new feather pillows I got – all wet. Skirt of her dress is sopping an' all.

Looks like someone's picked her up and dunked her up to her waist in stewed tea. Only it ain't tea, is it? It's piss. She's been lying there pissing herself for twenty-four hours. That's what accounts for the rankness of the pong.

She's a right horror. A right piss-soaked, pissed-up horror.

'Well, this time yow're too late,' she goes. 'Too sodding late.'

'Be fair, Miss E,' I go, in my most gentlest voice. 'We both said things we shouldn't of. I'm sorry, proper sorry, and I'm sure you are. Can't we forget what went down and start again?'

'Forget it?' she says, eyes widening. 'Never. Yow deserted me. Robbed me of everything. And yow expect me to forgive and forget. Get away from me, yow shit.' And she kicks out with her feet, winding the covers round her legs even more.

'Been thinking things over,' I say, meaning I been listening to what sensible Molly had to say on the matter. She'd told me, as we'd spooned, that I should go back, say sorry and admit I was in the wrong. Show Miss E I was taking responsibility for what I done. Be the bigger person.

The more I thought about it, them fairy lights twinkling above my head, the more I saw there was something in what she was saying. I promised I'd go back to Courtland Mansions first thing and give Miss E the speech me and Molly had worked out. I was keeping my promise.

'I shouldn't have taken advantage, Miss E,' I go, 'not after everything what you've done for me. I'll pay you back, every penny, I swear. And I'll work extra hard from now on. If you'll just give me another chance. You won't regret it.'

But Miss E is angry. And pissed.

'Don't yow come near me, yow shit,' she shouts. 'Yow made a monkey of me once but not again, Howie.'

Howie? Who's this Howie? Then I remember. She's that out of it, she's time-travelled back to when she was married. She's mistook me for her ex, Howard Haggarty. I play along, praying she'll come to soon.

'Yeah, well. Sorry about that an' everything,' I go.

She's looking at me out the corner of her eye. 'So, yow're not planning on running off again?'

'Course not. I'm gonna stay and look after you, like I said. Starting with your bed.'

That seems to change her mood, though I'm not sure it's for the better far as I'm concerned.

'Ooh Howie,' she coos, draping herself over me. 'Yow're so masterful.'

Somehow I get her in the bath.

'No peeking now,' she giggles, stumbling as she peels off her wet things. 'Yow're still in my bad books, remember.'

She's down to her gynormous bra and pants. Crinkly skin spills out over the top of her knickers and over the back of her bra, like she's wearing a punctured sumo suit. I look away as she struggles out of her underwear but I can't help but see her backside. It's bright and shiny, like two big red apples. Sitting in piss for a night and day will do that for you. Won't let me take that purple thing off of her, though. Hangs onto it for grim death, even in the bath.

'I'm never parted from my peignoir,' she goes. 'Never.'

Least the tatty old thing gets a rinse.

While I'm lathering up her hair, still looking anywhere but at her naked body, she's mumbling, 'Shits. Yow're all shits. Yow and yow.' She points and glares like there's other people in the room. 'Yow think yow've got away with it. Just yow wait.'

'I shall have my vengeance, in this life or the next,' I go,

Maximus Decimus Meridius-style, while I ladle water over her head. Flipping love that old *Gladiator* film I do.

I leave her to it while I strip the bed. Nothing for it but to hold my breath and lug the whole lot – pillows, bedclothes, an' everything – down two flights to the skip round the back.

Before long, she's tucked up inside my sleeping bag. Face washed, in a clean nightie and a fluffy dressing gown, towel round her head, looking like a normal, respectable old granny. I sit beside her. She gives a sigh, like she's shouldering all the cares of the world.

'I was so lonely while you were away,' she goes. A tear runs down, gets caught in a wrinkle, and drips off of her chin.

'I know,' I say, taking her hand. She squeezes it.

I clear my throat, embarrassed. 'About your book, Miss E. I'm sorry what I said. What do I know about writing? Been kicked out of school on and off since I was ten. Nor what I said about your daughter. I…'

A sound like a chainsaw rattles round the room. She's snoring. I get up to leave.

She stirs. 'Nighty night, Howie,' she murmurs and kisses the air. 'Love you.'

'Love you too,' I go without thinking. Not that she hears.

38.

BRADLEY

Best part of two days, she sleeps. Good. That gives me plenty of time to get busy. The more I think, the more I'm sure the answer to a lot of questions about Miss E is inside that digital recorder. To be honest with you, I ain't been paying that much attention to her tales – she does go on and on – but that's gonna have to change. I sneak the recorder out of her bedroom and settle down with it and a packet of Skittles.

Wow! The things she's seen. The things she's done. Looking at her now, it's hard to credit that she was like a Kardashian of the olden days, with a touch of the Katie Prices thrown in. You gotta respect that. She might be fat and old and shot to pieces now, but back then, she was an A-list influencer. Seeing her through new eyes, I'm telling you.

I go shopping. Got a surprise for her, something to cheer her up. I'm in the sitting room putting the finishing touches when she wakes up. 'Water, bring me water, Boy,' she shouts. 'My mouth tastes like an animal's shat in it.'

Charming. At least she don't think I'm her hubby no more.

'Sod me!' she goes when she eventually surfaces, all bleary-eyed. 'What have you been up to?'

Got the idea when I was up the shops. It's not even

December yet but the streets is already full of lights and the shop windows stuffed with Christmas decorations. So I think, *Why not?*

It starts off a mission to get back into her good books. As I'm hanging streamers across the ceiling, tinsel over the pictures and fairy lights, like Molly's, over the mantelpiece, it becomes more than that. I really do want to impress her, put a smile back on that wrinkly old face.

Am I going soft? No. I'm seeing things more clearer, that's all. Thanks to Molly, I'm realising getting buff down the gym, acting the tough nut – like Dom and his crazies – ain't always the way. Sometimes the smart way is to bite your tongue, let down your guard, and be nice.

That's what I'm doing. Being nice to Miss E, hoping, I suppose, she'll be nice back. Maybe even remember my name, once in a while, though I ain't holding my breath on that one.

'Thought we could celebrate early,' I say to her, turning on the fairy lights and watching them twinkle. 'Do it proper.' I stand back to let her see.

I'm trying to remember a proper Christmas when I was a nipper. Don't come up with nothing. Knees-up and a bottle of voddie – that was Ma's idea of a good Christmas.

It seems to be working. Miss E's eyes is twinkling like the lights, but she's not letting me off lightly. Not yet. Not her. I see it's gonna take more than a cotton-wool snowman and a plastic Santa to get rid of her grumps.

'Hmmm,' she goes. 'Don't think much of your tree. A Christmas tree should touch the ceiling.'

If my tree don't find favour, I'm hoping my Festive Feast will. 'Everything you need for a traditional Christmas dinner, including turkey, stuffing, roast potatoes and sausages' it says on the box. Looks dead tempting in the picture. And guess what – no washing-up – 'cause it comes with its own plastic tray to serve it on. Got two little Christmas puds and a tub of cream an' all.

She thaws a bit when I serve up the feast in front of *Judge Judy*. A time or two, I even catch her smiling at the divs they get on there. After our puds I break out the crackers. Try to make her laugh reading out them lame jokes. *What do you get if you cross Santa with a duck? A Christmas quacker.* I see her lips twitch but she ain't exactly splitting her sides.

I clear up, which don't take no time on account of them plastic trays, and settle down on the sofa. Some stupid advert is blasting out, horrible cartoon creatures dancing and singing like car insurance is the most excitingest thing ever invented. I've had enough. I punch the remote and the room goes silent.

'Here. Got you this,' I go, holding out a package done up in fancy paper and ribbons. Woman in the shop wrapped it.

Time was, she'd have gone bonkers over a present, snatched it out my hand, squealing and carrying on. Today she just blinks a lot and says, chin a-wobbling, 'Thank you, Boy. Thank you very much.'

'Shall I open it for you? It's a jigsaw,' I say. 'Lake District. We can do it together. Sheep and countryside an' that.'

'Sorry,' she says all of a sudden.

'For what, Miss E?'

'I didn't get you anything.' Reckon for two pins there'd be tears.

'Don't you worry about that,' I say. 'You've given me plenty.'

I pull off the cellophane and empty the pieces onto the table. I sort them by colour. Green stuff – grass and trees. Blue stuff – sky and clouds. Brown stuff – houses and walls.

She clears her throat. 'You're doing it all wrong. You need to separate the edgies from the middlies. Here, let me.' I sit back and let her take over. 'Where in the Lake District is this supposed to be?' she goes.

'Search me, Miss E,' I go. 'Only lake I ever seen was in Hyde Park.'

She don't ask but the memory pings back anyhow. It's a sunny day and Ma's took us to the park. That's a first. But it ain't for our benefit. Oh no. Turns out she's meeting a fella. Greasy-looking sort with a fag on. He spreads a blanket out under a tree and they lay down. Ma tells us to clear off out of it.

We wander off to the lake to chase the birds. Dom finds a squashed football, kicks it about a bit then lobs it into the water. Gets me to fish it out with a twig. Should of knowed he'd give me a shove. Soaked I am. Ma gives me a clip round the ear when she sees. She's fuming we have to leave early. I go home on the bus in wet trousers and socks. Spread them out but they's still damp in the morning when I put them on for school.

I look at the puzzle. Miss E's sorted out the pieces all right but she ain't put any in. Keeps picking them up, moving them over the table, sighing and putting them down again.

'Mind if I have a go?' I say, spotting an easy corner piece and an edge one with bits of a fence on them. I put them side by side and make a big show of not getting them to fit. 'Harder than it looks,' I say.

'Move over and let the expert show you how,' she says. She shoves me out of the way with her fat arse and slots the one piece into the other. 'Ta-dah!' she goes with a big, proud grin.

Think we're sound again.

I'm on the settee, laptop on my knee. Miss E's gone to bed. As predicted, she pulls a face when she clocks the new bedding with its nice bright cover, flowers an' that. She pulls at it and goes on about crisp white linen and a good woollen blanket. Never mind that she's gone and ruined the stuff she had. Minutes after she's snuggled down, she's revving up that chainsaw again.

Peace at last. Treat meself to a wildlife download. One I ain't seen before. It ain't Lord David. But it's still gold.

It's about these amazing fish. Snakeheads they're called. Ugly things what escaped from somewhere. They get everywhere. Golf courses. Gardens. Not only in water neither. 'Cause, thing is – get this! – they is fish but they can go on land as well. How cool is that?

Shows one of them wriggling through the grass to where some little Yankee kid is playing with his toys. You can tell it's America 'cause there's this big old swimming pool in the background. Don't show the snakehead nabbing the kid, though. Don't show it chomping chunks out of him with its razor-sharp teeth. That was a blow.

Cuts to it hunting other fish. Dead quick they is. One second this goldfish is swimming past, minding its own. Next second – whooompf! – it ain't got no arse end. It's wriggling like it's gonna swim away, but you can see its insides unravelling into the water an' everything. Hilarious.

Like I say, sometimes it pays to be nice, sometimes you gotta fight your corner. Knowing when to do what, that's the tricky bit.

'You, little fishy, ain't going nowhere,' I say to the screen.

39.

ELOISE

What's going on with the Boy? First he flounces out in a rage, then he's back, nice as pie. Can't keep up with him. Appallingly rude one minute, can't do enough for me the next. Bought me this sweet little Christmas tree and treated me to a slap-up meal, not to mention an impossibly hard jigsaw puzzle. I was quite touched, though I tried hard not to show it.

Called me a bitch, you know, when we were arguing. Me, a bitch? I was, of course. Known for it. Not anymore. Don't have the required energy for bitchifying these days. But that doesn't mean he can go around, Carte D'Or, abusing me with the truth.

At least he's lost that hangdog-in-a-manger expression. He's got some of his sparkle back.

He thinks I've forgotten about the money. I haven't. But it was never a big deal to me. Who cares if he treats himself to a coat and a few luxuries? I've never been poor myself, but I imagine it's not a bundle of laughs. Tabby took some persuading, storming about the apartment, threatening to call the police. After all it was, as she pointed out, her money he'd misappropriated. I managed to stay her hand with some well-chosen words.

'I've been working the figures out in my head,' I told her. I hadn't

but that's the sort of thing I know impresses her. 'I actually owe him more in back pay than he's taken. Also, he's tolerable company and almost house-trained. What use will he be if he's banged up in the clinker? Why don't we just let barking dogs lie?' I patted her hand and she didn't pull away. That's how I knew I'd get my own way.

40.

BRADLEY

Dom. I hear Dom's voice. Dream words snarling round in my head. I turn over and pull the sleeping bag up. 'I'm a firestarter, a fucking little git of a firestarter,' the voice goes. Hot breath blasts in my ear. I open my eyes. This ain't no dream. It's Dom. Here, at Miss E's. In my room. Next thing I know, I'm on the floor. I scramble to my feet.

'How did you…?' I stammer, cupping my hands over my privates.

'Winkle you out? Simples. Followed you, didn't I, that second week, just for the hell of it. Did you really think I'd let you head off without keeping an eye on what you was up to? Can't believe you didn't clock me but you was that keen to get to your poxy job, marching along like you was a proper bigshot. Never even looked round. What a prat.' Dom laughs. 'Ma went batshit, you know, when she seen what you done to the bedroom. What you hadn't set fire to, she smashed up. Priceless.'

'You ain't told her—'

'Where you are? Nah, your secret's safe with me. For now anyhow.' He looks round the room. 'Nice little set-up you got here. Been hanging round the area these last few days on the lookout for my long lost baby bruv. Almost give up on you. Then – bingo! – spotted you coming out the Tube yesterday afternoon, followed you here and… here we are now. Surprise, surprise! Oh, and thanks for leaving the front door key under the mat, by the way. Nice touch that. Very hospitable.' His eyes harden. 'Now we got the social chitchat out the way, let's get down to business, shall we? Give us it.' He sticks out his hand. 'Don't act more stupider than what you are. The key you was on about. To that room. Let's have it.'

'Keep your voice down. You'll wake her up.'

'Come on, Bradley,' he says, even louder. 'I know you got it. I can see it in your face. You owe me. I bin breaking my back kipping on the settee since you paid us a visit. Either you hand over that key or me and my mains is gonna kick that door in and that *will* wake her up.'

'Your mains?' I go, my mouth all of a sudden full of cotton wool.

'Yeah. Quiet ain't they?' At the doorway, two shadows shift. His homeboys. His mains. Hardeep and AJ. I look from one to the other. *Can I take on the three of them?* I'm pretty buff these days but even so. I seen them do the business before, when Dom had a ruck with some lad. They ain't big nor brave but they're quick and they're nasty. I play for time.

'Honest, Dom,' I go, hopping into my jeans and hauling on a tee. 'There ain't nothing worth bothering with in that room. I had a look. Only wish there was. It's all junk.'

'Don't give me that. If it's junk, why's she keep it locked? Spill, unless you wanna wake up in A&E with your plums tied in a bow on top of your bonce.' Hardeep and AJ split their sides at that. He grabs my arm. 'I'm losing patience here, bruv. Give us that key. This is your last ch…. what the fuuuuck?'

Out of nowhere, there's a shriek and a little fat Bellatrix with purple wings flings herself at him. It's Miss E, waving a rolled-up brolly, screaming, 'Scum, riff-raff. Get out of here! Go on, get out!'

For half a second, Dom holds his ground. Then she's driving him backwards down the hall. She's lashing out. He's swatting her away. Like they're in some sort of crazy swordfight. I stand there my mouth open. Unbelievable. The old dear's only got the upper hand. She's barely half his height but she's forcing him towards the front door. Then I catch Dom's smirky face and I look back at his boys. Hardeep's shoulders is shaking and AJ is bent over. They're just playing with her.

'Come on, old lady.' Dom flicks his fingers, egging her on. 'Let's see you kick some ass.'

All credit to her, she has a go. But realistically, I ask you? What blows she lands wouldn't trouble a butterfly and, anyways, mostly she's bashing fresh air. Next thing, the three of them is shadow-boxing round her, jostling and laughing like kids in the playground.

Dom straightens up. He's had enough fooling around. 'OK, you can stop now,' he goes, smile dropping away. 'Stop it, I said!' He grabs the point of the brolly and twists it. Whether he meant to or not, I don't know, but what happens is, the brolly opens up with a whoosh. Its spines scratch into the wall, gouging strips out the wallpaper. Miss E loses her balance and the tables, all of a sudden, is turned.

It's Miss E who goes backwards now, Dom driving her towards the sitting room with the open brolly. Miss E is snapping and snarling like a little Jack, but there ain't nothing she can do. He's got her pinned up against the wall.

While all this is going on, I grab my chance.

'This what you're after?' I'm standing in the hallway, holding up the dark green carrier bag. Dom's head snaps round. He's leaning over Miss E on the floor. She's trapped against the living-room door, brolly handle pressing into her side, tree-trunk legs scrabbling on the lino. Them morons Hardeep and AJ is killing theirselves.

'This'd better be good.' Dom backs off and swaggers towards me.

I see Miss E's eyes flit from the carrier to the door gaping open behind me. I upend the bag. Brooches, rings and necklaces tumble out onto the rug. Dom whistles. 'This is more like it,' he goes, eyes glittering. He kneels down to dig his hands in. My heart is thudding. Don't dare look at Miss E.

'Well done, Strawberry Face,' he goes. 'What else she got stashed in there?' He rises on his toes to gawp over my shoulder.

'Junk, like I said, old clothes and stuff. She's one of them crazy hoarders. I'm trying to sort it out for her. And that's God's honest, Dom.' He ain't about to take my word. He goes to push past. 'No,' I go, bracing myself. 'Don't go in.'

'Says who?'

'Says me.' I see him bristle. 'There's other stuff in there.' I close my eyes, thinking fast. 'If you must know, she uses it for her number twos. Bags it up and keeps it in the corner by the window. Been doing it for years.' I hold my nose. 'There's tons of it in there. The stink's unbelievable. If you don't believe me, you can...'

'No,' he goes, stepping back. 'No, you're all right. Long as you're not lying to me. You're not, are you, baby bruv?' He narrows his eyes, like he's trying to read my mind. I don't blink. He looks away. 'Come on, boys, let's bounce,' he goes, swinging the carrier over his shoulder. 'Can you believe that? She keeps her shits.'

Sniggering, the three of them swing down the hall. I shut the door behind them. The click is loud in the silence. Feeling like all the air's been sucked out my lungs, I lean against the door.

'That was a close one,' I say. Miss E's still on the floor where Dom left her, legs stuck out. Her head drops and she mutters something.

'What's that, Miss E?' I move towards her. 'You OK?'

She says it again. Still don't catch it.

'You'll have to speak up.'

'Traitor,' she says, quiet but clear. Then she lifts her head and raises her voice. 'You dirty, scheming little traitor.' She turns her face away.

41.

ELOISE

Traitors. Traitors on every side. I thought at last I'd found someone I could trust. I thought he was different from the others. I was wrong. He's like the rest. They all turn against me in the end.

42.

BRADLEY

I'm getting worried. Real worried.

It's the shock, I keep telling meself. *Just the shock.* Give it a while and she'll be right as rain. Back to her old self. Back to slagging me off all day long.

She's not talking to me, see. Not a word since Dom and his crew broke in. Won't let me explain why I had to give them the jewellery. Won't even look me in the eye. I have a go several times but she puts her fingers in her ears.

All she does is lie in bed, talking to that recorder. Wished I'd never bought the damn thing. Not eating. I try everything to tempt her out. All her favourites. Macaroons. Pop-Tarts. Cream of asparagus soup. Cheese toasties. She won't have nothing to do with them. Not drinking. Not even the gin.

This rate she's gonna make herself ill. What am I gonna do then?

Like I say. I'm worried.

43.

ELOISE

'Quick. Come on,' Bruno said, urging me outside. 'I've got four taxis waiting on meters.'

It had been more like two hours before Bruno collected me from the Adam and Eve, by which time I'd downed several double brandies and was feeling both sozzled and sorry for myself.

Even through my drunken misery, I was aware I wasn't the only one who'd been wounded that night. Bruno had championed Anti-Fashion Fashion like no one else. When they'd mocked our clothes, they'd been mocking him. Yet here he was, looking perkier than ever.

'Four taxis?' I slurred, stumbling out of the pub. 'Why four?'

'For the clothes.' Bruno opened the door of the nearest purring taxi. A heap of those lumpy, bumpy monstrosities spilled out. 'Do you think you could squeeze in amongst this lot?'

'What are you up to, Bruno?'

'What does it look like? I'm nicking the Anti-Fashion Fashion collection, of course. We can't let those two crooks get away with everything.'

Swallowing my distaste and a brandy-flavoured retch, I crawled into the taxi and curled up, taking care to keep well away from the clothes that had been the source of my humiliation. Bruno climbed in beside me, perching on a bulging cardboard box.

As the taxi drew away, Bruno eyed me. 'Why did you do it, Ellie? Sign your life's work away like that?'

'I didn't mean to. At least… Howard got me wasted, all right? And… oh, I don't know. I can't remember. But he showed me my signature, Bruno. Just now.' My voice faded. 'What can I say? I must have signed. What does it matter? The Heavenly Bodies label won't be worth a bean after tonight's fiasco.'

'Timing, that's the secret. It's not the right time for Anti-Fashion Fashion right now. But it's time will come, Ellie, I know it,' Bruno said. 'As for the rest of the label, that's still sound. Worth a small fortune, in fact.'

'And I've signed it all away?' I wailed, clasping my forehead.

'Don't torture yourself. We've all be made fools of by love,' he said wistfully. Then he squared his shoulders. 'Chin up. We've got Carnaby Street to burgle yet.'

After we'd ransacked the Soho boutique, we ferried the whole lot back to my flat. Bruno got the grumbling cabbies to fling everything into the guest room. When they'd gone, we trooped downstairs, spirits suddenly low again after the excitement of the raid. Bruno paused in the hallway, hand on the front-door catch.

'Not staying to drown our sorrows?' I invited.

'No,' he said gravely. 'I don't drink any more. Haven't for a while.' He paused. 'So, lass. This is it. I'm off.'

'Home?' I said.

'No, lass. For good.'

My world shifted on its axis. Bruno was leaving me.

'How will I survive without you?' I sobbed, clutching at his sleeve.

He shook his head wearily. 'Tonight has finished me off, lass. This is your world, not mine. You'll do fine. I'm too much of a Northerner.' He shuffled his feet. 'While I'm at it, there's more bad news.'

I didn't know how much more I could take.

'Trip and Dazzle,' he said. 'You won't be seeing them anymore. Tonight was the last straw. They're off to the Forest of Dean. Setting up on their own, making garden sculptures out of twigs. Should be a nice little business.'

Misery upon misery! My friends, all my old friends from the earliest days of Heavenly Bodies, were abandoning me. I was stunned. And tired. So tired. Too tired to argue. In any case, I could see by the set of Bruno's mouth that nothing I could say would change his decision. His mind was made up.

'Where will you go?' I whispered, defeated, deflated.

'I've got friends living in an ashram. They keep asking me to join them. I think I'll take them up on the offer.'

'Ashram?' I said, dazed. 'I don't even know where that is. Is it a very long way away?'

'Oh, Ellie,' he said, almost in tears himself. 'I'm gonna miss you so much.' He kissed the top of my head, pressed down the latch and was gone.

It was three days before I got out of bed. Three days during which the gutter press constantly hammered on my door and rang my phone. There had been Rottweilers roaming loose at the show, you see. By which I mean, tabloid snappers and scribblers. I was all over the papers. It was that 'Elephant Woman' line. They loved it: 'HB trumpets fantuskically bizarre Elephant Woman fashion.' That sort of thing.

Besieged in Lowndes Street, I lived like a mole, groping about in the gloom behind closed curtains, or scurrying out after dark to do my shopping. Another flurry of press persecutions came with the divorce from Howard several months later, provoking more so-called witty headlines: 'Elephant Woman fashionista gets peanuts, while ex walks off with jumbo pay-out.'

I almost died laughing.

I had to get away. Somewhere I could hide.

Once more, for a final time, I turned to Bruno. The last favour he did for me before flying off to Ashram was to sell Lowndes Street and, with the proceeds, buy this Courtland Mansions apartment, a much more modest pad.

'It should leave you enough to live on – *if* you're careful,' he warned me over the phone. 'You will be careful, Ellie, won't you?'

I wasn't, of course. Careful, I mean. Well, I was lonely. And bored. What with the cruises and the entertaining, the greedy so-called friends and the grasping so-called boyfriends, the money dried up remarkably quickly. What I would have done after that if dear Tabby hadn't stepped in with a monthly allowance, I don't know.

'Just as long as I don't have to visit you every month to hand it over in person,' she said. Joking, of course.

Thirty years – more than thirty, in fact – I've been here now. How fly times! All those years living with the Heavenly Bodies relics locked safely away in the box room. I've never even looked at them. Just closed the door and turned the key. There they stayed – until *he* came along.

Shitterty shit, shit, shit! The whole shitting world's gone to shit.

44.

BRADLEY

Crash! The sound of smashing china jolts me awake. Overnight, she's gone from silent to violent. I've drifted off, fully dressed on my bed, earbuds in, listening to her voice. Bringing meself up to speed. Another crash, coming from the kitchen. I follow the sound.

She's standing, knuckles on the table, panting. Around her, the cupboard doors is open, the drawers hanging half off. I step forward. There's a crunch. A sharp pain goes through my foot. Piece of glass. I hop back just as a saucepan clangs against the wall, making a big old dent in the plaster. Lucky for me she's a rubbish shot.

'If you was to let me explain…' I go, but I can tell by the way she picks up the colander and aims it at me that she ain't in no mood for explanations. She lets fly with a grunt, hitting the picture of a café what hangs on the wall – or used to. She works her way down a stack of side plates, launching them over-arm at me, then, as her arm gets tired, chucking them any old how onto the floor. When they're all smashed, she looks around for something else.

'Listen, Miss E,' I go, seizing the opportunity. But listening ain't on her radar. A cup flies through the air. 'Not the bone china, please!' I reach up and catch it in my open hand. Always was pretty fair at cricket. She keeps the missiles coming. I skip about doing my best to wicket-keep, catching some, missing others. All of a sudden she stops. Out of ammo and breath. She plonks down on a chair, sweat on her top lip.

'You done?' I go, puffing myself. 'Look at this mess.' I get the dustpan. 'Now you've got that out your system,' I go, on my knees, brushing up the broken pieces, 'how about if I explain?' She gives a snort. I take that as a yes. 'I'll put the kettle on. If you've left us any cups, that is.'

We're sitting at the kitchen table, steaming cuppas in front of us. Neither of us is drinking. She still ain't spoke, though the stink-eyes she's giving me say more than enough.

'OK, I can see how it looks,' I start. 'Me handing over your stuff to Dom. But I done it with the best of intentions.' Another snort. 'It got rid of him, didn't it? It was all I could think of. Believe me, Miss E, you don't want him and his mates anywhere near you.'

While I'm talking, I'm thinking, *What's to stop him from coming back? Bringing more of his mates? Would a coupla bolts on the front door be enough?* I push the thought away. Right now, I gotta convince Miss E I'm one of the good guys.

'Them jewels I give him – I don't mean no disrespect nor nothing – but they ain't… aren't worth anything.' I picture the man's face, the man in the jeweller's, as I'd tipped my haul out onto the counter. I can still hear him laughing.

'Nothing but cheap costume jewellery,' I tell her, repeating word for word what the man said. 'Not worth a tenner for the lot.'

What's Dom gonna do when he finds *that* out? Another worrying thought.

She still don't say a dicky. She folds her arms and is

pretending to look out the window but I can see by the way she keeps narrowing them eyes that she's taking it all in.

'Except for this,' I go, reaching into my back pocket. 'This is worth a bit.' Victorian, the arsey jeweller told me. She turns her head. I dangle it in the air. Steam rises. She focuses on the swinging chain. 'Spotted it straight off,' I go on. Her eyes follow it like she's hypnotised. 'Real gold.'

'Terry's locket,' she breathes, grabbing it.

Yesss! I take a slurp. 'Kept it to one side, didn't I? I would of mentioned it before but you, well… you wasn't yourself.' She's staring up at me through her lashes. 'So,' I go, 'this Terry? He an old boyfriend?' Though I know full well who he is, from her recordings.

She works her lips. She don't wanna speak. I can see that. But she can't stop herself. She's gotta put me straight. 'My daddy,' she mumbles.

'Your doggy?' I go, still playing the dumb-arse. 'Terry was a dog?'

'No, idiot boy,' she snaps. 'Terry was my daddy. My father.'

'My mistake,' I go. 'Present was it?'

'For my sixteenth birthday. I thought I'd lost it for ever. Oh, you darling, darling thing.' It's the locket she's talking to, not me, of course. She's clicked it open and is gazing at the pictures inside. Her face flushes.

'Who's that?' I ask, though I already know that too.

She holds the locket so's I can cop a look at the two faded black and white pictures. In the one, there's this little girl with blonde curls. Pretty, even though she's done up like a dog's dinner in a ballerina dress I've seen before, with floppy ribbons in her hair. In the other, it's the same girl, only older, this time wearing a funny sort of a straw hat. Both of them smiling the same wicked half-smiles.

It's a smile I know. I see it every time I walk down the

hallway. Because it's not some seventies supermodel, the blonde stunner hanging on her walls. It's her, when she was young and happy, when she hadn't got so many miles on the clock and kilos round her middle. It's Miss E.

And when I say, 'It's you, isn't it, in the locket?' I see her break into the same mischievous half-smile. A bit frayed round the edges, but the same smile.

'It's the bone structure, isn't it, that gives me away?' She pats her face. 'Even as a girl, I had the cheekbones of a film star. I was twelve when this one was taken, sixteen in this one.' She heaves a long sigh. 'Aren't I adorable?'

She takes a sip of her tea, then spits it out, splattering the kitchen table. 'Eugh! Stone cold. What are you thinking? A fresh pot, Boy, chop chop.' With that, we're back on track again. No more talk about the jewels.

She hangs the locket round her neck and keeps kissing it. I spend the next coupla hours putting the kitchen back to rights. Later, while she has a long nap, I catch up with more of her tales.

45.

ELOISE

I had to trust him dear reader. Who else was there? He gave me back my locket, after all. Never thought I'd see that again. And he was being so very enterprising. With the collection and everything.

Strange how things work out, isn't it? One minute you are the energetic, vibrant centre of a fabulous fashion universe, then in the blink of an eye, or so it seems, you can hardly summon the energy to get out of bed in the morning. That's me by the way. One minute he's a common little council house rat with no ambition and nothing to say for himself, then all of a sudden, he's bursting with ideas and won't stop talking. That's the Boy.

Role reversal, you see. I could no longer be bothered – 'arsed' he would say – while he'd become Captain Unstoppable. Always in my box room, labelling things, wrapping them, putting them in neat piles, like a meticulous little squirrel. I watch, intrigued, from afar. And phone calls. He never had any calls before, suddenly he was Mr Popular. And always smiling, as if he knew something I didn't.

It came totally out of the blue. 'How do you fancy an outing?' he chirruped one afternoon, breezing into the drawing room, disturbing me at a particularly tricky grassy stage. 'Tomorrow? Take you out of yourself?'

'Too cold,' I mumbled, trying a piece.

'Rubbish. It's lovely out there. Nippy but the sun's shining fit to singe your lashes off. We wrap you up warm, you'll be fine. What do you say? Nice trip up West? Take in the sights? Drop in on an old friend?'

'Don't have any,' I said.

'That's what you think.' He grinned in a most disconcerting manner. 'Come on, you can't stay hidden away for ever. There's a big old world out there.'

That was the trouble. It was a big old world. A big old, hostile world, full of traitors and cheats, a world I had no desire to encounter. Let me confess, dear reader, the very idea of leaving the sanctuary of Courtland Mansions was terrifying. Apart from the odd dash for cash – and even that hadn't been necessary of late – I hadn't stepped outside for months, who knows, perhaps years.

He persisted. 'We'll make a thing of it. Get your hair done. Get you dolled up.' He looked away, embarrassed. 'I gotta friend, see? She knows about make-up and that sort of thing. I could give her a bell? Get her to come over first thing?'

Aha, no wonder he's so chipper, I thought. *He's got a bird on the go.*

'No disrespect,' he said, looking me up and down, 'but we can't have you going out like that, can we?'

The cheek of it. 'What's wrong with what I'm wearing?' I said, glancing down at the informal loose top and harem pant combo I'd put together.

'Your nightie's got tea stains down the front. The knees of your trackies is all holes and that purple thing is filthy.'

I drew the peignoir closer. 'This is a classic piece. I've had it since *that* night in 1988.'

'Looks like it, an' all,' he said. 'Come on. Let me take it down to Sketchley's.''Over my dead body!' I cried, clutching it even tighter. 'This garment and I are never parted.'

Even as I yelled, I could feel a knot of excitement beginning to fizz in my innards – if knots can fizz, that is. A trip to the West End! Maybe I could face it after all. I softened my voice to a persuasive purr. That always used to work. 'Perhaps if you told me where we're going, I could choose clothing more appropriate to the occasion.'

The Boy was not susceptible. He wouldn't be drawn. I tried a different tack. 'What's she like, this girlfriend of yours?'

'She isn't my girlfriend,' he said, somewhat surly.

'I get it. Your fag hag, then,' I said, noting in passing the welcome use of that 'isn't'.

Fag hag or not, she was quite a sweet little thing. Lovely smile. Soft hands. Molly, she was called. Helpfully, she wore a badge with her name on it. Shiny blue-black hair past her shoulders. In awe of me, of course. Her eyes were on stalks as the Boy introduced us.

I put her at her ease. 'The Boy tells me you're a student of fashion. This must be quite an honour for you.'

She blushed prettily. 'I can't believe I'm in the same room as *the* Eloise Slaughter. Did Brad tell you, I did this course on the history of fashion? Our teacher was always on about Anti-Fashion Fashion. She said – I can remember exactly – she said it "redefined women's self-image, lighting the beacon for feminism". That is so cool. And here I am, standing here, talking to you in the flesh,' she ended breathlessly.

I accepted her compliments with a regal nod.

Then she had to spoil it. 'The following week, we did a whole module on your friend Kristina Krabtree.'

'Never,' I said, a picture of dignified fury, 'mention that arseless bitch's name in my presence again.'

The girl recoiled. Gallantly, the Boy stepped in, steadying me. 'Sorry, Miss E. Molly's not acquainted with the history. It won't happen again. She's ace with the old powders and paints, though. Show her, Moll Doll.'

The girl heaved up a rectangular cerise box with ugly silver metal corners. She flipped the lid. 'My beauty case. There's plumpers, fillers, serums,' she said, taking various tubes and jars from its many compartments and showing me. 'Anti-shine, anti-red and anti-spiderthread cover-ups. Blushers, bronzers and illuminators. Everything you could possibly need.' She looked at me uncertainly. 'At least, I think so.'

'Indeed?' I said. True, she was a sweet enough thing but I wasn't about to lose face to a young flippertigibbet not long out of her pram. 'It takes more than creams and lotions, my dear. It takes flair. That is why they're called make-up *artistes,* not dabber-onners of illumination creams and anti-spider lotions.'

The girl shrank back. Instantly I regretted my harsh treatment.

'It is not my wish to be critical,' I soothed. 'I simply mean to point out the significance of the occasion. This is a very big day for me. Nothing less than my return to public life. I shall be under scrutiny as never before. I need to look nothing less than sensational.' I waved a finger in the direction of the sofa. 'Pass me that *Radio Times*, Boy. There's a picture in there that might help you visualise the effect I'm seeking.'

Opening up the magazine, I held the pages for him to see. 'Is she up to it?' I challenged, pointing to a photograph. 'Can your fag hag make me look like her?'

The Boy paused. 'But Miss E,' he said, 'that's Cheryl Tweedy.'

After a good, long soak in the bath, I presented myself, wrapped in towels, damp and smelling delicious, for the transformation. While he fed me tea and Cameroons, Molly set to work.

First came the undergarments. A body for my body, as she explained. A revelation, I must admit. Light as a feather, but firm – like the best of spankings. Surprisingly comfortable too. Once I'd stuffed handfuls of my flesh into it, the effect was remarkable. I stood before the mirror mesmerised, running my fingers over the cannonballs of my bosoms – they hadn't been up so high since the last time I did a handstand – across the curve of my stomach and down the smooth expanse of my thighs.

Then I spotted a flaw. 'I can't wear this, idiot girl,' I frowned. 'What if I need a wee?'

Molly flushed. 'You can un-pop it,' she explained, gesticulating, 'down below.' After some contorting I did indeed find two rows of ingenious crotch poppers.

Next she turned her attention to my face. I settled myself down and prepared for a mega-pampering. Dozing, I was transported back to the old days when we'd spent many a happy hour in beauty salons being buffed and primped in readiness for some red carpet occasion or other. Those were the days!

'All done!'

I woke with a start to find Molly, smiling nervously and

inviting me to admire myself in the mirror. I leant forward, scowling. Where were the Jersey cow lashes, the razorblade cheekbones, the cherry tart lips? My disappointment, I fear, dear reader, was written plainly across my face.

'You don't like it, do you?' Molly was on the brink of tears. 'I went for the natural look.'

'Natural,' I bellowed. 'Who in sod's name wants to look natural at my age? Natural is wrinkly. Natural is blotchy. Natural is saggy. I want fake. Fake hair, fake nails, fake tan, fake lashes, fake lips, fake face. Fake everything. I want Cheryl. Give me Cheryl.' I beat out the rhythm on my dressing table. 'I want Cheryl. I want Cheryl.' Backing away, Molly sent the Boy out for reinforcements.

'Wig,' I commanded. Closing my eyes, I savoured the moment, as the weight of the chestnut creation pressed down on my scalp. I opened my eyes. This time, I was not disappointed. The face that looked back from the mirror was… well, astonishing. Lips glistened, eyes smoked, hair glinted like the rippling flanks of a thoroughbred. I looked amazingly, fabulously Cheryl-like. Molly and the Boy were so overwhelmed, they couldn't speak.

'A little better,' I conceded. It never does to let the help get too cocky.

We argued for ages over what I was to wear. My 'clobber', as the Boy so vulgarly put it. Molly and he had brought a selection of clothes on approval. He and the girl had obviously been planning this trip for a while. As each garment was revealed, my spirits sank lower and lower. Tailored suits, dress and jacket combos, and staid wraparound dresses in shades of mouse-grey, taupe, powder blue and lavender. Yeuk!

I was adamant. None of their pallid choices would do.

'Hang on a bit,' the Boy said. 'I've had a brainwave. Don't

know why I didn't think of it before.' He was back in a trice. 'Here. Wear this.'

I was horrified, dear reader. It was the purple bridal gown. I hadn't seen it since that night in the Hot Spot. Let alone touched it. The thought of actually putting it on made my flesh crawl.

'You don't understand,' I whispered, backing away in terror. 'I couldn't. I simply couldn't.'

'Go on,' the Boy said, undaunted, taking a step forward. 'It can't hurt you. It's just a frock. You're not scared of a frock, are you?'

Reaching out, I touched it with one hesitant finger. What was I expecting? A jolt of electricity? A jet of flame? A serpent's bite? I don't know. This dress, more than anything else, had come to symbolise my downfall. For years it had trapped me under its evil spell. Yet, when I placed my hand on its lumpy surface, I felt… nothing. The Boy was right. It was just a frock.

'There you go,' he said, pride in his voice. 'You're stronger than you think. Molly'll help you into it.'

It was strange to be outside again, feeling the wind on my face, the dust in my eyes. Had the streets been so raucous and confusing before? The hammer of pneumatic drills. The shouts of coarse workmen. Traffic grinding and squealing past. People bumping into one, when one is standing in plain view on the pavement as one waits for a cab to be hailed.

When a cab did pull over at last, I was forced to cover my ears against the machine-gun rattle of its engine. I don't mind admitting, dear reader, I'd have given up there and then if it hadn't been for the friendliness of the cabbie. Obviously taken with my eye-catching appearance, he ushered me aboard with a broad smile and a wink. Good to know I've still got it.

46.

BRADLEY

We do our best, that's about all you can say, me and Molly. We do our best with the resources at our disposal, as Miss E would say. The three hundred quid, I mean. Let's face it, no matter how much we'd spent, she's never gonna be no Cheryl Tweedy. Mrs Brown would be a stretch. And she would shout at Moll: 'More lashes. More lippy. More everything.' Put her right off, it did.

Sorting her shoes gave us more grief. She's crammed her feet into bright pink sandals she's had me dig out of her collection. Bunions bulge and fat toes escape between the straps. Can't hardly stand in them, and as for walking, a wobbly waddle is about the best she can manage.

'You got any flats?' Molly goes.

Miss E looks around like a pair of kicks is gonna materialise out of nowhere, then her eyes light on Molly's shoes. 'What size do you take?' she goes, eyeing up Molly's DMs. Molly ain't so keen. The boots is new but she's wasting her breath. Five minutes later Miss E is striding about happy as anything in Molly's black patent Doc Martens, while Molly's lumbered with the sandals. She gives me a look. I shrug. It's usually better to let the old girl have her way.

'Half a mo,' I go. Got a little business to take care of before we set off.

Miss E tuts and taps her foot, impatient to get going. I duck into the kitchen. Got this new mousetrap, see? KillEm this one's called. No messing. Gonna put it behind the fridge, and leave it to do its stuff while we're out.

I bait it with chocolate and pull the spring to set it. Balance it on my palm, giving it one last once-over. Picture the mouse's neck squashed, eyes bulging, brain squirting, three little legs hanging limp. I make a decision.

Snap! The spring goes and the chocolate shatters in the bottom of the bin. Then chuck the trap away. 'You've had a lucky escape, Stumpy, my friend,' I say.

'Oh, come on, you can tell me now,' Miss E goes, settling herself into the back of the cab.

I shake my head. 'Told you. It's a surprise.'

Safe and sound in the cab, she's all talk. But outside on the pavement, it was a different story. She's terrified. Fast as she backs out the way of one dude, deep into his texting, she crashes into another. Thought she'd have a heart attack when the cab drew up.

I look over at her. At that frock. Molly was all for getting her into something more mainstream, but the more I think about it, the more I know this is the right outfit. It's way over the top and I daren't catch Molly's eye or we'll lose it for sure, but it's what she has to wear.

What does it look like? Well, to me it looks like she's wearing an unmade bed. Too loose in some places, too tight in others, bumps and bulges all over it. Purple it is, same colour as the thing she always slings round her shoulders. She's got that on an' all, over the top. Good job she does 'cause she can't do the frock up at the back. She's too chubby. The whole thing keeps slipping off of her shoulders. To cap it all, she's got me to loop that old bike chain round her neck like a necklace.

All the way there, she's going on and on and on, like she's four years old. Coming up with ideas where we might be going. Places I've never even heard of. Dinner at the Top of the Tower, she says? Tea with the PG Tips Chimps? Gambling at the Playboy? I just do the zip thing across my mouth. By the time the cab pulls up at the kerb, we're up to yachting in the Caribbean with Noel Coward – whoever she is.

'Elegant but unexciting,' she goes, gazing up at a grey-stone building. 'I'm disappointed. I was hoping for fun and frolics.'

'I'm expecting it to be lively,' I go. 'Do you know where we are?'

'Somewhere near Park Lane?' she says, giving a yawn. 'An expensive but dreary part of town, I always think.'

'Twenty-seven Upper Brook Street. Headquarters of Hotspot Productions.'

She looks up. 'Hotspot?'

'Listen to this.' I take a paper out my pocket and read out what I downloaded off of the net. '"British film producer, Howard A. Haggarty' – Miss E gasps – 'and fashion designer Kristina Krabtree' – she gasps again – 'co-founded Hotspot Productions in 1989…'

She groans, doubling up like she's got gut-ache. 'The bastards. They had the nerve to call it *that*. How could they, rubbing my face in the salt like that?' She drops her head into her hands and rocks. Molly pats her shoulder.

There's a photo of Howard Haggarty. I show it to Miss E. She takes a quick glance. It's of a fat man with stupid hair and very white teeth. Not much of a dreamboat, you ask me.

'You up for it?' I go.

'Up for what?'

'Going in there and giving that bastard Howard Haggarty a taste of his own medicine?'

'You mean he's… in there? Right now?' She looks up again at the building, truth dawning. 'Try and stop me,' she goes, pushing Molly aside.

'Hold on, hold on,' I go. 'You can't just go in. I've got a plan.'

All credit to the old girl, after I explain, she's all for it.

'This is how we get ourselves into the building,' I tell her. 'After that, we'll have to just wing it.'

She's our gran, is the story, and we're on our way to the Hilton for cocktails, when she's taken poorly right outside their door. I wanted to say on our way to Pizza Express. Miss E won't hear of it. It's the Hilton or nothing. We're celebrating her fiftieth birthday. (Guess whose idea that was?) Can we come in and sit down for a minute or two till she's herself again?

Like I say, that's the plan. What actually happens is this: Miss E sails in, frock-thing dragging across the floor, marches up to the snooty woman at reception and says, 'Three teas, if you please, young woman. Pronto. It's sodding cold out there.'

The woman makes like a goldfish. I step forward, doing my best to speak proper. 'Sorry. What my gran means is, she's had a funny turn, her weak chest, see? If it's no trouble, we wondered if we could sit here, just for a few minutes, till she's feeling better?' I treat her to one of my twinkliest smiles.

The woman's not buying it. She's straight out of *Made in Chelsea* with her big hair and long red nails. She wrinkles her nose. Can't say I blame her. What does she see? An old girl in a weird dress and a cheap wig clinging to the arm of a boy what's putting on airs and graces, and a girl too terrified to open her mouth. It's not gonna work.

'Leave this to me,' Miss E hisses behind her hand. She steps in again, all charm and chat.

'What marvellous offices,' she goes, waving her arm. 'What is it you do here?' Before the woman can answer, a row of framed posters lining a wall catches Miss E's eye and she goes over for a closer look. She fumbles in her bag for her specs, puts them on, peers, frowns, takes them off and puts them on again, this time the right way up. I wish she would get a move on.

Walking down the line, she examines each poster. They're all pretty much the same. Monsters and zombies in the foreground, leering out the frame, claws dripping blood. Girls in the background, screaming, tattered clothes falling off.

Miss E turns to the receptionist woman. 'You're a film company, I see. How thrilling. I used to be big in the media myself you know. You don't mind if I sit, do you, my dear?' She lowers herself onto a white leather settee. 'Would I have heard of any of your productions? *Alien Vampires vs. Robot Virgins,*' she reads out. 'That rings a bell. I've a fancy I caught it on *Afternoon Movie* a few weeks ago. Marvellous performances.'

I'm getting fidgety. But Miss E, as I'm learning, has her ways.

'Have you worked here long?' she goes on, looking over at the woman. 'Only, take it from one who knows, with your classic Grace Kelly looks you won't be slaving behind that desk for long. It can only be a matter of time before some big Hollywood producer sweeps through that very door' – she points – 'astrakhan coat over his shoulders, and snaps you up for his next big bust-blocker.' Miss E beams.

The snooty receptionist puts her head on one side and says, 'Bless', like Miss E's a fluffy kitten. 'That is so sweet. Please, make yourselves at home. I'll get you those teas.'

'Lady Jane Grey if you have it, my dear,' Miss E calls out. I glare over at her. She's pushing it. She winks at me.

As soon as the woman's in the little kitchen behind her desk, we head for the old-fashioned lift. It's that small, we can't all fit in. Not the three of us, not with one of us being Miss E, round as a bowling ball and dressed in something wider than a *Big Fat Gypsy Wedding* dress.

'One of us will have to stay down here, to keep a lookout,' I whisper.

'Well, *I* can't stay. I have to go upstairs and confront that shit,' Miss E says. 'And *she* can't stay on her own.' She points to Molly, white-faced and silent. 'She's scared out of her wits. It'll have to be you.'

'*I* can't stay,' I go. 'It's my plan. I gotta be there.'

'Sorry,' Miss E goes, pulling Molly into the lift after her. She clangs the metal gates shut in my face and jabs at the button. 'See you on the other side. Bye-eee.' She wriggles her fingers through the diamond holes in the rattling doors. With a whirr, the lift rises.

'Try and keep her out of trouble, Moll,' I call up the lift shaft.

'Here you are. Three teas. I'm afraid we didn't... oh.' The receptionist is back. She freezes when she sees the room is empty. 'Cause by then, see, I'm crouched behind the settee. 'That's odd,' she mutters and puts the tray down. She goes outside to look up and down the pavement. That's my chance. I leg it up the stairs.

I know where to go 'cause of the racket. A man and a woman – that's gotta be Miss E – are shouting at the tops of their lungs. Then there's a scream and a thump. *No*, I'm thinking, *please don't let her kill him.* I follow the sounds into a big old office. It's bedlam. There's a body on the floor all right but it ain't him, it's Miss E. And she ain't dead. I can tell that by the way she's struggling with the two office drones trying to heave her onto a chair. Her performance is attracting an audience. Nine-to-fivers appear from nowhere.

Where's Molly? I see her, beside a filing cabinet, trying to look as if she ain't there. 'What's been going down?' I whisper. 'What's she done now?'

'I don't know,' she goes, on the verge of tears. 'As soon as we got up here, she gave me the slip.'

'Moll Doll, you was supposed to be keeping an eye.'

'I know,' she sniffs. 'But she's surprisingly quick. I heard raised voices then a loud bang. I found her flat on her back. Someone's phoned for the ambulance.' There's more shouting. Miss E's in a chair now, clutching her arm while some poor soul is trying to give her a glass of water.

Molly's chin wobbles. 'I think she's broken something.'

That's all I need.

'Where's Haggarty?' I say. 'I don't see him.'

Molly looks around. 'He *was* here.'

I hear the siren, as I go hunting.

47.

ELOISE

Did I startle you, Howie? Had you been having a nice snooze, feet on the desk, daydreaming of your next million? And I spoiled it for you. Poor baby. I bet it's a long time since anyone dared disturb your afternoon nap.

You've got to admit, I was magnificent. I've been remembering every little detail: you opening one eye as I stood in the doorway, waiting for a spark of recognition; your feet crashing to the floor, when I strode in and said, 'Glad to see you're keeping busy'; you reaching for the phone on your big, shiny desk, then having second thoughts and withdrawing your hand.

You know what? Even after all these years, I could tell exactly what was going through your mind: *I don't need help. I can deal with this*. You yawning, saying, 'Can't you agency cleaners ever get it right? Come back later, woman, when the offices are closed.'

There I stood, in a Heavenly Bodies original with a genuine Cheryl Tweedy wig on my head and you took me for a cleaner. You swinging your legs back onto the desk with a grunt, relinking your fingers, each with a fat ring on it, and closing your eyes.

Me saying, 'I'm not your skivvy, Howie. I'm your nemesis.'

Your eyes snapping open. Was your irritation turning into a prickle of uneasiness, Howie? Or didn't you know what 'nemesis' means? Allow me to assist. Nemesis: the inescapable agent of a downfall. I had the Boy look it up on his internet. Inescapable. That was me. A downfall. That was what you had coming to you.

Where was I? Oh yes. 'I'm not your skivvy, blah, blah, blah…' That shut you up.

Cutting, I fancy, a striking figure, I crossed to a display of small, round ornaments. I picked one up. A painted rural scene. Trees, a river, horses drinking and so on. Charming, quite charming. It fitted neatly into the palm of my hand.

'Careful with that,' you spluttered, waddling over, hands flailing. My, how you've piled on the pounds! 'That's early Prattware.'

'How appropriate,' I said, hurling it at you. Remember?

Moving, I may say, surprisingly niftily for a man of your bulk, you caught it. I went over to a glass cabinet, enjoying the way my new black boots – where did they come from? – crushed your carpet, leaving a trail of bruised footprints in its too-perfect, creamy pile. What did I find in the cabinet? More knickknacks, so ugly they must have been worth a fortune and, lurking at the back, a strangely-shaped plastic object.

'What do we have here? Some sort of trophy? Could do with a dust by the look of it.' I read the engraving: '"The Golden Raspberry Award for the Worst Picture, 1992." 1992? Nothing since then, Howard? You must be losing your touch.'

'If you don't leave right now, woman,' you said, sticking out your chest, 'I'll call security and have you dragged out.'

I weighed the trophy in my hands. 'I'll leave when I'm good and ready, you shit,' I said and lobbed the Raspberry at your head. This time you missed. It hit the carpet, bounced and snapped in half. The plastic raspberry landed at your feet.

'Who… who are you?' you said, bending to pick it up.

'You still don't know? Take a closer look.' I attempted a heel spin, catwalk-style. 'You must get it now, for sod's sake.' I was growing impatient. 'What about this?' I opened the purple peignoir to show off my lumpy, bumpy bodice.

'Those old tatters?' you scoffed. 'They look like—'

'That's right. The bridal gown.'

The colour drained from your face. 'Good God.'

'Penny sinking in, is it?' I crowed. 'What about this?' Dragging it off, I thrust the peignoir in your face, my voice rising. 'Remember this? This is all that remains of the velvet cloak the bride wore *that* night. That night you stripped me of everything. The night my life ended. I wear it always,' I gritted my teeth, 'to remind me of my rage.'

'Plumpkin?' you squeaked.

'Don't you dare call me that, you shit! Yes, it's me. Come to see how you and your rich bitch are doing.'

'After all this time. I can't believe it,' you said, lowering yourself onto the creaking Chesterfield, hand to your brow. 'Krissie? I haven't seen Krissie in years. Don't see anyone from the old days, in point of fact. Remember Fergus Machin? Poor Fergie ended up in clink. Unfortunate that. Krissie went the other way. Got involved with those pompous United Nations types. It didn't last, her and me. Fizzled out soon after—'

'You got your hands on my company.'

'After you signed it over to me, you mean,' you smiled. 'There've been others since, of course. Three wives and numerous others. None like you. You really were quite something.'

Always susceptible to flattery, I'm ashamed to say, even then, even after everything, your words touched me. Maybe there was some good hidden deep inside you after all, I thought. Maybe you did care for me a little, once upon a time.

'No, unlike you,' you went on, smile twisting into a smirk, 'the others were more or less sane.' You pushed yourself up and stood over me. 'Whereas you, you've always been an overweight, selfish, deluded, amoral, manipulative witch. Now, get out!'

That hurt, Howie. That really hurt. Overweight? Me? In my youth I could give Twiggy a run for her money. Even today I'm only *that* much away from a perfect twelve. But I wasn't to be cowed. Oh no, not this little miss from the Midlands. I came out with the killer line I'd rehearsed.

'Leave?' I told you, drawing myself up to my full height. 'Not on your nelly. Not until I have had my revenge – in this life or the next.' Oh yes, magnificent!

'What?' you barked. 'You're quoting Russell Crowe at me now? Are you completely deranged? This farce has gone on long enough.' You reached again for the phone.

I put out my arm to stop you. If you remember, I was quite calm. Dignified even. 'I deserve something, Howard, for what you did to me. You owe me that at least.'

The shaking began at your head and worked down your body, until the whole blubbery mass of you was vibrating. You bent over and small hiccoughing sounds came from your mouth. Do you know what I thought? I thought: *Oh goody. He's having a potentially fatal stroke.* No such luck. You were laughing.

'You expect me to give you compensation?' you wheezed. 'That's a good one. You always did make me laugh – even when you didn't mean to.' You mopped your streaming eyes. 'You are such a joke.'

That did it. I'd promised the Boy I'd keep my cool, but he wasn't there, was he? I'd endured enough insults. Like a saucepan of milk, my anger, simmering gently up until now, frothed up and boiled over. And just like in the kitchen, things got messy.

'The only compensation I want from you,' I howled, wrestling the bike chain from my neck, 'is your dead body stretched out at my feet.'

You must remember what happened next? I swung the chain, once, twice, three times, then let go. It whipped through the air with a whirring that thrilled me to my core. My aim was true. If only you'd kept still, your ridiculously quiffed skull and my greasy chain might have connected – crunch, splat. Your brains on the shag pile. But no, you had to dodge, didn't you? You had to move. The weight of the chain and the momentum of the swing were too much for me. I overbalanced.

You must have heard the crack. It echoed round the office like a pistol shot. You didn't even wait to see if I was all right. I saw you, wobbling out, bellowing for security. You shit.

How many times did I tell them I wanted to go private? How many times did I stress I had the wherewithal? Or Tabby did. Or would have. The King Whatsit the Whatsit, I said. Where the Queen goes when she has the trots. Would they listen? Would they buggery? Four hours I was on that trolley. Four hours. I insisted the Boy and his fag hag stay. Why should I be the only one to suffer?

I go vague after that. I remember an X-ray and a child doctor with an earnest face and a high voice – boy or girl, it was hard to tell – informing me what I knew already. I'd broken my wrist.

'So, plaster me up, bung me full of morphine and send me on my way,' I replied, not unreasonably. It wasn't as simple as that, he – or she? – said. Due to my advanced years, they had to keep me in.

So here I am, stuck in a public ward, with only my little digi-whatsit for company. On one side there's a bag lady, coughing out a steady mist of National Health germs and on the other an old tramp, flashing his wanger every time he turns over.

Nurse, where the sod are you? I've been pressing this sodding bell for ages. Drugs, I need more drugs. Nurse!

48.

BRADLEY

I find him in the gents. Haggarty. Recognise him straight off from his Wiki picture, though the photo don't do justice to what's on top of his head. It's quite a construction. Snow-white hair streaked with brown dye, fancied up into a big old Elvis wave set solid like concrete. Looks OK-ish from head-on but when he dips his head to rinse his hands, I can see right through it to the pink of his scalp. He looks put out when I stand at the sink next to him. Does a double take when he clocks the thing on my face. I eyeball his reflection. Cool. Steady.

I turn on the tap and say, 'Quite a to-do out there.'

'Poor old dear,' he goes. 'Makes you think, doesn't it?'

'Think what?' I go, squirting the soap.

'You know.' He waves a wet hand in the air. 'There but for the grace of whatever.'

'You don't know her?' I soap and rinse.

'Me? God, no. Some homeless woman who wandered in off the street.' He frowns, all of a sudden realising he don't recognise me. 'You with the paramedics?'

I ignore his question and walk over to the roller towel to dry my hands. 'So, you wasn't never married to her?'

I turn my head the same second he does. Our eyes lock. He makes a dash for the door but I'm too quick. Block him.

'She didn't come alone then,' he goes. 'If you—'

'Shut up,' I go, grabbing him by the tie. 'Shut your fat face and sit down.' I tug on his tie, hard, like I'm yanking a ripcord. He collapses like a sack of spuds, his tie twisted over his shoulder, the knot tight. I'm getting that feeling again. That feeling like in the park hut. Or when I tossed the lighter.

'Listen, Mr Howard Haggarty,' I go. 'I'm here representing the interests of Miss Eloise Slaughter. I got a proposition to put to you. Stay where you are.' He's trying to scramble to his feet. 'She told me – that is, I heard – what you done to her. Destroyed her business. Run off with that woman. You put her through hell. Left her with nothing. Nothing.' I raise my voice and he cringes. 'I'm here to make you pay.'

'I don't carry much cash,' he goes, groping in his inside pocket, fingers trembling, 'but it's yours. Just don't hit me.' He offers his wallet up like an open book.

I laugh. 'Miss Slaughter's not interested in your small change, Mr Haggarty. Let me tell you how it is.' I walk up and down, hands behind my back, like a copper on the beat. He slumps back against the tiles, listening hard. I tell him about the collection she's kept stashed away all these years, about how I stumbled upon it, about what I reckon it's worth.

While I'm talking, a sneaky look is creeping into his eyes. 'Heavenly Bodies originals?' he says. 'I thought they were lost for good. Well, well, well. You're not wrong there, kid, they could be worth a bob or two – in novelty value if nothing else. There's only one problem.' He gives a smug little laugh. 'Those clothes don't belong to Eloise. They're the property of Fashion Inc. You may not know this but Fashion Inc bought out Heavenly Bodies way back in the eighties and Fashion Inc is owned by—'

'A Monaco holding company set up in your name. Yeah, I know. It's all there on the internet if you know where to look. That's why I'm here, to— '

'Let me guess,' he interrupts, getting cockier by the minute. 'To negotiate her cut? Am I right?' He tugs his tie round to the front, loosening the knot, fussing with it. 'As the legal owner of the items, I'm prepared to be reasonable. Shall we say, ten per cent of whatever they make at auction?'

I grab his ankles and yank. 'Legal owner? That's a laugh! You stole that company from her.' His mouth makes a comical 'O' as he slides down. The crack as the back of his head hits the floor echoes round the room. 'No, you slimeball, you're gonna give it back to her. All of it.' I press my foot into the hard balloon of his belly. 'Every frock, every shoe, every bag, every hat. The whole collection. The whole company. Got that?'

He's got a bigger pair than I bargained for. 'Or what?' he goes, rolling out from under my foot, running his hands through his ruined quiff.

'Or I go to the coppers and tell them how you tricked her out of her business with this.' I slap a wad of yellowed papers in his face. 'Recognise it? It's the contract for the sale of Heavenly Bodies to Fashion Inc dated the third of March, 1988.'

For a second he looks flustered, then he smiles the smile of a great white. 'So what? She signed it. She may have been off her tits at the time but her signature's on that document. You don't have a leg to stand on. And nor does she.'

My heartbeat speeds up. Now we're getting to it.

'You see, I know her, Mr Haggarty. I know her better than what you do, it seems. She would *never* of signed her company away. No matter what lies you and your bent lawyer mate told her. No matter how stoned you got her. She loved it too much. You couldn't get her to sign, so you forged her signature.'

'Prove it.'

'Ever heard of forensics, Mr Haggarty? Won't take the Serious Fraud Squad more than ten seconds to prove this ain't Miss Slaughter's writing.' I see his shark-smile fade. 'Know what sickens me most? For years she's been blaming herself, thinking she was weak, that she'd let you talk her into signing this thing.' I prod him with the rolled-up papers. 'When all the time…' I take a breath, struggling for control. I need to keep my cool. 'Still, it's up to you. If you want to put it to the test, we can get a handwriting expert in.'

'What do I care?' he goes after a pause. 'It's a piss in the ocean. The zombie adult film scene has been kind to me, after all's said and done. I can afford to indulge the old slapper. Help the aged, eh?' He has a go at a smile.

Ignoring his cheap shot, I take a white envelope out of my jacket and hand it to him. 'Just one more thing,' I say, still playing it Mr Coolio. 'Some insurance.'

I make him stay down on the floor while he reads what it took me practically all night to write. He only looks up once, a sneery smile on his face. 'This is full of spelling mistakes.'

'A confession's still a confession.' I say, handing him a pen, 'even if it's spelled wrong.'

Leaving the gents, I almost walk slap-bang into Molly. It's obvious she's been earwigging. I try to hide it but I know she can see in my eyes how pumped I am, how much I'm getting off on this.

'Was that really necessary?' she goes, nodding towards Haggarty, who's dragged hisself to his feet and is splashing cold water in his face. 'What are you, some sort of animal?'

'Not just an animal, Moll. A predator,' I go, my mind going back to that snakehead fish. I link my arm through hers and walk her out. 'You see, girl, in this world, there are two kinds of animal. There's your predators and there's your prey. We humans, we're lucky. We can be either. We get to choose. And I, Moll Doll, have chosen to be a predator.'

She don't say nothing but, when we get in the lift, she hunches in the corner as far from me as she can.

49.

ELOISE

The years haven't been kind to you, Howie, have they? Not kind at all. That belly and that hair – dear God, that preposterous hair. You look like Elvis Presley if he'd *really* let himself go. If it hadn't been for those almost-black eyes, I wouldn't have…

Why hadn't I noticed before? While I was swooning into your eyes, why hadn't I seen the nothingness behind them? I didn't see it then, but I saw it today all right. It was like staring into a mineshaft. Perhaps I'm being unfair. Maybe they weren't so empty back then, so dead. Maybe you did have feelings. Not at first, perhaps. But later, over time. It couldn't all have been fake, could it? You did care for me. You must have.

Why-the-bloody-why, Howie? You could have had me *and* the company for the asking. We could have made our fortunes together. But no, you couldn't share. You had to take it all. Who am I kidding? You didn't take it. I *gave* it to you, wrapped up in tissue paper with a big red ribbon round it.

Whose idea was it? Be honest. Yours or hers? Was she your partner in crime or your victim? You certainly dumped her quick enough afterwards. Oh Howie, to run off with her. That cocktail stick on legs. That simpering skeleton. That sexless sack of spanners.

You see how bitter you've made me? I don't want to be like that. I don't. It's just, I've lived with this ache inside me for so long, it's become a habit. A habit I should break. Turn over a new slate.

Because, you see, even if you never cared for me, I loved you Howard Arthur Haggarty. There, I've said it. I loved you. I loved you from the first night and – fool that I am – I've loved you all these years. Though I pretended to myself I didn't. Does that surprise you? Love, real love, is strong, you see. And betrayed love is the strongest. It stays with you. It stays and it curdles inside you, infecting every part and turning you into a sad, bitter old woman.

Do you want to hear something funny? Despite everything, despite all I've suffered, if you'd smiled at me today and opened your arms, I would have melted into them. Yes, I would. You could have told me any old story, made up any excuse and I'd have forgiven you. 'Just like that!' as Henry Cooper would say. Oh yes.

But you didn't. You insulted me.

When I saw you, when I peered into those deep, dark pools, you know what? I had a whatsit… a revelation. My heart didn't skip a beat like it used to. Oh no, Howie, my gorge rose. As the Boy would say, 'I could of vommed in my mouth.'

So, I'm cured. You cured me, Howie. My heart is no longer broken and I'm flying. Weeeeeeeeeeeeeeeeeeeeeeeee!

I take it all back. These NHS drugs are bloody marvellous.

50.

BRADLEY

We follow the ambulance by taxi to St Mary's. They've already took her away by the time we get there. Me and Molly is left stuck in the waiting room. We try to get comfy on them orange plastic chairs but it's mission impossible. Nothing to read. Nothing to do. People rushing everywhere but no one's got time to tell you anything.

It's quiet when we get there but it gets more fuller by the minute. In they come, hopping, limping, holding their arms and their heads. Old, young, drunk, sober, whatever, they end up parking it on them chairs, giving each other the evil eye, wondering who's gonna get seen first. All except one old lady. She's got a corner to herself. Curled up over three chairs, head on a battered handbag, blanket over her legs. She's sorted.

Blood drips from the head of a bloke in a muddy footie kit. The kid next to me coughs into the cardboard bowl his mum's holding. I point all this out to Molly but she's still not speaking. I've had enough. Go for a stroll, leaving Molly to her strop. Find a shop and stock up on snacks. I'm on my second can of coke by the time they call us through.

Pull back the curtain and there she is, lying there, eyes shut, face sort of collapsed.

'She dead?' It's the first words Molly's spoke since we left the gents.

'Course not,' I go, thinking, *What if she is?*

Molly starts to cry. 'Look at her. All that work.' She's talking about the makeover, in ruins now. Lashes hanging off, black smears down her cheeks, Cheryl Tweedy wig lying on top of the sheet like a dozy moggy.

I touch her arm. 'Miss E? It's me. Bradley.'

Cracking out a gynormous snore, she opens one eye. Next thing, she's struggling up, yelling, 'Nurse, help! I'm being kidnapped. Nurse!' No one comes, of course.

'Ssshhh, it's all right. It's only me, Bradley.'

Her eyes soften. 'What a start you gave me, Boy. So kind of you to visit.'

She's being nice to me. She must be feeling bad.

'Got you something.' I waggle the string of the 'World's Best Granny' balloon I got from the shop. It bobs up and down. 'What do you think of that then, eh, Gran?' I go, thinking she'll find it funny, me calling her 'Gran'.

'Very thoughtful,' she goes, closing her eyes.

Nearly have thirty thousand fits when a small Asian doc asks me to step into a side room for a talk. My first thought is, she's gonna tell me Miss E's dying. Then I'm sure they've found out she ain't my gran and I'm breaking all sorts of rules. Next I just know they're onto me for dipping into her bank account. A police car wails outside and I feel the panic building. It passes and I relax. Then the doc tells me they wanna keep her in, and I start to panic all over again.

'Why?' I go, worrying what she'll go blabbing to all and sundry about stuff. 'It's only a busted arm.'

'Your concern is understandable, Mr Slaughter,' she goes,

coming over all social worker. 'But we have to be cautious with someone of your grandmother's age, especially as she's experiencing a certain amount of confusion. As soon as we have a bed, we'll be admitting her.'

You'd think, it being a hospital an' all, that beds is something they'd have plenty of. Seems not. Me and Molly is left kicking our heels some more while they search one out. It's dark outside by the time we finally get the go-ahead. Miss E ends up in a ward of six beds. In some of them, there's blokes. *Uh-uh*, I think, *she's gonna kick off for sure*. But she's out for the count. Must be strong, the drugs she's on.

They've scrubbed the muck off of her face and combed her hair back. OK, so now she seems ancient, right, and her eyes and mouth sort of disappear into them wrinkles, but I reckon she looks better.

I get chairs for me and Molly – them blessed orange things again. I sit down and Molly does the same. She places her feet careful so's her leg don't brush against mine. We watch in silence as Miss E's chest goes up and down. After a bit, I feel the weight of Molly's head on my shoulder.

My mind is buzzing. What if the hospital get on to the authorities and the social, and the Old Bill come sniffing around? What if she don't make it? Will they blame me? Then I go all sentimental. OK, so she's a nutjob but life's never dull living with Miss E. Keeps me on my toes. She's got some bottle. Look how she stood up to that Howard Haggarty. And her stories, her crazy stories. Fact or fairy tale, you have to laugh. And we did. We had some great laughs.

I wake with a jolt, pins and needles in my legs. Molly's standing up and stretching. Miss E's still sleeping. 'I'm going home,' Molly says, not looking me in the eye. 'Mum and Dad will be going spare.' She holds up a hand. 'And before you ask, no, I don't need walking to the bus.'

Weird, it is, leaving Miss E with a load of strangers. Even weirder still, letting myself into her place. Walk from room to room, plumping up the cushions, squaring off the mags, collecting up the mugs. Stand for ages staring at the stuff from this morning's make-up session – seems like such a long time ago – before I clear it away.

My mind keeps going back to lard-arse Haggarty squirming on the bog floor. His face when I flashed that bunch of old papers under his nose! Can't help but grin. What would he say if he knew that they wasn't the takeover contract? They was the deeds to Courtland Mansions. That I don't have the foggiest where the real contract is. That I wasn't even sure he *had* forged her signature, not until I clocked his guilty face. Just a hunch, a real strong hunch. And it paid off.

That's it, though. No more lies. All above board, that's me from now on. Proper papers wrote up by a proper solicitor.

I go to bed, mind still racing round the track like an F1 car. I hardly get a wink. First it's the tick of the heating and the creak of the boards what keeps me awake. Then I get to imagining stuff. The crackle of the electricity through the wires. The gurgle of the water in the pipes. The whispering of the people in the flats above and below. Soon as it's light, I'm up, dressed and off to Macky D's for a sausage, egg and cheese bagel. Feel better after that, well set up. Spend the morning back in my room on the laptop. Tons to do.

When visiting time kicks off, I'm there, ready and waiting. Miss E's still in bed, only she's awake and there's a bag of clear liquid hanging from a hook, and a tube in her arm.

'What they doing to you, Miss E, pumping neat Bombay Whatsit into your veins?'

She gives a poor excuse for a smile. Severely dehydrated, she is, a doc tells me. Another one, full size this time. He frowns like it's my fault or something.

On the third morning, this is what I hear as I walk into the ward: 'In sod's name, will someone tell that man to adjust his pyjamas? I don't want to see his shrivelled ding-a-ling.'

She's in a wheelchair, arm in a sling, attempting to throw one-armed wheelies, going round in circles, bumping against the beds. No one takes any notice, not the patients snoozing in their chairs or laying in their beds, not even the nurses. They just walk round her. I call out and she careers over and comes to a crashing stop.

'What's with the wheels?' I go, rubbing my shins. 'Thought it was your arm that was broke, not your legs.'

'I'm test-driving it for that poor old soul opposite. She can't get the hang.'

'You're feeling better, I take it. Here.' I hold out a packet. 'Brung… brought you something.'

'What's this? Gypsies?' She looks suspicious. 'I thought you said one couldn't get them.'

'Romany Creams,' I tell her. 'Similar. But I'll leave you to be the judge. Tracked them down on the net. Got a box delivered yesterday, so's you won't run out, not for ages.'

I tear open the packet. She takes a nibble of one, chews, pauses, takes another and, with both hands, posts the two of them, whole, into her mouth. Crumbs go everywhere. Reckon they pass the test.

51.

ELOISE

I didn't take to David at first. A nice enough name in itself – but for a *woman*? But David it was. I got her to repeat it several times. There was no doubt.

I was resistant, I must confess, when the Boy first suggested it.

'Been doing some digging,' he said over breakfast, 'on the laptop.' Or it could have been high tea. Toast was at any rate on the menu… or crumpets. I remember distinctly because of that wretched plaster cast. Whatever it was, I was struggling to butter the bread one-handed. So engrossed was the Boy in his news, he didn't notice my predicament.

'Turns out,' he went on, 'stuff from the olden times, your times, people can't get enough of it. Ugly old chairs, naff ornaments, horrible clocks, even tatty posters, you name it, if it's old they'll shell out for it. And guess what's real hot at the moment? Old clothes. Only they call them vintage.'

'Would you mind?' I said, giving up on the butter and pointing with my knife to the honey pot. He didn't even hear.

'I was thinking,' he said, taking a bite of toast… or crumpet. 'What if you was to sell your collection, put it up for auction? You'd get bare money for it, going by what I been reading, you being the first celebrity queen of fashion an' all. No need to mooch off of your girl.' He chewed. My mouth watered. 'The beauty of it is, you wouldn't have to do nothing… anything. You could sit back and let that wrist heal up while me and Molly, we do it all.'

I was, dear reader, dumbfounded. For not only had he called me 'the first celebrity queen of fashion', he might actually have come up with a Bobby Darren of an idea.

'Hmmm. I used to have connections at Christie's,' I began, recalling a dashing, moustachioed lover.

'No need. I already belled the auction people. Vintage clothes specialists they are. They was snotty at first, of course, but after I emailed them some pictures, they soon changed their minds. Reckon they'll bite your hand off.'

'Are you telling me,' I said, skewering him with my most severe glare, 'that you've been talking to complete strangers behind my back about auctioning off my pieces, you presumptuous little urchin? Selling off my memories? Trading away my history? Making capital from the precious objects that for thirty long years have been my only companions?' I sniffed. 'More comforting than any family. More loyal than any friend.'

'Come off of it,' he huffed. 'Till I come along, you never even looked at them.'

He had a point. So I changed the subject. 'Bare money in your ridiculous slang means…?'

'Multo sponduliks,' he grinned. 'What do you say?'

I chewed my lip. I lifted my head to the heavens. Since he'd talked me into touching that gown, into wearing it, for sod's sake, I'd felt different about the collections, as if a spell had been broken, a curse lifted. Could I cope with liberating the rest of them? Of course I could, especially if multo sponduliks were involved.

I delivered my verdict: 'I'll agree on one condition.' He lifted a questioning eyebrow. 'Make some fresh toast and, this time, spread it for me.'

Or it could have been crumpets.

So that's how I came to be sitting among my now immaculate collection, while David, the auctioneer – extraordinary name for a woman! – looked it over. That's right, dear reader, I was actually *inside* that room after more than three decades.

Having braved the bridal gown, it wasn't too difficult. Not after the Boy persuaded me that I would need to be hands-on if the auction were to be a success. The box of doughnuts he provided helped. Krispy Kremes they're called. He enticed me in like a shy fawn, waving their delicious scent under my nose. Once I'd crossed the threshold, I relaxed. Sitting among my creations, we consumed the whole box. Scrummy. They might even pip Cameroons.

Where was I? David. As I may have mentioned, I didn't take to her at first. Not my type. Sturdy legs, long horse-teeth and a whinnying voice. Reminiscent, now I come to think of it, of my dear, galumphing sister. I quizzed her mercilessly – David, that is; the Carthorse doesn't know one end of a raglan sleeve from the other – determined to establish her credentials for the job.

Generations of auctioneers in the family before her, she reassured me, though she was the first filly to take up the reins. It was her idea to specialise in vintage fashion. A lucrative *quiche* market, she told me, no doubt attempting to bamboozle me with her absurd management-speak. I remained above such tactics. In fact, I rather enjoyed the intellectual challenge of negotiating with an equal once more.

To mix my semaphores, we sparred like prize-fighters; me the ring-hardened – but thankfully unmarked – champion; she the brash new contender. It brought it back, the old days when I was such a formidable negotiator, getting up to all sorts of tricks. Different times, different ethics, you see. (Remember those fleas?)

A quick look round and she would know, she assured me, the auctioneering woman. David. Yes, really. She perused while I sat in queenly splendour on a kitchen chair, my face giving nothing away, my carefully catalogued collection arranged around me. Who did that? It couldn't have been me. I hadn't been in that room for years.

She prowled and poked, pretending only mild interest. Where was the Boy? Oh yes, he stood at the door, head bowed, hands clasped like a junior Jeeves.

'You're sure they're Heavenly Bodies originals, straight off the catwalk, not mass-produced high street?' David asked, rubbing an organza and denim shortiskirt between her fingers. 'Only with this eccentric stitching, it's hard to tell.'

'Each garment is individually numbered, as you'll note,' I told her. She looked inside and found the label. 'Bruno was a stickler.' He was a complete pain in the arse about it, in fact. I could never see the point. Now I do.

David picked up a pair of fur and rubber shortishorts. 'Still, it's strange these pieces haven't come under the hammer before. No one even knew they existed.'

'That, my dear young woman, is because they've been here in my private collection,' I told her. 'As for hot off the catwalk, they're still soaked in the sweat of illustrious coat hangers. Eau de Shrimp. Essence of Twiggy. Parfum de Veruschka. It's all there. Have a sniff.'

To my amazement, that is exactly what she did. She put the crotch of the shorts to her nose and inhaled.

'Ah, vintage supermodel DNA. You can't put a price on that,' I said.

We got on better after that. I told her how I was present when most of the pieces were created. I was there as Trip and Dazzle scribbled designs on the back of menus. I watched as they whizzed the garments up on their rickety sewing machine. 'You can be sure, these are the real McDonald's,' I told her.

'Oh yes. O'Grady and Pinkerton.' David looked thoughtful. 'What happened to those two?'

'They went abroad. The Forest of Doom, I believe,' I told her. 'Artistic differences.'

'Do you, by any chance, still have those menus?' David said, oh-so-casually. 'Or the sewing machine?'

I didn't. But I couldn't help wondering where the Boy could lay his hands on some old menus and a second-hand Singer. Still playing it cool as a cabbage, I lobbed a grenade into the conversation.

'You're rather assuming I will sell. I haven't actually decided on that yet. You have to understand, David, these dresses and handbags have great sentimental value. They are my… erm.'

'Your memories and your history?' the Boy supplied. 'More comforting than any family? More loyal than any friend?'

'Precisely,' I said, grateful for the intervention.

'Oh, but you must sell, Miss Slaughter,' David insisted. 'These pieces are part of our social history. The world deserves to see them.'

'I may decide to exhibit them in my museum,' I said airily. Then I remembered and I clapped my hands over my mouth. 'Sod it! That's supposed to be top secret information. Don't go blabbing, David, or *she'll* find out.'

David gave a low laugh. 'Your secret's safe with me.' She threw a glance round the room. 'In any case, there are more than enough items here for an auction *and* an exhibition.'

'How much money are we talking?' The Boy stepped in again, cutting to the quick.

David turned to him and said, 'When a vintage Krabtree collection' – I gave an involuntary shudder – 'came under the hammer in New York a year ago, one dress alone, a peach ball gown of flounced tulle and chiffon, if you remember, the so-called Billy Fury dress with the handprint…?'

I got to my feet. 'For the love of sod, woman, how much?'

She flushed. 'Well, the hammer price on that piece was seventeen. And vintage KKs are, let's face it, ten a penny.'

'Less your ten per cent?'

'Our buyer's premium is twenty.'

'Outrageous. How many pieces?'

'We don't want to flood the market,' she said, casually picking up a lobster-shaped shoe. 'Say, fifteen or so, to begin with.'

I was calculating furiously in my head. *Fifteen times seventeen, minus the cost of a premium hammer, multiplied by ten a penny. That came out at…*

'Erm,' I said, 'are we talking dollars or pounds here?'

David threw back her head, raised her top lip and, exposing alarmingly pink gums, uttered a sound like a donkey dying. Which is to say, she laughed.

'Believe me, you stand to do quite well, Miss Slaughter,' she said, running her hand down a rail of plastic-covered garments. 'If I'm any ju… Good God!' She froze, mouth open, eyes goggling. 'Are these…?' she stuttered. 'They couldn't possibly be… could they?' She closed her eyes, collecting herself. 'Miss Slaughter, are these…' she gulped, 'are these Anti-Fashion Fashion originals?'

'Yes. Those sodding things are—'

'The pick of the bunch,' the Boy butted in smoothly.

'Oh my giddy aunt!' David exclaimed. 'May I?'

I nodded permission and she removed a dress from the rail and pulled off the plastic. It was one of those awful flower girl monstrosities. She gasped. 'One had heard rumours, of course… and there were those sketches. But to see them… to touch them… Oh, Miss Slaughter, I feel like Howard Carter entering King Tut's tomb. I see wonderful things.'

Then, to my astonishment, she burst into tears.

52.

BRADLEY

This auction can't come soon enough. Fifty-odd quid, that's all we got left. Not that it'll be easy money, mind. Might of thought twice about kicking this whole thing off, if I'd knowed just how much there was to it.

So much to organise. So many people to talk to. Miss E, of course, tries to muscle in on everything, making things ten times more complicated. And asking for cups of tea all the while. One time, she asks Davina – who she calls David for some reason – to make her a round of cheese and pickle. And Davina's the boss of Davina Lawton Auctions, Specialists in Antique and Vintage Fashions. Davina just smiles and gets her intern to run round to the Marble Arch M&S.

She reckons social media's gonna go mad for it. She's got her people tweeting and 'gramming all day long. Even got me to pose for some of pictures. Seems like, before she's finished, everyone on the planet's gonna know about Miss E and the auction.

Not that I'm complaining. Not really. It's hard work but, I'm telling you, this is the biggest rush. I'm proper psyched. You know what's the best part? Everyone comes to me when they got a question. They might say, 'We should run it past Miss

Slaughter before we green light it', but that's just for show, to keep her happy. They know the real score all right. I'm the one who calls the shots. The main man. That's a first.

And while they're firing their questions at me, do they talk to the place just above my left eyebrow? And while they think I'm not looking, do they cop a sneaky gawp at the thing on my face? Truth is, I'm that busy, I can't say as I notice.

53.

ELOISE

I hadn't been so nervous since *that* night. You know, at the Hot Spot. Jolly good job I had the Boy and his girl. I don't think I'd have made it otherwise. They'd spent days closeted in my box room with David and her crew, choosing from the collection, photographing chosen pieces, tenderly wrapping them in tissue and laying them in cardboard cradles to be transported to the auction house. Such a fuss. Sometimes I had to ask three or four times for my tea to be served.

On the morning of the big day, butterflies in hob-nailed boots were dancing a fandango in my guts. 'What are you going to wear?' the Boy asked. 'You need to make a proper entrance. Dignified – for once in your life.' He was getting cheekier by the day. Somehow I didn't mind.

I knew what he referring to: the mouse-grey wraparound. Though I pulled a face, this time I went along with it. Why? Don't let on, dear reader, but Molly's more subtle style was beginning to grow on me. I liked its flowing lines and I especially liked the wide-brimmed black straw number she'd added – shades of St Jude's – and the Golly Holightly tinted specs. There was only one word for it: classy. Yes, after a lifetime of jaw-dropping entrances, I, Eloise Slaughter, was embracing the Muted Look.

That's why it had to go. It didn't chime with the new, restrained me. Too purple-y. Too peignoir-y. I folded it carefully and put it… I forget where. I cannot be expected to remember every minor detail, dear reader. All I know is, I set forth for the auction *sans* peignoir.

What's your idea of an auction house? Wood-panelled Edwardian premises somewhere near Bond Street, the sort of place where Charlie Dickens might feel at home? Mine too. But we'd both be wrong. Our cab took us south of the river, through the backstreets of Wandsworth and decanted us outside a stark three-storey, yellow-brick dockland warehouse.

I was all for turning tail right there and then. If it hadn't been for the delicious prospect I saw waiting for me at the door, I might well have done so. The young man had just the right combination of pale skin and dark eyes that has always been my downfall. Smart too, with a crisp, grey-striped shirt, silver tie and a well-cut dark suit. If that sounds somewhat funereal, the stubbly chin and the welcoming smile added a friendlier touch. The whole package was totally irresistible.

'Welcome, Miss Slaughter,' he said in a rich voice that recalled Mr Featherstone-Leigh. 'My name is Marcus. What a very great pleasure it is to have you.'

'Saucy!' I said with a giggle.

We shook hands and he gave a slight bow. This was more like it!

Heads turned and the murmur of conversation died away as I entered the salesroom on Marcus's arm. He stood back, beaming. 'Our guest of honour, Miss Eloise Slaughter,' he announced.

Smiling faces thronged around me. Who were these people? Who cared? They were fans of some sort and I was more than ready to accept their adulation. The warmth of their welcome was in contrast to the starkness of the room. Nothing but concrete pillars and shiny grey industrial flooring.

Bestowing an air-kiss here and a 'Hello, darling' there, I was in my element. This was *definitely* more like it. There was a tug on my arm. Just when I was enjoying myself.

That wretched Boy. 'You gotta see this,' he said.

I hated to desert my fans but he insisted. Taking his arm, I made my way across the drab flooring towards... oh my! There they were, my pieces. A group of Heavenly Bodies creations, displayed simply on headless silver mannequins.

David had had the good taste to let the pieces speak for themselves. And, oh, how they spoke. There was the lime and orange jumpsuit I'd worn the first day I'd met Mr Featherstone-Leigh. And Trip and Dazzle's original Rag Bag pieces – the scrawled-on blouse, the safety-pin trousers, the badge jacket and the rubber skirt. Not to mention, several of the first patchwork shortiskirts.

Other clothes hung from a rail in plastic garment bags or were laid out on shelves, patiently waiting their turn. I spotted the chicken hat, the lobster shoes, the testicle handbag and so many more.

But it was the main display that was grabbing the attention. Roped off on a low dais, turning slowly under soft spotlights, was the wedding tableau, recreated from that night at the Hot Spot. They were all there, the lumpy, bumpy bridesmaids' and flower girls' dresses and – at the centre – the Elephant Woman wedding gown. All beautifully arranged and lit. All perfectly hideous.

Standing before the slowly revolving dais, I put my head on one side, struggling once more to see what was so special about

Anti-Fashion Fashion. What did Bruno – and now David and all these people at the auction – see in it? What was I missing?

A voice broke into my thoughts. 'Didn't I tell you people would get it one day? It brings a lump to my throat, lass.'

I turned to find an elderly gent in a snowy-white Indian shirt smiling at me. The hair was peppery and the beard white, but there was no mistaking Bruno. Then, two tall women, one pale and delicate as a May dawn, the other dark and menacing as a midnight in Manchester moved forward. I knew them immediately. Trip's hair was still thick, though the black was streaked with grey. Dazzle's white teeth still beamed out like a lighthouse.

'Isn't this marvellous?' I cried. 'My three best friends in all the world. But how did you know…?'

'It was me,' the ever-present Boy said. 'I tracked them down. I invited them. I knew you'd want them here.'

'And you came. You, Trip and Dazzle,' I said, taking their hands, 'all the way from the Forest of Doom – where is that, by the way? Transylvania? And you, dear, dear Bruno,' I gave him a hug, 'making that long trek from Ashram. You know, I looked but I couldn't find it in the atlas.'

To my astonishment, the whole lot of them burst out laughing.

'When this shindig is over,' the Boy said, with an air of authority, 'Miss E has instructed me to engage a lawyer to work out how we can ensure you get a fair share of the proceedings. Isn't that right, Miss E?'

I, dear reader, just gaped. Both at his presumption and his improved grammar.

Bruno smiled. 'Aren't you going to introduce us?'

'Bruno, Trip, Dazzle. This is my new business manager… erm. He's called…'

'Bradley McCreedy,' the Boy supplied, leaning forward to shake each one of them by the hand.

Just as I was beginning to feel all warm and glowy inside, as if everything was going to work out for once, a piercing voice rang out. 'Do I look to yow like the kind of person who needs yower 'elp?'

A wheelchair hove into view, a skeleton inside it. Could it be? Surely not. ''Ello, ower Elaine,' the voice said. 'We en't missed the sale of the century, 'ave we?'

'Surprised to see us, Mummy?' Tabby grinned. 'I thought, since I'm not working at the moment, Granny and I would come along to check out how much lolly you make.'

Indeed, dear reader, the skeleton with the crocheted blanket over her knees was my ancient mother, 104 years old and still refusing to croak. The woman pushing the wheelchair, who'd earlier sprung her from a nursing home in Bentley Heath, was my daughter Tabitha. Both had a glint in their eyes.

'Elaine? Ower Elaine?' Urse screeched. 'Are yow listenin'?'

'For the last sodding time,' I muttered weakly. 'It's not Elaine. It's—'

Bang! – the double doors at the far end of the auction room crashed open. I looked up. Silhouetted like Alan Ladd in that western, were three figures: the bullying brother, Dominic, and his two leering cronies.

54.

BRADLEY

An envelope. Just a boring white envelope. Who'd have thought it could do so much? There it lays snug as, locked in the safe of Smith and Smith, Business and Personal Solicitors, Marble Arch, London, keeping Miss E safe and helping me sleep sound in my pit.

Here's the thing, see, letting your fists speak for you can only take you so far. I get that. OK, I had that Howard Haggarty on the floor, pleading eyes looking up – *Please don't hit me!* – agreeing to do almost anything, but at the end of the day, can I trust him? No, is the answer to that one. I need insurance.

I go there a month before the auction: Smith and Smith's, above a wine shop on the corner of Great Cumberland Place. I ring the buzzer, speak into the squawker and go on up. Don't look much from the outside but turns out it's a Tardis. Top of the stairs it opens out into a huge reception, with doors what whisper open when you walk up to them and offices with frosted glass walls.

I'm sitting in one of them glass offices, across a wide table from Mr Alan Wisdom, senior partner. Secretaries is chattering and down below the traffic is grinding past, but once them glass doors whoosh shut behind you, it's like you've gone deaf. Like the outside world's on mute.

On the phone I've said I'm Miss Eloise Slaughter's business manager, come to discuss a confidential matter. I see the look on Mr Wisdom's face. Even though I've put on a new dark green shirt, even though I make an effort to talk proper, the set of his mouth, the dull look in his eyes tell me loud and clear what he's thinking. Why is this yobbo wasting my time?

He shuffles in his seat, anxious to get the meeting over with. Dissing what I got to say before I've even said it. I keep my cool. I got it worked out in my head. First I gotta get something clear.

'What I tell you today, that's confidential, right? You can't go running to the Old Bill with it?'

He clears his throat and straightens his already straight tie. 'Client confidentiality is an important principle of law in England and Wales. Except in certain circumstances – if disclosure is required by the law, for instance – what you tell me will remain between these four walls.'

'Yeah, glass walls,' I say, looking through to the drones in the offices, busying about like actors in one of them old-time silent films. Then I tell him the story. Her story. All he needs to know, at any rate.

As I'm talking he leans forward. Surprised, interested, then impressed. By the end, he's so far forward, he's practically toppling off of his seat. Don't know what he was expecting to hear when I come... came in, but I'm guessing a tale about dirty deeds in the fashion industry wasn't top of his list of possibilities.

I bring him up to speed on Heavenly Bodies. How Miss E made her fortune. How Howard Haggarty cheated her out of it. How she's been living with the consequences ever since.

I end with my plans for the auction and the small matter of settling legal ownership of the company once and for all. I stop talking and wait. He sits back, tips of his fingers pressed together.

There's a long pause. 'Quite a story,' he goes at last. 'If it's true, my professional advice is, go to the police. Let them deal with it. Thirty years ago or last week, fraud is still fraud, forgery is still forgery. Let the law take its course and, if justice prevails, this man Haggarty will serve his time and Miss Slaughter will be compensated for her losses.'

I shake my head. 'Not an option, Mr Wisdom. Too long-winded and too risky. She'll be pushing up daisies before she sees a penny. Any case, she's still soft on him even now, I reckon, though she'd kill me if she heard me saying so. It'd be just like her to refuse to press charges at the last minute. He'd get away scot-free. No, I've come up with another way to get Haggarty to toe the line. I've come up with this.' I tap the envelope against my fingers. 'Can you have a ganders and tell me if it's kosher. If it is, I'd like you to look after it for me. Keep it safe.' I lean forward, keen to explain my plan. 'See, I got Haggarty to—'

'For God's sake, man!' Mr Wisdom leaps to his feet and starts pacing. 'What did I say just a moment ago about certain disclosures being required by law? Don't tell me what's in it. I don't need to know. I don't *want* to know, especially if it concerns an alleged offence. If I know what's in it, that could put me in a very sticky position, very sticky indeed.'

That makes me sit back. 'I see. But you can still take care of it?' I go, offering him the envelope again. 'That's not against the rules, is it? Holding a signed conf… a signed statement in your safe as insurance?'

Mr Wisdom moves to the window. He stands, hands behind his back, looking down over Great Cumberland Place. 'Was the, erm, statement freely obtained?' he goes, sounding troubled.

'How do you mean?'

'It's a straightforward question, Mr McCreedy. Were threats or violence employed in obtaining it? Any hint of violence could render the document inadmissible as evidence.'

I go red, thinking of that gents toilet. Have I stymied everything? I open my mouth to say something. Mr Wisdom holds up his hand. 'On second thoughts, Mr McCreedy, forget I asked. Your face speaks volumes. Let's cross that bridge if and when the case ever comes to court.'

'Thing is, I don't think it'll ever get that far.' I walk over to the window to join him. We stand side by side, looking down on the buses, cars and taxis cruising silently past. 'Haggarty likes to keep his name out the papers, not draw the Revenue's attention, if you know what I mean. I don't think he'll contest it. And what we're asking for won't hardly make a dent. This envelope's back-up. Just in case. So, what do you say? Will you look after it?' I hold it out.

Mr Wisdom rubs the bridge of his nose. 'It's unconventional but…' He takes it.

'Yesss!' I punch the air. 'Now, there's something else I want you to lawyer up for me.'

The day Howard Arthur Haggarty sails into Smith and Smith's is one I'm gonna remember for a long, long time. He's late and I'm wondering if he'll turn up at all or if he'll bring along his own brief to argue the toss. But no, he keeps us waiting half an hour, but when he does turn up, he's alone. I figure he doesn't want no one… anyone knowing what a dirty little shit he is. That's fine by me and Mr Wisdom. We handle him great.

Haggarty plays the bigshot, saying 'good morning' to all and sundry as he follows Mr Wisdom into the glass-walled meeting room. Mr Wisdom, in his dark three-piece pinstriped, won't meet his eye. I do the exact opposite. Togged up in a new dark red shirt and navy tie, and a leather-look jacket, my eyes never leave Haggarty for a second.

Mr Wisdom's voice is cold. 'Sit down Mr Haggarty. There's a contract on the table. Read it carefully and if you agree with its terms, sign where indicated.'

'What's this about a contract?' says Haggarty, dragging out a chair at the head of the table. 'At least do me the courtesy of explaining what the hell is going on.'

Mr Wisdom takes up a position right behind Haggarty. He stands feet apart. Strong. Unmoveable. 'It's quite simple,' he goes. Haggarty squirms in his seat, trying to look over his shoulder at Mr Wisdom. 'It's a legal contract signing over to Miss Eloise Slaughter the business known as Heavenly Bodies, the intellectual property rights on that brand label, and any goods and products appertaining to that business, including original garments produced when the business was actively trading.' Haggarty looks like he did when I yanked him down onto the floor of that gents. Gobsmacked.

'Furthermore, it requires you to renounce all claims on the business, the proposed Eloise Slaughter Museum of...' – Haggarty coughs out a dry laugh; Mr Wisdom sails calmly on – 'the Eloise Slaughter Museum of Fashion History and any subsidiaries thereof, now and in perpetuity. Take your time, Mr Haggarty.'

It's so quiet as Haggarty reads, I can hear the expensive tick-tick of Mr Wisdom's wristwatch. Haggarty finishes and looks up. 'And if I don't feel like signing?' Lifting the contract, he lets it fall. The pages flutter in the air conditioning. He twists awkwardly to fix Mr Wisdom with a look. 'What'll you and this little thug do then, eh? Duff me up again?'

Mr Wisdom's voice is smooth as velvet. 'You'd be within your rights to refuse, of course, but I wouldn't advise it. Mr McCreedy?'

Time to up the ante. I gather up the scattered pages and stack them in a neat pile in front of Haggarty. 'Remind me, Mr Wisdom,' I go, looking up. 'What time did that inspector at the Serious Fraud Office say he could see us?'

Behind Haggarty, I see Mr Wisdom's eyes flicker, but he's cool. 'Three-fifteen,' he says.

Silence hangs in the air. Mr Wisdom's watch tick-ticks. Haggarty rubs his neck, like the twisting and turning has give him a crick. Then he pulls the pages towards him and picks up the pen. His hand is shaking. 'Anything to get that bitch off my back,' he spits.

He scratches his name in big loops and chucks the pen down. Mr Wisdom carefully adds his own small signature. The chair scrapes. Haggarty stands, smoothing his hands over the sides of his hair, doing his best to look like a big-time suit. Only round his mouth he's gone an unhealthy greenish colour, as if a puke might be on the cards. 'Thank God that's done with,' he goes and catches a little burp in his hand.

We see him off the premises, Mr Wisdom and me. Arms folded like bouncers, we watch as he struggles into his mac. Ignoring me, Haggarty bares his teeth at Mr Wisdom in a quick, nervous smile, and sticks out a paw. 'All's fair in love and business, eh?' Mr Wisdom looks at it, like he's being offered a cockroach, and turns on his heel.

From the window of Mr Wisdom's office, we watch Haggarty clamber into a taxi, hair streaming in the wind. The taxi drives off and poker-faced, we look at each other.

Mr Wisdom cracks first. He grins and grabs my hand, almost shaking it off at the shoulder. I give a whoop. We hug. Then we dance round the table, laughing and slapping each other on the back, the fancy solicitor in his pin-stripes and the boy from the estate in his leather-look jacket. Through the glass walls, the secretaries glance up pop-eyed.

55.

BRADLEY

We did it. Smashed it right out the park. Totally cleaned up. Two hundred and seventy-four thousand quid. Oh my days!

The money's not even the best bit. That was giving Dom the hiding he deserves.

This cannot be happening, I thought when I saw him standing in the doorway with his crew, giving the room evils. *Not today of all days.*

Dom spots me straight off and comes swaggering over.

'What the fuck do you mean,' he snarls, shoving the green Harrods bag into my chest, 'fobbing me off with this load of old crap, you cheating little shit?'

'Please, Dom,' I say, keeping my voice low and trying to move him towards the exit. 'Let's keep it civilised. The auction's about to start.'

'Oh yes. Your precious auction. Fed up of seeing your ugly mug plastered all over Twitter and Insta, going on about it. And it's about to start, is it? We'll have to see about that.'

He marches over to the chairs set out in rows and starts kicking them over, one by one. His homies look at one another, give a grin, then join in. Posh heads turn as chairs crash to the floor. All conversation dies.

'Stop that, you fuckwit!' I shout.

Dom freezes, leg raised for another kick. 'What did you call me?'

'Sorry, Dom,' I say. 'Didn't mean to call you a fuckwit. I meant to call you a shit-for-brains, meat-headed fuckwit.'

With a roar, Dom charges. But I'm ready. I sidestep, nimble like. Catch him off balance. Do it exactly like he taught me.

Blindside him. Quick jab to the face, in, out and away, before he knows what hits him. From somewhere behind me I hear Molly scream. Down on his knees Dom goes, squealing like a stuck pig in front of his mains and all those people. Mint, it was.

'You bust my nose, you little bastard!' he snivels, through a mixture of blood, snot and tears. Reckon I did an' all. There's blood everywhere.

I hear the sirens and before long the Old Bill comes striding in. One of them lends Dom a hanky and gets him to tip his head back, while the other takes me aside.

'Well, my lad,' he goes, the copper, 'this is a right to-do and no mistake. Your brother tells me he slipped and banged his nose on the floor. So we're gonna put this down to an unfortunate accident – this time. But watch those fists in future, eh? If you don't want to end up like him.' And he gives me a wink.

To me that's as good as a 'Cheers, mate. We owe you one.'

Feel ten foot tall.

The police cart Dom off, a bloody hanky stuffed up his nostrils, and we get back to the business of the day: the auction.

The sun's come out by now, making white squares on the grey floor. They have to pull down the blinds to protect the clothes. Davina's girls have been handing out sales catalogues.

At the bottom of each page is printed: 'Provenance: the Eloise Slaughter Private Collection.' Her spare room, in other words. Miss E's stoked about that. Paws through the pages, checking the printer hasn't missed one by mistake.

I have a read meself. 'Unconventional cut and disquieting colour combinations... random and refreshingly naïve... extending the imaginative boundaries of fashion.'

Is it only me what sees them for what they really are? Old rags I wouldn't use to clean the windows. Not that anyone's likely to ask my opinion. Too busy taking it serious, murmuring politely to each other like they're in church.

Davina sweeps in at 12:30, looking sharp in a black frock. The murmuring falls away. She takes her place at a lectern thing and looks down on us. 'Welcome all,' she says, raising her hands. 'Thank you for your patience after the earlier unfortunate intrusion. I think you'll find it was well worth the wait. We at Davina Lawton Auctions are extremely proud to be holding this sale of some of the most rare and important fashion finds of the twenty-first century.' She smiles. 'I hope you have deep pockets because I've a feeling we're going to see some astonishing prices.' She takes a deep breath. 'So, to business. Lot number one.'

And we're off. In a matter of seconds, the first bids have climbed into the hundreds. 'Four? Do I have five? Thank you, sir. Six at the back. Six-fifty on the phone. Seven on the net. All done at seven? Eight? Just in time, madam. This unique piece sold at eight hundred pounds.'

Eight hundred for a handbag in the shape of a melon! As fast as a picture is flashed up on the screen behind Davina, the bids come in, some on the phones, some on the laptop her assistant crouches over, and some from in the room.

I've sat Miss E near the back, in case she kicks off and I have to bundle her out. But no, today, the biggest day of her life, the one we've been working on for months and months, and what does she do? Give me strength! She wriggles her bum on the hard wooden chair, drops her chins to her chest and, before the second lot is gone, she's zizzing.

No skin off of mine. Gives me a chance to take in the surroundings. In front of me, there's this tall, slim blonde, sitting very upright, long legs crossed neatly at the ankle. A model for sure, I'm thinking – until she stands up and turns round, checking out the room. Maybe she used to be a model, maybe even one of what Miss E calls her coat hangers, but that was a long time ago. She's eighty if she's a day.

Over by the window, sitting cross-legged on the floor and getting in everyone's way, is this scruffy, student type. Dirty hair, ripped jeans, heavy metal tee. I'm about to lean over and tell him to park it on a chair like the rest of us, when he goes and waves this numbered card in the air – paddles, Davina calls them – and parts with five hundred smackeroonies for a pair of punk sunnies in the shape of handcuffs.

Two rows from the front, there's this shy young Chinese couple, sitting huddled together, whispering to each other, like children who've sneaked in and are waiting for a grown-up to spot them and throw them out on their ears. Next minute, bold as, the girl lifts up her paddle. Twenty-five K she bids for a jacket covered in badges. Don't know what she'll do with it, mind. She can't hardly lift it, let alone wear it. It takes three of them to carry it to the taxi.

So it goes on. Forty-eight lots there are in all. Forty-eight lots sold in a few hours. The biggest bids come at the end, when we get to the wedding frocks. Seven of them, there are. Each one uglier than the last. The bride's dress, the purple one Miss E wore to deck Haggarty, that went for fifty grand. Fifty! That is just mental.

You've got to give it to that Davina. She's got some stamina all right. She goes at it like a train, rattling through the bids so fast, I can't keep up with who's bidding how much for what. All I know is, every single thing goes. Every stupid frock. Every crazy shoe. Every bonkers hat. Every screwy handbag. All sold.

We tot it up in the back office, do the calculations and the result is: two hundred and seventy-four grand heading for Miss E's bank account. Two hundred and seventy-four grand! And all this time, Miss E's kipping. I figure it's about time me and Molly woke her up.

'I can't believe you dropped off,' I tell her, shaking her arm. 'It's over. You missed it. You slept through the whole thing.'

'Missed what?' she goes, blinking in the sunlight.

Davina breezes up. 'You must be so thrilled,' she croaks – she's been talking that much, she's lost her voice. 'Europe, China, America, Japan – they can't get enough of Heavenly Bodies. And the Anti-Fashion Fashion pieces set new international records. It's an absolute triumph.' She pumps Miss E's hand, then stands back, beaming, waiting for her to spout her piece in return.

Miss E turns to me. 'Quick, Boy, the lavvies,' she hisses, loud enough for Davina and half the room to hear. 'Before I wet myself.'

The hoo-hah starts the next day. Suddenly there's pictures of Miss E and her mad old frocks everywhere. 'Time-warp fashion hoard found in Paddington home of faded fashionista makes record prices' I read on the BBC website.

'Faded, indeed!' Miss E goes when I tell her. 'And I distinctly told the young man, Bayswater. That Lionel Blair lives just up the road, you know?' She clocks my blank expression. 'Lionel

Blair? Don't you know anything, Boy? Used to be prime minister.'

So, she's got what she wants. She's a celeb again. Double-chuffed about that, she is. Lets me tag along when she's invited on the *One Show*. While we wait for their car, she's that hyped, skipping round like a two-year-old, in her new DMs. She's got loads of pairs now. Pink flowers, puke green, shiny red, camo pattern – she's got the lot. Just like wearing slippers, she tells me again and again.

When we get to the studios, they hoik her off straightaway to make-up. Reckon they figure it'll take a while! I tag along. She loves it. Hairdressers and the rest flapping round her.

'Ah me, how this takes me back!' she keeps saying. And off she goes, rabbiting on at anyone who'll stand still long enough. Loves a new audience, Miss E. Telling her stories, acting them out, doing the voices. Like she used to do for me.

They let me watch from the control room behind the glass, with the director and the rest of the crew. In the studio, she's in her element, cracking lame jokes and chuckling at them herself, lifting her skirts to show off her boots. 'You should try them,' she tells that Alex Jones. 'It's just like wearing slippers.' For some reason, everyone falls apart at that.

There's some Paralympic woman on with her. She's mad for Anti-Fashion Fashion. Makes a speech about how Miss E led the way, making clothes that didn't hide imperfections, they celebrated them. 'Way before anyone else,' she says into the camera, 'this pioneering feminist used her talent for fashion to champion equality, diversity and inclusion. We owe her so much. She raised the banner. It's up to us to carry it forward.' She shook her fist in the air and everyone in the studio cheered. Everyone, that is, except Miss E.

Celebrating imperfections? I can relate to that. But Miss E doesn't get it, you see, especially not if it means sharing the spotlight with someone else. She reaches over and touches Matt's knee, starts batting her lashes, and sure enough, it works. The camera cuts back to her and she launches into one of her tales.

I roll my eyes, as she starts on about some drummer she slept with. I'm that embarrassed. But when I look round the control room, they're all smiles, lapping it up. 'Telly gold,' I hear the director mutter.

56.

ELOISE

I had a money bath. That's right, dear reader. The first thing I did, after David had transferred the proceeds into my account, was to withdraw two Waitrose bags-for-life-full from the bank, tip them into the bath and, stripped to my undies, roll in them. I rubbed them over my face, in my ears, under my arms and into my hair. I kicked my legs in the air and laughed for pure joy.

'Boyeee,' I called. 'Come on in, the lolly's lovely.'

'It's your dosh, not mine,' he said, leaning in the doorway, looking impassively on at my antics. That was the first time I noticed the sadness in his eyes.

I, on the other hand, was a new woman. It was as if I'd been slumbering under a log and woken up to find a host of spring sunbeams dancing around me. I was alive again. And it wasn't only the money, though that helped, naturally. It was the adulation – and that's not an exaggeration.

One was in such demand, you see. Newspapers, radio and, of course, the old jellybox, which – without being immodest – I quite unexpectedly found to be my natural medium. The small screen loved my colourful stories as much as I loved telling them. Everyone wanted to hear about my exploits. The only drawback was, they also wanted to hear about Anti-Fashion Fashion.

On and on they would bang about the place of its lumps and bumps in history, their role in society. Blah, blah, blah. Then it was the handicapped – if that's the right phrase? What did Anti-Fashion Fashion have to say about people with disabilities and real lumps and bumps? How the sod should I know? But I didn't let on. Anything to get on the old jellybox.

Not that being a media personality isn't without its complications – which is to say, it has its complications. There's my image to think of, for one thing. It needs a considerable brush-up. The Boy and his girl were all very well, but I quickly found that a national treasure – that's me by the way – required skilled professionals. Urgent action was needed – and taken – on the hair, the nails, the eyebrows, the skin and the bunions.

What with the beauty appointments and the interviews and the many telephone calls it took to arrange both, I hadn't much time for the Boy. I assumed he'd be as elated as me. He had good reason to be. I would never have said it outright to his face but he knew how I felt: I couldn't have done any of it without him. The holding of the auction, the rebirth of my career, the putting in his place of Howard the shit Haggarty, that was all him.

But it seemed to give him no pleasure. On the contrary, he seemed to be experiencing a drastic come-down; the sick headache after a particularly good party, if you will. He was, dear reader, down-in-the-mouth.

I was puzzled. Why, when it had all gone so well? Then it came to me. After the excitement of the past few months, he was bored. Intellectual challenge, that's what he needed. I, of course, had my media career to keep me busy. He had no such distractions. His grey cells needed stimulation. I wracked my brains for the answer.

'What's this?' he asked when I handed him the package.

'A book of Sudoku,' I explained. 'To stretch your brain.'

He flicked through the pages. 'Never was one for sums,' he said, putting the book down. 'Thanks anyway.'

How stupid of me! How ridiculous to think the Boy's deep malaise could be cured by a book of simple – or even super-fiendish – puzzles. I needed to think bigger.

'When did you leave school?' I asked, one sunny afternoon before setting off for my Nifty Fifties Pilates class. (David's idea. She signed me up. Said it would help tone up my core, whatever that means.)

The Boy was up to his elbows in soapy water, listlessly washing dishes and staring out of the window, even though a dishwasher was one of the first luxuries we bought when the lolly arrived.

'Hard to say,' he replied, wiping the suds from his arms. 'Started bunking off big time when I was still in the juniors. By the time I was thirteen or fourteen, I pretty much only went in if Ma marched me up to the front gates – and even then, I was usually down the rec by morning break.'

'Have you ever thought about resuming your education? Getting some qualifications under your skin.'

'Go back to school?' he snorted. 'Don't think so. It was bad enough first time round.'

'Further education isn't like school. No playground bullies for a start. And you're more mature now, more focused. Look what you've achieved since I took you under my wing. You've got a brain. Shame to see it go to waste. Or do you want to end up like your brother? No job. No prospects. Just killing time until you get caught and banged down in gaol.'

'Up,' he said, shifting in his seat. 'It's banged up, Miss E.'

Five thousand pounds. Quite a chunk of money to invest but, thanks to him, I could afford it. I got David to do the necessary. Make the enquiries, fill in the forms and so on. I wanted it to be a surprise. It was all booked. All I had to do was write the cheque.

He'd been out all day, where I don't know. He went out most days and I didn't like to question him. Eager to pass on the good news, I pounced as soon as he was through the door and gabbled it out. His response was not as I'd expected. No hugs and thank-yous, no tears of gratitude. My gift in fact had the opposite effect: his drooping face drooped even lower.

'Regent Street Business School,' I repeated. 'All booked and paid for. PA, secretary and administrator course.' I laughed. 'Might have to pay you a proper salary, once you're a fully qualified amen… amen… What is that sodding word?' He didn't laugh at my little jest. 'Anyway,' I went on, 'you start next month. You don't have to pay a thing. It's all on me.'

His shoulders sagged. Why was he so lukewarm? Was he worried he wouldn't be able to measure up academically?

'You'll walk it,' I said. 'The others may have more conventional backgrounds, but I doubt any of them have had the practical experience you have.'

'The thing is…' he began.

'The thing! What thing? When will you ever learn to express yourself clearly?' I couldn't help it. I wanted to be nice to him, I really did, but he could be so exasperating. I took a calming breath and began again. 'Look, it's just up the road. It couldn't be handier. You take the Central Line and—'

'Yeah. Regent Street. I know. You already said.'

He was staring at his feet, like he used to in the early days. So annoyingly subservient. So stubbornly unimpressed.

'Most people would be grateful,' I snapped.

When he spoke again, his voice was firmer. 'Sorry,' he said, lifting his eyes, 'but I can't.'

'Why not?'

Then I knew. It was as if everything in the room – the William Morris wallpaper on the walls, the Chinese rug beneath my feet, even the velvet sofa under my backside – had floated away into the distance, leaving the two of us suspended there. Just me and the Boy. I put my hand out to steady myself. He moved to help but I waved him away.

'You're going, aren't you?' I said, voice breaking. 'Leaving me. Sodding off.'

His head dipped. 'Going to Brighton.'

'That's an interesting choice,' I said, mustering up a thin smile.

'They got good access courses there. Went down yesterday. Saw this bloke. Reckons I might have a chance. Have to do some exams first, of course, then I could apply for a foundation course. After that, who knows? Maybe even a degree. I was thinking, you know, one day, maybe I could study law.'

'Law,' I repeated, my eyes swimming in tears. I cast my eyes up to the ceiling. It seemed important not to allow the tears to spill.

'I'll keep in touch,' he went on anxiously. 'You won't get rid of me that easy.'

I blinked and two fat tears rolled down. He offered a tissue – he always had a tissue or a wet wipe, like magic, to hand – and blotted my damp cheeks. 'Sweet of you, Boy, but you'll have forgotten me before you get as far as Victoria Station. I'll be just some silly old biddy you once knew.'

'You'll never be that, Miss E.'

'When were you…?' I cleared the frog in my throat. 'When were you thinking of leaving?'

He looked back down to his feet, then up at me from under those long, dark lashes. 'That's the thing, see?'

'What?' There was a small silence while he waited patiently for me to catch his drift – and then I did. At least I could get this right. 'Oh, of course,' I said. 'You'll be needing money. Find my handbag and I'll write you a cheque. Would five thousand help?'

57.

BRADLEY

After the rush comes the downer. Can't seem to shake off this mood. Everything's dench, everyone's happy, except me. I can't settle.

Who'd have thought Davina and Miss E would get on so well? Not me for a start. Don't get me wrong. I like Davina. She's switched-on, knows her stuff. Posh without being stuck-up, if you follow. But Miss E can be so off with new people. Luckily Davina isn't the sensitive sort. Comes with dealing with awkward clients all day long, I suppose. She doesn't even mind when Miss E calls her David and orders her about.

Anyways, in double-quick time Davina's mastered the tricky art of brown-nosing Miss E just enough to make her feel special but not so much as to get on her nerves. Took me weeks to get that one right.

Reckon I can trust Davina. She might need a top-up, see, one day, Miss E. Might need to sell more stuff. There's still plenty. If she was to auction the purple thing, for instance, Davina told me it could make a tidy sum, 'cause of its history. But could she ever bring herself to part with it? At least she's given up lugging it around with her everywhere, like a comfort blanket. I put it in her bottom drawer, folded and wrapped in tissue.

One good thing, Haggarty won't trouble her. Mr Wisdom and the white envelope took care of that. The others, they turned out to be sound. The two weird women, batty though they looked, didn't want a penny. Seems they'd made a fortune knocking out little statues of deer and pigs and suchlike made out of sticks. You see them all over the place in garden centres. They just wanted recognition, their names on their designs – which, after pulling a few faces, Miss E agreed to. They're on the phone to her almost every day, though how she makes head or tail of what they're on about, I'll never know. They yak over each other so much, interrupting, contradicting. Miss E doesn't seem to mind. Used to it, I suppose.

That old hippy Bruno called round to visit, bunch of flowers in his hand, big box of chocs under his arm. He was bit stiff-necked at first, when he clocked I was living there. Jealous, see? Of me! Can you believe that? I opened the chocs, poured the gin and left them to it. Put my head to the door later and heard them laughing, so he must of thawed out. After he'd gone, Miss E was flushed and skittery for hours. I reckon there could still be some mileage in that relationship.

As for the money, the five grand, that was more than I was expecting. One per cent is what we agreed – though she won't have remembered. That would have been less than three grand. You could say, I made a profit on the deal. She never even mentions the money I'd creamed off. And I don't remind her.

I'm cheeky enough to ask for a souvenir. The photo hanging in her hallway. The hot one.

'That old thing,' she goes. 'Of course. I've got dozens of copies… somewhere.'

So there we are. From now on, Bradley McCreedy's legit.

And if I'm short, there's bound to be plenty of old ladies down in Brighton needing taking care of.

The days are getting warmer. The nights lighter. Just think, summer by the sea. Magic. They reckon it could be a hot one this year. I might even have to get meself some swimmers. That'll be a first. Bradley in a cozzie.

So you see, it's not like I'm leaving her in the lurch. She's got plenty of visitors these days. That Molly, she's round two or three times a week. Though she can hardly bring herself to say a word to me, she and Miss E chin away for hours. Last time she came she brought Miss E a onesie. Leopard print. Miss E flipping loves it.

I feel bad about Molly, to be honest with you. Was going to have it out with her face to face, but what would have been the point? She'd have acted upset and I'd have acted sorry and we'd both have been faking it. Truth is, she went off of me big time ages ago when I came over all Jason Statham. She didn't like that side of me. Not used to people using their fists to put across their point of view. That's another thing I should probably turn over a new leaf on.

I'll text her when I'm well on my way. Won't mention Brighton, just in case. Anyways, Molly will be all right. She's a good kid. She'll end up with a nice, steady bloke. Nicer and steadier than what I'll ever be. Yeah, Molly will be all right.

So, that's everything. Except the note. Gotta find the right words.

'Cheers for everything, Miss E. Enjoyed being your amanuensis. Looked that one up for you. Ha, ha! Hope you get your book published. Least you got it all down on your digi–whatsit. Look forward to seeing it in WHSmiths. Anyhow, take care and make sure you keep rocking that ponytail. Love, Bradley.'

58.

ELOISE

'Love, Bradley' indeed. The cheek. Such vulgar familiarity. But at least it's grammatical.

What to say? What to say? Should I mention the bunions? Probably not. Keep it short. I'm definitely getting myself one of those wheelchair thingies, though, for when they flare up. That was such fun in the hospital. I can get the new one to push me around. Yes, better put that in.

The thing is, how's one supposed to exist without live-in staff? My wrist is throbbing again, the cupboards are full of tins I can't bloody well get into, and I've got no one to talk to. I'm in pain, I'm starving and I'm bored, bored, bored.

Why did he go? We were getting on, weren't we? He was getting used to my funny little ways. I was doing my best not to throw the crockery. We could have continued working together. Like Dr Holmes and Mr Jekyll.

Silv's been in touch. Saw me on the old jellybox. Nice letter, wishing me well and filling me in on the family news and so on. Good old Carthorse. Still not going to the sodding Algarve, though.

Time to get dolled up and find a newsagents. The response is bound to be excellent, now I'm a household name. What a delicious prospect. A long line of them, young and eager, snaking down the stairs, agog at the chance to meet the celebrated Miss Eloise Slaughter. Must dig out something special to wear.

His name was Bradley. I used to call him 'Boy'. He never minded. At least, he never said. Ah me, how will I rock the ponytail without him?

'Wanted!!! Urgent!!! Refined, respectable lady authoress, pioneering feminist and famous fashionista, seeks full-time amanuensis and occasional pusher. Usual rates.'

Acknowledgements

The writing and publishing of a book is not a solitary exercise. If it takes a village to raise a child, it takes a supportive family, a host of patient friends, and a lot of clever professionals to make a book. *Note to Boy* is no exception.

First and foremost, I thank my family. Michael, Matthew and Ben, and Naomi, Ian and little Bethany – none of you are lampooned within these pages, I promise. I don't say enough how much I love and appreciate you all; now you have it in black and white.

To everyone who read early versions of the book and generously and honestly shared their thoughts, my thanks. Honourable mention must go to my good friends and fellow writers Lesley Bootiman, David Byrne and Mike Coleman; to my talented sister, Jude Fowler; and to my Summertown writing group buddies and lunch companions, Anna Pitt, Imogen Matthews, Gill Lane and Louise Ludlow.

Special thanks to my wise and wonderful friend Carol Watts for her legal know-how. Any mistakes of a legal or other nature are, of course, mine.

Thanks also to Jane Bidder, whose creative writing course at

Oxford University Department for Continuing Education set me off on the path that led to this novel.

I owe a particular debt to Maureen Lee and Juliet Burton; Maureen for her advice and encouragement since we first crossed words many years ago in the letters pages of the *Observer*, and Juliet for her stalwart endeavours on my behalf.

Then I come to Unbound. It's safe to say, this book probably wouldn't have seen the light of day if I hadn't happened upon an Unbound novel when shopping in Waitrose one day. You see, it does sometimes pay to shop upmarket.

So thank you, Kwaku Osei-Afrifa, Xander Cansell, Caitlin Harvey, Georgia Odd, Anna Simpson and everyone else at Unbound who gave me a chance, answered my questions, and nursed me through. I would be very remiss if I didn't single out for thanks editors Craig Taylor, Sue Lascelles and Andrew Chapman – you saved me from many an embarrassing blooper and made this the best book it could be – and the design genius Mark Ecob, who created the cover.

To the gaggle of disparate (occasionally desperate) souls who make up the online Unbound Author Social Club, I wouldn't have got this far, this sanely, without your cheerful and knowledgeable encouragement, many kindnesses, and occasional gentle bullying.

To my patrons – some I know but many I do not – thank you so much for having faith in me and pledging so generously to enable this book to reach publication. I hope the resulting tale gives you some laughs.

Lastly, I must mention Andrew Crofts, whose writing competition first spawned the short story that was to develop into *Note to Boy*. Sadly, he didn't award me first prize (I was a robbed runner-up) but it was his phone call that spurred me on to create the Eloise and Bradley who exist within these pages today. So you could say, it's all his fault.

PS. I've learned a lot while writing Note to Boy. *One thing is book reviews are like gold dust to authors. Good, bad or indifferent, we love them all – though we prefer the good ones. If you've read this book, please take a few minutes to post a short review. I value your comments.*

Unbound is the world's first crowdfunding publisher, established in 2011.

We believe that wonderful things can happen when you clear a path for people who share a passion. That's why we've built a platform that brings together readers and authors to crowdfund books they believe in – and give fresh ideas that don't fit the traditional mould the chance they deserve.

This book is in your hands because readers made it possible. Everyone who pledged their support is listed at the front of the book and below. Join them by visiting unbound.com and supporting a book today.

Will Adams
Tim Atkinson
Zena Barrie
Rhianwen Beint
Jerome Braud
Fiona Bray
Heather Brebaugh (AfterSixtyClub.com)
Stephanie Bretherton
Nicola Brookes
Professor Liz Browne
Erica Buist
Marcus Butcher
Kathy Calmejane
Anne Carr
Lina Carr
Jacqui Castle
Philippa Challenger
Cheryl
Mark Ciccone

Andy Clark
Jason Cobley
Anthony Colclough
Stevyn Colgan
Rachel Connor
Janet Cooke
Mark E Cooper
Heather Coull
Jane Davis
Amanda de Grey
Alison Dewar
Joyce Doughty
Jessica Duchen
Jane Dulieu
Ember
Zazarina Ferguson Hemmings
Antonia Fleishman
Trupti Gardner
Alan Gillespie
Heide Goody
Paul Green
Josephine Greenland
Petra Greenland
Claire Handscombe
Victoria Harvey
Sally Hathaway
Alexandra Hay
Jennifer Hay
Grace Helmer
Monika Horcickova
Jeff Horne
Jeanne Jackson
Oli Jacobs
Elena Kaufman
Dan Kieran
Susan A King
Shona Kinsella
Maureen Lee
Kathryn Little
Lety Lozano
Andrew Marks
David Marsh
Karin Matthews
Roger Maynard
Emma Miller
John Mitchinson
Susan Moore
Carlo Navato
Sarah Nelson Smith
Carol Parke
Carol Pearce
Justin Pollard
Nikki Pryke
Robert Purbrick
Sobia Quazi
Sue Read
Simon Reap
Mark Sawyer
David Schofield
Jan Scott
Mike Scott Thomson
Tara Shah
Deena Sherman
Wayne Smith
Sue Spokes
Dee Szymura
Alexandra Turney
Paul Waters
Carol Watts
Susie Wenman
Jessica Williams
Caroline Wood
Laura Wood
Robert Woodshaw
Lucien Young